Simon Grave
and the Drone of the Basque Orvilles

Len Boswell

Black Rose Writing | Texas

The author grants the final approval for this literary material.

First printing

This is a work of fiction. Names, characters, businesses, places, events, and
incidents are either the products of the author's imagination or used in a
fictitious manner. Any resemblance to actual persons, living or dead, or
actual events is purely coincidental.

ISBN: 978-1-68433-416-2
PUBLISHED BY BLACK ROSE WRITING
www.blackrosewriting.com

Printed in the United States of America
Suggested Retail Price (SRP) $18.95

Simon Grave and the Drone of the Basque Orvilles is printed in Palatino Linotype

*As a planet-friendly publisher, Black Rose Writing does its best to eliminate
unnecessary waste to reduce paper usage and energy costs, while never compromising
the reading experience. As a result, the final word count vs. page count may not meet
common expectations.

To all I love without condition,
To all I love without omission.

Never doubt.

And to my dear sister, Nancy,
Victoria's new BFF.

Simon Grave
and the Drone of the Basque Orvilles

"The scary thing about the future . . . There will be tiny cameras everywhere, and they'll be flying around like mosquitoes and drones. That will be bad. Drones are scary. You can't reason with a drone."

—Matt Groening

"Drones overall will be more impactful than I think people recognize, in positive ways to help society."

—Bill Gates

"You need to put drones under control; you need to lay out certain rules of engagement in order to prevent or minimize collateral casualties. It is extremely important."

—Vladimir Putin

"Drones can be useful tools, and I am all about useful tools. One of my mottos is 'the right tool for the right job.'"

—Martha Stewart

1

Whir, whoosh, zoom! The sound was near deafening as forty-three drones, one for each diner at Le Crabe Bleu, tested the limits of synonyms as they hovered, bustled, scuttled, scrambled, scampered, and generally fluttered about overhead. Some went this way, some went that, and still others just hovered. But all had the same goal: fussing over their owners. The result was a pulsating din of humming, droning, whirring, and buzzing, with an occasional hiss or fizzy lifting sound thrown in.

It was a wonder that diners were able to eat at all, so distracting was the chaos in the sky. But eat they did, feasting on the upscale fare of the only French café in Crab Cove. A few blocks away, at Bob's Crab Shack, tourists were hammering away at blue crabs steamed in Old Bay Seasoning, but here in the faux-French café, as the drones weaved and wobbled, the diners nibbled daintily at minuscule portions of Crabe Impérial and the café's signature dish, Crique de Crabe, a dish named after the town and featuring a piquant blend of lump crab meat, scallions, and New Bay Seasoning. Oh, you could get a steamed crab at Le Crabe Bleu, but the waiter would present it to you on a silver tray and dismantle it for you right at your table, with the feigned panache and swooping arm movements of a master of magic and prestidigitation.

Detective Simon Grave stared down at his now-empty dish, which the waiter insisted on calling a *plah*—the sound suggesting that the waiter was about to heave—and then turned his attention back to the drones. On an ordinary day, he wouldn't have noticed them at all, so commonplace were they now—just another part of daily living—but his own personal drone, Barry, had made a point of commenting extensively on them.

"Do you know, sir, that there was once a time in Crab Cove when carrier pigeons filled the sky in such numbers that they blotted out the sun? Why, getting lunch would require nothing more than to point your shotgun skyward, in any direction, and you'd soon have a feast at your feet."

Grave looked down at his *plah*, which was so small he could blot it out by just putting his thumb between it and his eye. "I suppose a lot of other less desirable stuff fell from the sky as well."

Barry was a bit taken aback. "Er, yes, but that's not my point, sir."

"Well, what *is* your point, Barry?"

"So many drones sir. So much noise. Wouldn't it be better to find a smaller, more accommodating restaurant where conversations did not require some familiarity with lip-reading?"

Grave shrugged. "I see what you mean, Barry, but this is actually perfect for my meeting."

Barry fluttered down to eye level. "With the retective?"

"Yes, an annoying buzz might be just the thing to cut this meeting short."

Barry tilted his rotors down by way of nodding. "I sense a certain reluctance on your part to participate fully in the retective's investigation."

"You think?"

If Barry could have smirked, he would have, but like all the personal drones, or PDs, flying about, he had no means of physical expression. However, he was a master at intonation. If a smirk was called for, his voice software would provide just the right intonation to simulate that smirk.

"Come now, Simon, you know that retectives are a wonderful resource for detectives, providing detailed analyses of past cases, from process to logic to every aspect of a case. What you detect, they retect. It's a win-win."

Grave offered his own smirk, which had more years of experience. "Second-guessing is what they do."

"Call it what you will, Simon. Their goal is to make you a better detective."

"Whatever," said Grave, glancing at his watch. "Tell you what, Barry, we have a few minutes. Do you see that young lady at the table near the sidewalk?"

"Yes, quite beautiful, but perhaps too young for a man in his forties."

Grave offered a more nuanced smirk. "Spare me the commentary. Go have a chat with her drone, do a compatibility test, and so on. If things are simpatico, see if she might be interested in dinner."

Barry issued what his programmer proudly called "Sigh 67," and buzzed away, leaving Grave to survey the scene, and what a scene it was.

A year ago, in 2052, this same Crab Cove café would have had a similar group of regulars and tourists, but unlike today, they would have been talking to one another or, more likely, talking *with* someone on their *cellphones*. That had all changed. Cellphones were now as dead as rotary phones, replaced by personal drones that offered so much more than phone service, internet access, and a dizzying variety of apps. Yes, a cellphone could do many things, but it couldn't get you a beer when you were too tired to leave the couch.

The switchover had been abrupt. Apple had simply announced that it was no longer making cellphones, and that was that. After a brief period, during which people chained themselves to cellphone towers, cellphones were no more. People of means lined up to buy expensive Apple "Flutters," which featured a combination of ionic-wind, zero-gravity, and dark-matter propulsion that made them nearly silent, in a variety of sizes from gnat-like swarms to larger, cat-sized monodrones. Other manufacturers had to scramble to keep up, their early models nothing more than slightly enhanced delivery or military drones featuring batteries and noisy rotors. And Crab Cove being Crab Cove, the preponderance of models hovering over Le Crabe Bleu, including Barry, were these old clunky types that were largely responsible for the high-decibel aural attack. They even drowned out the screaming of the seagulls.

Grave could see from his vantage point that the meeting of drones was not going well. The young woman's drone kept backing away from Barry, who persisted, chasing it around a nearby tree before giving up and returning to hover above Grave's table.

"Her drone, Maureen, a SimSat 111 if you didn't notice, says she's available, but not for the likes of you."

Grave cringed. "The likes of me? Ouch."

"I persisted, of course, pointing out your broad shoulders, considerable height, and Dudley Do-Right charms."

"Jesus, Barry, how many times do I have to tell you to not mention that dolt?"

"Sorry, sir, but the image provides a helpful shorthand to anyone considering you as a likely mate. It can be crucial when time is of the essence. Moves the negotiations along."

"But I'm *nothing* like Dudley Do-Right. I'm more handsome, smarter, and vastly more charming."

Barry just hovered silently, as if he were trying to ride out the storm of misplaced boasting. Clinically speaking, Grave was *almost* handsome, just north of nondescript, with an IQ that suggested "C" student, and a charm that fluctuated between blunt and not so much. As for social skills, well, think minimal.

Grave knew Barry was suppressing a smirk of enormous size and complexity. "Oh, all right. Any more feedback?"

Barry hesitated.

"Well?" said Grave.

"Um, well, the word "geezer" was used more than once, and she thinks your Hawaiian shirt is at best gauche. Her words, not mine."

Grave sighed. "Oh, terrific."

"Well, you *are* in your forties, sir."

"So that makes me ancient?"

"To an eighteen-year-old, yes, *emphatically* yes. You really need to adjust your sights, sir. Besides, the young lady is only here for today. She leaves for the Mars Colony on the morrow, from the new Mars Terminal."

The Mars Terminal was the talk of the town. No one could figure out why a town as small and backward as Crab Cove would need, or even want, a gateway to another planet. Crab Cove, a town where time passed but never said howdy, was already strange enough. Still, the terminal brought more people to the town, people looking for their last taste of steamed crabs before a flight to a planet the same red color, but without Old Bay Seasoning.

Grave couldn't believe it. "Mars? How can an eighteen-year-old afford a trip to Mars?"

"She mentioned someone named 'daddy,' I believe. And as I'm sure you're well aware, Mars needs women, sir."

Grave nodded. "Yes, I've heard that."

Barry spun slowly in a circle, scanning the café. "Let me see, let me see. Ah, perhaps the woman in the blue jumpsuit?"

Grave didn't see her. "Where?"

"There, sir, by the hostess station. She's just arriving."

Grave spotted her and groaned. "Oh, shit, it's her."

"Her who, sir?"

"Tilda Must, the retective."

"*Must?* Oh, dear, a Determination Series simdroid? Yikes."

"Indeed, she's been programmed to be bulldog-like. Lucky me."

Barry waggled in the air, trying to assess the situation. "Well, at least she's modeled after actress Tilda Swinton, in her younger years, of course. Beautiful, don't you think, in a severe sort of way?"

Grave nodded. She was beautiful, and like all simdroids, a perfect replica. "Well, there's that."

Grave started to say more, but he had caught sight of someone else entering the café, an old man who could save him from Tilda's clutches—Captain Henry Morgan, his boss—who rushed past Tilda and raced toward Grave's table, "raced" being a relative term for a balding, overweight police officer approaching retirement. His drone, an old noisy model named Rum, made it to the table long before the captain, who had stopped halfway to catch his breath.

"Grave, there you are," said Rum. "Come with us, there's been a murder!"

Grave didn't need coaxing. He pushed back his chair and followed the drone to Captain Morgan, who attempted a smile. "Down by the marsh, Grave. Come along."

"Yes, sir."

They made their way out of the café, Barry and Rum trailing. Grave paused briefly as he passed by Tilda to give her a shrug and a wink. "Perhaps tomorrow."

Tilda just stood there with her mouth open, watching them leave, then shouted after them. "I must *insist*, detective."

Grave turned and shouted over his shoulder. "Tomorrow morning, at the station. I promise."

Grave knew she had said something else in response, perhaps a well-reasoned expletive, but he was well out of earshot by then, climbing into the captain's police hovercruiser.

He couldn't help smiling. *A murder!*

2

The police hovercruiser sped on. Grave and Captain Morgan sat silently, Morgan staring into space absently, exhausted by all the running, Grave hypervigilant, uncomfortable driving in a driverless car.

Morgan stretched out his legs and groaned. "I'm getting too damned old for this shit, Grave."

Grave knew he was right, but you don't just point that out to your boss. "Not at all, sir."

Morgan gave Grave an appraising look, sensing his true feelings. "Believe it or not, Grave, there was a time when I could leap fences and wrestle the biggest, fastest perps to the ground."

Grave winced at the word *perps*. He hated abbreviations. To him, they were nothing more than the skeletal remains of words that once roamed free in full syllabic grandeur. Give the perpetrators their due with four syllables well earned.

"You still can, sir, I'm sure."

Morgan laughed. "Nonsense."

They fell silent again, Morgan continuing to groan and stretch as Grave glanced nervously about, looking for the car or tree he sensed they'd crash into. But there was nothing. Just their cruiser and their two personal drones speeding along just behind the cruiser. They seemed to be having a heated exchange about something.

Grave turned to the case at hand. "Captain, any information about the murder?"

Morgan let out one final grunt and sniffed himself erect, assuming the position and the role of stiff-backed leader of men, or as best as he and his potbelly could manage. "I got a call from Polk, who's already at the scene. Some confusion about cause of death."

Grave had to smile. With Jeremy Polk, ME, there was always confusion about cause of death, or at least Polk played it that way. Forensic science had taken so many technological leaps in the past two years that medical examiners were approaching the status of ox-drawn carts. Polk had to throw some mystical nonsense into the mix just to justify his considerable salary. That, and he loved to tease Grave, withholding information until the final second, making Grave work for it.

"How *unusual*," said Grave.

Morgan chuckled. "Yeah, right. Anyway, he mentioned something about dog bites and lacerations."

"So this could just be a dog-bites-man thing?"

"Could be. We'll find out soon enough. Only a few more minutes. This car is pretty fast. Speaking of which, why aren't you driving your Sprite today?"

Ah, the 1965 Austin Healy Sprite. Grave's pride and joy. On any normal day, Grave would be behind the wheel, the sports car's radio cranked up to eleven—in fact, stuck on eleven.

Grave sighed. He would have loved nothing more, but ever since the death of the Reverend Bendigo Bottoms, driving the Sprite was no longer fun. Grave had been an avid listener to the reverend's radio gospel hour, the Sprite's radio stuck on that one station, at full volume. He and the reverend had developed a friendship over the years and would often meet at the Skunk 'n Donuts on Main to discuss religion and the meaning of life. His death had been a blow. And now all Grave's radio produced was deafening static.

"The Reverend Bottoms," said Grave, and nothing more.

Captain Morgan nodded solemnly. "Damned shame. What a way to go."

The reverend had choked to death on one of Skunk 'n Donuts signature donuts, the Little Jimmy Cruller, named after a certain body part of the town's founder, James Skunkford, famous for its small size.

"I must have spent hours with that man discussing the meaning of life."

"You mean like, life is like a bowl of cherries?"

"Yeah, something like that, although the reverend thought that life was like a tuna fish sandwich."

"A what?"

"Sandwich. Tuna fish specifically."

Captain Morgan leaned forward in his seat. "Interesting, but hold that thought. We're here."

Grave could see the marsh ahead and the crowd of officers and forensic specialists standing near the body of what looked like a man in a bathing suit. The smallest man among them, Jeremy Polk, already clothed in his pristine white jumpsuit, was walking toward the cruiser, waving his arms and directing them with white-gloved hands to a parking spot outside the crime scene, which was already marked off with yellow crime-scene tape rippling and fluttering in a breeze blowing in from the Chesapeake Bay, where clouds as white as snow and tall as buildings were scudding along the horizon.

Slightly apart from the others was a large man in kilts, walking back and forth, playing a bagpipe. A dog as tall as Polk trailed behind him, trying its best to howl along with the tune, which Grave recognized immediately: "The Itsy Bitsy Spider."

It was going to be an interesting day.

3

Jeremy Polk greeted them curtly as they stepped from the cruiser into a stiff breeze. "A word, over here," he said, motioning them to a slight rise in the land.

Captain Morgan got right to it. "What've you got?"

Polk wringed his hands, a mannerism familiar to both of them. It was just Polk's way of formulating a response. "It's complicated."

Morgan slapped his arms to his sides. "Shit, man. It's always *complicated* with you. What have you got?"

Polk rolled his eyes. He was not sure how much longer he could work with the captain, who seemed to be losing his filters if not his marbles, turning into an even more irascible version of his already cantankerous self. Polk imagined the captain's retirement as one filled with spit-filled harangues and the caning of passing cars. "I don't make this stuff up, Captain. This one's *truly* complicated."

"And?" said Morgan.

"Well, firstly, we're dealing with three possible manners of death: a vicious dog attack, an equally vicious knife attack, and a garden variety heart attack."

Grave looked back at the man in kilts and his dog. "Is that the dog?"

"No," said Polk. "I'll get to that."

"How is that complicated," said Morgan. "We've had plenty of cases involving multiple manners of death."

"Yes, yes, we have," said Polk, "but nothing quite like this. I mean, yes, we'll sort out manner of death, but I was really referring to the murder scene itself. Manner of death was my *firstly*. You never let me get to my secondly."

"All right, I'll bite," said Morgan. *"Secondly?"*

Polk imagined that biting would be part of the captain's retirement repertoire as well. "So, *secondly*, there's no human or animal DNA within twenty yards of the body. Our scanners picked up nothing, nada."

Grave leapt to the obvious conclusion. "So the perpetrator used one of those new DNA blocker gizmos."

As far as forensics had advanced—the new instant-read DNA scanners being just one of many new tools—crime had kept pace, creating counter-tools to confound the police.

"Exactly," said Polk. "Usually with these blockers, we pick up at least a few segments, but whoever the killer is, he has one fine piece of equipment."

Grave looked back at the scene. A dozen simdroid officers, all modeled after the late actor Morgan Freeman, were fanned out, looking for clues in the grassy areas along the marsh. Police drones, all named Larry and featuring the exact same voice of Morgan Freeman, flew overhead, scanning the entire area.

"But you're still looking, I see."

Polk nodded. "Of course. You never know. The murderer may have dropped something or thrown his knife into the marsh. I doubt that, of course, given his use of the blocker, but we must be thorough."

"Precisely," said Morgan. "Now, back to the body. I know you'll want to slice and dice him back at your place, but what's your gut feeling?"

Polk bristled at the captain's crude description of his job. "Captain, you know I don't like to just guess at things."

"I'm fully aware of that, Polk, but guess away anyway."

Polk sighed. The captain really was becoming impossible. "As you wish. My gut feeling, as you say, is that he was frightened to death and that the wounds were postmortem. There simply isn't enough blood for any other conclusion."

"So," said Grave, "he was frightened by something and then bitten *and* slashed?"

"Yes," said Polk, "but don't press me on the order of events—or even the timeline—quite yet."

Grave turned to Morgan. "A vicious dog and a man with a knife are both good reasons for a heart attack, but why do we have both?"

Morgan seemed confused. "What do you mean?"

"I mean," said Grave, "and correct me if I'm wrong, Polk, but it seems we would have either a frightened-to-death man followed by a dog attack or a frightened-to-death man followed by a knife attack. One or the other, but not both."

"Unless," said the Captain, smiling, "unless we're dealing with more than one potential killer. Is that what you're saying?"

"Yes, perhaps." Grave just wasn't sure. His mind, which was never noted for speed, often went blank after a particularly cogent statement.

Polk shook his head. "Yes, that's always possible, perhaps even probable, but we could also be dealing with a murderer who just happened to have a vicious dog along for the ride—or the killing."

Morgan huffed. "About the knife wounds. Do you think?"

Polk knew exactly what he meant. Were the wounds consistent with those typically inflicted by the elusive and prolific Chester Clink, serial killer extraordinaire? Clink had run up more than a hundred kills, mostly young women, along the Eastern Shore of Maryland and up and down the coast from New Florida to Newest England.

"I'll have to see what I see back at the morgue—the slicing and dicing as you call it—but yes, the wounds look at least fairly consistent with the Clink signature."

Morgan nodded and looked down the road that led to the crime scene, where not a single car seemed to be approaching. "So did you call Holmes and Watson?"

Polk chuckled. "You mean Charlize and Smithers? Yes, sir. It seemed appropriate."

Grave groaned. "Surely you're not giving her the case, sir."

Morgan bristled in his usual pre-retirement way, which was at least one notch above normal. "That's up to Polk. If we've got a Clinker, the case is hers. You know that."

"But otherwise?"

Morgan clenched his teeth. "Otherwise, I'll decide later. Maybe you'll *both* work the case. I just don't know at this point, all right? As Polk says, it's complicated."

"And speaking of Ms. Sherlock," said Polk, pointing toward the road, "here she comes."

Her vehicle was easy to spot. No hovercraft for her. No flying car, either. Detective Charlize Holmes, a simdroid modeled after the younger version of now-elderly actress Charlize Theron, was so fixated on her hero Sherlock Holmes that she preferred something older, classier. In truth, if town ordinances hadn't prohibited it, she would have been arriving in a horse-drawn carriage, calash, or landau, or at least something clearly evocative of the nineteenth century.

As it was, she was not far off in the vehicle she had chosen, a jet black 1929 Duesenberg Model J, which combined the look and ample accommodations of a carriage, complete with decorative landau irons and the muscle, flow, and sparkling chrome that came with a new century, albeit the early twentieth century.

She had built the car herself after an upgrade to her software, changing the original design only slightly to accommodate an efficient and utterly quiet electric motor quite unlike the throaty rumble of the Duesenberg's original straight-eight internal combustion engine.

When you looked at the car as it approached in eerie silence, you had the feeling that a ghost car had separated itself from the fabric of time and was headed directly for you. Your first instinct was to turn and run.

But Grave and Polk and Morgan just stood there. They'd seen this before, and they knew what was to come.

4

A truly beautiful woman can get away with wearing anything, from a sack to the most outrageous designer clothing, and still come off as beautiful. Such was the case with Detective Charlize Holmes, whose clothing of choice these days conformed strictly to the wardrobe of Sherlock Holmes, from his brown tweed suit to his caped Inverness coat, to his deerstalker cap. She was overdressed for this fine summer morning, of course, but simdroids being simdroids, ambient temperature was never a concern.

Combine such beauty with the luxurious Duesenberg, and you have a combination that will stop traffic, or in this case, a police investigation. Everything came to a halt. Detectives, simdroid patrolmen, and CSI technicians immediately dropped what they were doing to stare as Holmes stepped from the car, puffing on her meerschaum electro pipe, which created smoke without the use of tobacco.

She scanned the scene and the assembled onlookers, gave a brief nod to Captain Morgan, and then turned back to the Duesenberg. "Watson, I need you."

Grave had seen this little bit of theater many times over the past two years. Charlize, once his personal simdroid and auto mechanic, had been instrumental in solving a particularly complicated case involving ten men named Jimmy. Morgan had been so impressed he had hired her on the spot as the first simdroid detective in the Crab Cove Police Department. A lover of the works of Sir Arthur Conan Doyle, Charlize had been quick to adopt the persona and mannerisms of Sherlock Holmes.

She also knew that every Holmes needs her Watson. Charlize had selected another simdroid, Smithers, the former butler at the Hawthorne Mansion, and turned him into her own Doctor John H. Watson, or in this case, Doctor Smithers-Watson. After some supplemental programming, the two of them had set about solving case after case, from missing kittens to crimes of every type and severity. They were quickly becoming a legend, and Grave was more than a little bit jealous. He also missed having a personal simdroid to come home to.

Smithers Watson stepped from the Duesenberg as stiffly and as country doctorly as he could manage, as if he were arriving at the most ho-hum event imaginable. Like Holmes, he was dressed in a tweed suit, although it had a more military cut and seemed a better fit. His designer had modeled him to look exactly like the late actor Peter O'Toole, but with the voice of Richard Burton. Somehow, the combination worked well, both for a butler and for a close personal assistant and confidant of the great Charlize Holmes.

Watson glanced at the crowd and offered his best response. "Well, then."

The words were as effective as a cattle prod. Everyone except Grave, Polk, and Morgan broke from their reverie and returned to the work at hand. Simdroids shuffled to and fro, drones whizzed overhead, and the CSI technicians, both human and simdroid, poked and prodded at things approaching invisibility. All the personal drones, who had assembled on orders under the one lone tree along the edge of the marsh, buzzed with renewed energy.

"Good afternoon, Captain," she said.

"Yeah, hi," said Morgan, not one for formalities. "Let's get to it, shall we?"

The captain, with occasional amendments by Grave and Polk, did his best to explain what they knew so far. Charlize listened patiently, expressionless, and then held up a hand to stop Morgan's further ramblings.

"I see," she said. "Let's have a look at the body." She began walking toward it, all of them following. "Do you have a name?"

"No," said Morgan. "No personal effects."

"Ah," she said, stopping at the edge of the blanket. "A human, male, about forty-five years, three months, wearing only a bathing suit of shockingly bad taste. Married but no wedding band. Six feet tall, pattern balding, never had a manicure. The look on his face suggests severe shock. He saw something quite terrible. Bite wounds consistent with a dog the size of a mastiff, like the one over there with the bagpipe beginner. Also a series of slashes suggesting a Bowie knife or small machete. Time of death approximately 1:07 a.m. this morning, give or take."

She reached down and touched the man's foot. "Make that 1:11. The body is warmer than I first surmised. Watson, a scan if you please."

Smithers stepped forward, opened his ever-present black bag, and pulled out a DNA scanner.

Morgan interrupted. "We've already scanned the scene. No DNA whatsoever."

Charlize smirked. "Yes, I remember you saying that. We're interested in the *victim's* DNA."

"Ah," said Morgan, stepping back.

Smithers scanned the body and held its viewing screen up so Charlize could see the results.

"Interesting," she said. "The person lying before you is none other than Wright Orville, CEO of C3 Corporation, makers of modestly priced, modestly engineered and executed personal drones."

"Wait, what?" said Morgan. "How did you get that from a DNA scan?"

"Elementary, my dear captain. Heritage readings indicate that his ancestors were principally from *Euskal Herria*, an area of the western Pyrenees, straddling the border between France and Spain on the coast of the Bay of Biscay."

Morgan squinted at her. "Euskal what?"

"Herria, sir. You may know it simply as *Basque Country*. And with that heritage and what we know about the residents of Crab Cove, the victim here can only be Wright Orville."

Polk chimed in. "But there must be more than fifty or so people here with that heritage."

"Ah, Polk," she said with a dismissive wave of her hand, "as my friend Sherlock always says, *you see, but you do not observe.*"

Polk winced. He hated when Charlize quoted Sherlock.

Charlize continued. "Now, *observe*. Look closely at this man's musculature. You will see that he is in excellent physical condition, suggesting participation in strenuous activity, rare for a CEO. And what is more strenuous than the traditional Basque Trials of Strength? Cutting tree trunks with an axe, stone dragging, stone lifting, tug-of-war—sixteen different disciplines in all."

"You're right," said Grave. "I watched the events last year, and the winner was Wright Orville."

"Of course he was, and of course I am," said Charlize.

"So here's what we do," said Captain Morgan, but Charlize held up a hand to stop him from talking further.

"No, I'm not finished, captain. Look at the bottoms of his feet, sir. They're stained with grass and something else—dandelion blossoms."

Polk leaned down to take a closer look, then shrugged. "So?"

"So," she continued, "you have to be running at great speed, for some distance, to get stains like that."

Morgan wasn't following. "And that's important because?"

"I'm not sure," said Charlize, "but it suggests that he first saw the murderer some distance from here and thought his only avenue of escape was toward this blanket, and—"

She suddenly stopped and looked around. "Where's his car?"

Grave offered a solution. "Perhaps far away, as you said."

Charlize rolled her eyes. "Simon, Simon, Simon. No, if the car was where this all started, he would have run to his car to escape, but he ran to this blanket. Why? Was his car here? And if so, where is it now?"

Morgan shrugged. "Maybe he had a weapon here?"

Charlize shook her head.

"Or maybe he was trying to warn someone else, a companion perhaps?" said Grave.

"Maybe," said Charlize.

"His wife, perhaps," said Polk.

"Or *not* his wife," said Charlize.

She bent down and examined the victim's hands and lips, then sniffed at the edge of the blanket. "Ah, as I thought, traces of red wine. Yes, there was definitely another person, a woman, probably not his wife, given the strength of the perfume. A romantic liaison."

Morgan was shaking his head in awe. "Wow, your deductive powers amaze me."

"Well, sir, I do appreciate the compliment, but I think you'll find that my demonstration of the facts here, as it always was with Sherlock, is more a result of *abduction*. That is, *inferring* an explanation from observed phenomena."

"Whatever," said Morgan.

"One question," said Polk. "Would you agree that the slash marks are matches for a Clink killing?"

Charlize laughed dismissively. "Of course not. Not even close, but you can tell that whoever did this was not slashing violently. With force, yes, but more slowly, with great intention, to fool us into thinking just that."

"Even so," said Captain Morgan, "I'd like you to work the case with Grave."

Charlize shook her head. "Captain, if you don't mind, I'd like to finish my current case."

Morgan was incredulous. "What, the missing cat?"

"Precisely, sir, and I'm sure Detective Grave can handle this case without any help from me."

"But we're talking about a murder, Detective Holmes. Would you really rather be investigating the disappearance of a *cat*?"

Charlize rolled her eyes. "Murder is easy, sir. Cats are hard."

Morgan relented with an appreciative sigh and the beginnings of a smile. "Very well, but I want you on call as needed."

"As you wish, sir."

"Okay, then," said Morgan, addressing them all. "We know the known knowns and the known unknowns and maybe a few of the unknown unknowns. All we need now is to address the unknown knowns."

There was an uncomfortable silence as Grave, Polk, Charlize, and Smithers tried to parse what Morgan was saying. Smithers was the first to realize a change of subject was in order.

"Sir, if I may," he said. "I'd say the first order of business is for Grave to interview the gentleman over there in the kilt and his singing mastiff."

"Oh," said Morgan. "Let's do *that* then."

"And let's confirm the identity of the victim," said Charlize.

"Of course," said Polk. "Grave, I'll give you a call when I know for sure."

"Right," said Grave, eager to get to the bagpiper. "Well, then, I'll just get to it."

The others stood there for a second, watching him go, then looked from one to the other, not sure exactly what should come next, until the captain shrugged and walked away, giving them their cue to disperse.

The team had quickly dispersed, leaving the knowns and unknowns to roam free in each person's and simdroid's brain to cavort and perhaps form hypotheses big and small, simple and complex, ridiculous and sublime, and so on in never-ending combinations of conjoined opposites. Grave had waved goodbye to each of them in turn, the last being Charlize, who offered up a parting comment that made Grave cringe. "Tilda sends her love."

Then she had turned on her heels, climbed into the Duesenberg, and speed away. Looking at the departing elegance of the Duesenberg, which Charlize had built thanks to a lottery win, Grave briefly wondered why simdroids were permitted to play, let alone win, the state lottery. But that's the way things were these days as the Simdroid Suffrage movement gained more and more concessions and rights.

The shrill wheeze of the bagpipe drew his attention back to the task at hand: interviewing the witness without being eaten by his dog.

Grave caught sight of Barry and summoned him with a flick of his hand. "Come on, Barry, we have work to do."

Barry hovered near Grave's shoulder as they made their way to the man and his dog. Grave loved dogs, both real and simdroid, but this man's mastiff, a hulk of a dog with a mouth that could accommodate a man's head, gave him pause.

"Ach, pay Fred no mind," the man said, sensing Grave's concern. "He's a puddle of love that one."

Grave took a step closer, allowing the dog to sniff him up and down. "Quite a dog."

"That he is," the man said. "Probably the best example of a brindled mastiff you'll find, at least in America."

"Brindled?"

"Yes, you know, his coat, mottled like, with gray and black."

"Ah."

"A yard high at the shoulders, two hundred pounds, and a right healthy appetite." He reached down, which was not far, and patted the dog on the head. "And sweet as pie."

Grave looked the dog in the face, which was much bigger than his own. Folds of black flesh flowed downward to the dog's jowls, making its head look like a cooled lava flow or a mudslide in progress.

"Quite a dog," Grave said again, stuck on his initial analysis. Grave, who had been staring exclusively at the dog, turned to the man. "I'm Detective Grave, and I'll be working the case. Anything you can tell me would be greatly appreciated."

"Hello," the man said, offering his hand, which seemed to go well with the rest of his hulking body. He was the perfect match for a mastiff: tall, broad, and heavy. His pale white legs emerged from under his kilt like hairy marble columns. And like Grave, his hair was black as midnight, though the man had the edge on hair length, his locks flowing down over his shoulders. He looked like a Scot from another age. A companion to William Wallace, perhaps.

"I'm Lachlan McLachlan." His Scottish accent was so thick the sound of his name reminded Grave of a man preparing to spit.

McLachlan pointed up the hill. "I run a kennel and training center atop the bluff. It's where I saw what I saw, so I suspect you'll want to take a look. It was the damndest thing."

A dirt path of sorts ran from the crime scene across the grassy flats near the marsh, twisting and turning as it climbed to the top of a bluff, which was easily a hundred feet above the marsh and the bay. Grave could see the roof and one wall of the man's house, an old white clapboard structure, probably once the home to a crabber or fisherman.

"Lead on," said Grave, motioning Barry to follow.

Grave decided to wait until they had reached the promontory before beginning his official interview, which gave him time to talk about other things.

"I see you're a bagpipe player."

Lachlan McLachlan looked down at the bagpipe he was carrying as if it had just suddenly appeared. "Oh, that. Well, yes, of sorts. Just a beginner. Just started lessons with Lenny the Git down at The Pickin' Crab music store. It gets a bit lonely here, even with all my dogs, and the sound of the bagpipe just takes me home. You know what I mean?"

Grave's first thought was Reverend Bendigo Bottoms, whose voice and gospel hour, propelled from the Sprite's radio at full volume, had a similar effect on Grave. He made a mental note to visit the man at the Crab Cove Cinema Cemetery. "Yes, of course. So, what brought you to Crab Cove?"

"I came because of the sea and in spite of the sea."

Grave could guess at the first part. "Yes, I hear Scotland has been especially inundated by the rising seas, but we've had the same problem here. Two of our most famous islands—Smith and Tangier—are gone, and parts of Crab Cove as well. I think we'll probably be a tiny island before I die. So, why come here for the same fate?"

McLachlan stopped for a moment to catch his breath. "This is one bloody climb."

Grave agreed. His legs were burning, and he was panting as hard as the man's mastiff, although not with his tongue hanging out. "I'll say."

"Anyway, I've always lived near the sea, so when I saw this property up here on this high bluff, I knew I'd be safe." He swept his arm toward the bay. "And the view is *spectacular*."

Indeed, it was. The Chesapeake Bay stretched to the horizon. On a clear day long ago, you could see the western shore, but no more. The rise of the oceans and the bay had greatly increased the bay's width, even inundated Baltimore, which was trying its best to advertise the city as "Venice on the Bay."

"That it is," said Grave. He pointed up the path. "Shall we?"

"Yes, of course, but let me warn you. When we reach the top, we'll be greeted by my drone, Haggis. I kept him away from your crime scene. Didn't want to distract your men."

"Oh?"

"He's a bit imposing. My own design, actually."

As they crested the hill, Grave understood exactly what McLachlan meant. Haggis was heading toward them at ground level, at full speed, a mouth at his center opened wide, exposing what looked like razor-sharp teeth.

"Fiddle-de-dee!" McLachlan shouted, and the drone slowed and came to a stop right in front of Grave, who was frozen to the spot. "Guard mode off, phone mode on, hover, and follow."

The terrible aspect of the drone suddenly changed. It could have been any drone now, albeit a very large drone with a central core that resembled a mastiff's head. All Grave could manage was, "Whoa."

"Sorry," said McLachlan. "He wouldn't have hurt you. In guard mode, he's all bark, unless someone makes the mistake of attacking him."

"Then what?"

"Well, initially, he'll retreat, then stop and try barking again. But if the attacker persists, well, Haggis is programmed to bite in nonlethal parts of the body. Arms, legs, and so on."

"Even so, those teeth looked razor-sharp."

McLachlan seemed to take pride in that. "Oh, yes, surgical steel, like scalpels."

"But surely that can't be legal."

McLachlan shook his head vigorously. "No, no, it's perfectly legal, detective. I checked all the codes and ordinances."

Grave looked up at Haggis, who was now hovering next to a clearly frightened Barry. Grave briefly wondered if a drone could shit its pants, even if it had neither because the way Barry was hovering suggested just that.

"Mr. McLachlan, I have questions. Many questions." He looked over at Barry, who nodded back, knowing his job was to record everything and stream the data back to Crab Cove's latest technological advancement, a central computer where all data from all sources could be stored, sorted, and analyzed. "But first, tell me what you saw and heard."

McLachlan sighed. "Again? I already told your officer."

"Yes, I'm afraid so. It's important." Important, Grave knew, because any variance from what the man told the officer would be highlighted and reported by the central computer.

"Ach, very well."

He motioned Grave to a nearby bench that overlooked the bay. "I don't know about you, but I could use a good sit-down."

Grave joined him on the bench and tried his best to ignore the view as sailboats and crab boats and large freighters passed by in the distance. McLachlan had other thoughts.

"Just look at those seagulls hovering over that crabber there," he said, pointing at a small boat off to the west. It seemed to be lost in a swirl of seagulls. "What beautiful birds they are."

Grave thought of them as flying rats. "Beautiful?"

"Ach, yes," said McLachlan. "And smart as all get-out."

"Smart? I think of them more as scavengers and pests."

McLachlan gave him a disapproving look. "You are so wrong about that. If they could speak, they'd set you straight."

Grave chuckled. "Yeah, if you say so."

McLachlan's reply was stern. "I do."

Grave knew he needed to change the subject. "So," he said, "how did it begin, the murder?"

McLachlan sighed and then launched into his story. He had been awakened the previous night by barking. His first thought was that his kennel was being attacked "yet again" by a stray dog that McLachlan referred to as the "demon dog," a dog so fierce it had attempted to chew through a chain-link fence surrounding the kennels, trying to get at one of his dogs, a bullmastiff in heat.

"But he was more than randy, that one," McLachlan had said. "I think he meant to kill her. Kill them all. "

McLachlan had raced to the kennel but quickly realized that the barking was coming from the marsh below. From his position atop the bluff, he could make out the shape of a man running away from a dog. The man was screaming, clearly "terrified."

Grave had stopped him at that point. "It was dark. How can you be sure of what you saw?"

McLachlan had pointed out that it was a clear night with a full moon. "Nothing more lovely than the moon reflected in the sea, but nothing more horrible than what I saw. The dog glowed like a right demon, and caught him, tore into him, and it was done, quick as that."

"And what time was this?" said Grave.

"About one o'clock or thereabouts."

"And yet you waited until near noon today to report it?"

"Yes, yes," said McLachlan, looking nervous, "I explained that to the officer. Haggis was in pieces, you see. I had his head off, working on some nuances."

"Nuances?"

"The way his lips curl when he growls. I wanted them a bit fiercer. So, as I was saying, he was in pieces, meaning I couldn't send or receive calls until I put him back together, which took the rest of the night. Haggis is a complicated bit of machinery, detective."

"And you didn't think to check on what had happened down there?"

"I was afraid of that hound. It was so quick and so violent, I just knew the man was dead."

"In the moonlight?"

"Yes."

"And did you see which way the dog went after the kill?"

McLachlan trembled. "No, it was there one minute, bright and glowing, and then it just *vanished*, like some demon, some *demon dog* from Hell."

Grave gave the man a moment to recover before proceeding. "What a wonderful view you have here. I could sit here for hours."

McLachlan took a deep breath. "I sometimes do."

"So," said Grave, "did you see anything else? A woman, and perhaps a car?"

McLachlan brightened. "Yes, yes, I had forgotten about that. There was a car, but no woman."

"And yet the car isn't there now."

McLachlan's eyes grew large. "No, it isn't. Is that important?"

Grave shrugged. "Well, the body didn't drive away in it."

"Maybe the woman you mentioned? I don't know. I didn't see one."

Grave sighed. *Yes*, he thought, *this case is* complicated.

The driverless taxi had taken its own sweet time getting to the crime scene, the sun already beginning to set as Grave climbed in, setting Barry down next to him on the seat.

Grave wondered what to make of the man's story. A demon dog? Probably just a big dog looking for love. And given the ferocity of the dog bites on the victim's body, what about Haggis and his scalpel-like teeth? Surely, he must be involved somehow. And then there's the missing car. Whose car was it? Who drove it away? And what was Wright Orville doing there in the first place?

Grave smiled. He loved this part of a case, the early hours when you tried to make sense of an overload of information.

"Any thoughts, Barry?"

Barry whirred briefly in contemplation. "None to speak of, sir. I was just recording and transmitting, as usual."

"Right."

"A couple of thoughts, though," Barry said. "First, I don't trust the man. I think maybe he's covering up something. And second, if Haggis is what the man says he is—a watchdrone—he may have recorded something."

"But he was in pieces, remember?"

"Well, was he? I think we should check, don't you?"

Barry was right. Grave added another note to his already overflowing mental notepad and changed the subject.

"So, any calls?"

Barry whirred again, then added a series of clicks. "Yes, you had a call from your father, three calls from Tilda Must—who seemed quite insistent, I must say—a call from my namesake and your partner, Barry Blunt, and six calls from Woof. It seems your dog, Lucky, is begging for bacon and the lack thereof.

Grave had made the mistake of giving Lucky bacon, and now that's all the little dog wanted. His pet drone and dog expert, Woof, should have taken care of this, offering astute veterinarian counseling to the dog.

Grave sighed. "Okay, erase all the calls from Tilda Must—I know what she wants—then play the others in order. No, wait. Erase the calls from Woof as well. I'll deal with that when we get home. Just play the calls from Blunt and my father."

"As you wish, sir. Here's your father's message."

The senior Grave, Jacob Grave, a former Crab Cove detective, now retired to curmudgeonhood, seemed more out of sorts than usual. "Answer dammit! Aw, shit. Look, Simon, I'm here with Ida, and she's receiving something, some fucking image or other that suggests to her that a murder has taken place out near the marshes. Please call. No, come over. She's in quite a state. All right, bye."

Grave sighed. The elder Grave's fiancé, Ida Notion, was a psychic whose skills were at least suspect. Still, she had hit the crime scene on the noggin, so he knew he'd have to hear what she had to say.

"Okay, Barry, delete that one but put a note on my calendar for tomorrow morning. We'll go to dad's and see what's what."

"Yes, sir. Here's the message from the other Barry, meaning not me."

Each Barry referred to the other Barry as the Other Barry, which was becoming annoying. A name change for one of them might be in order, but he hadn't decided whether to change the name of Barry or the Other Barry. "Yes, I understand that, Barry. All right, let's hear it, then."

Sergeant Barry Blunt's voice sounded strained. "Grave, I'm sorry I can't be there today. It's Rip again. A major hassle at the daycare center. I'll be in tomorrow, and we can catch up. Again, sorry sir."

Grave chuckled. Rip was Blunt's two-year-old daughter, Rippley, who supplemented her "terrible twos" with a clear and often frustrating advantage: she was completely invisible, a genetic gift, or perhaps fluke, from her parents, who were both so nondescript they were "almost invisible."

"Okay, you can delete that one, too. I'm sure Barry will fill me in at tomorrow's meeting."

"Yes, sir. That's all, then."

"Wonderful."

Grave settled back in the seat and closed his eyes, and immediately thought of the Reverend Bendigo Bottoms. He remembered their long-ago conversation on the meaning of life. If life really was like a tuna fish sandwich, as the reverend had said, Grave wondered whether that applied in a driverless car speeding along at ninety miles an hour, on a highway with a dozen other driverless cars, some so old he knew they didn't have the latest no-crash software.

He thought not. In this case, life was surely more like a mystery meat canapé: soft and gray and tasty in a strange way, but brief.

7

Woof greeted him at the curb with news of the latest lamentations of his bacon-deprived dog, Lucky. "Sir, he's just being *impossible*."

Grave stepped out of the car and gently lifted Barry into the air. "Barry, why don't you just go in and say hello to Lucky while I talk with Woof here."

Barry nodded, then sped away up the sidewalk and into the house.

"Now, Woof, what's going on?"

"I can't get him to do anything. He just lies there in your chair, curled up into a ball, moaning."

"And you're sure it's about bacon?"

"Well, of course I am. I ran a full medical scan, even did a psychological workup, and the result is that you have a dog unwilling to do anything without first receiving bacon."

"But you didn't give him bacon, right?"

"Yes, no, no bacon at all."

"Well, you're the expert. What should we do?"

Woof whirred in a way that suggested seething anger. "Sir, I'd like to suggest *once again* that we replace that intractable ball of fur with a simdog of similar aspect, one that has no need of bacon."

The appeal was nothing new. "I'm sorry, Woof, but I much prefer an actual dog over a simdog, and besides, you know that simdogs are prohibited from having pet drones."

Woof emitted a nuanced harrumph. "Well, I'm sure the Simdroid Suffrage movement will have a say about that, sir, and soon."

Grave shook his head. "Perhaps they will, perhaps they won't. Now, let's get inside. Did you do the usual?"

"Yes, sir, I fried up a pound of bacon."

"Good. Shall we?" He pointed Woof toward the door.

"Oh, very well."

Grave and Woof headed for the front door, Grave glancing wistfully at his Austin Healy Sprite, which sat at the top of the driveway, covered in a form-fitting metallic silver tarp. He wondered whether Charlize could fix the radio's tuner, so he could receive other radio stations.

He turned back to see Lucky framed in the open front door, his tail wagging wildly, the look in his eyes suggesting but one thing: bacon.

Grave sighed. *I'm such a pushover.*

8

The evening had gone about as expected, Lucky polishing off a pound of bacon and then curling himself around Grave's neck like a furry boa, one of the most endearing traits of Chesapeake Crab Retrievers, a relatively new breed cobbled together and downsized from the intermingled blood lines of Chesapeake Bay Retrievers, Rat Terriers, and Dachshunds. The result was a small, medium-haired dog with the head of a retriever, the speckled body of a rat terrier, and the exaggerated body length of a dachshund. Thus conceived, the breed was particularly suited for capturing crabs, swimming eel-like at great speed and to great depths to grasp and retrieve crabs, even softshell crabs, without doing them harm, despite the motivation the crabs provided with their claws.

Grave had no interest in Lucky's crabbing abilities. He just liked the goofy look of the dog. And besides, he was much better than those new vegetable-dog hybrids. He just couldn't see himself in the company of an emerald green Mint Terrier or a Brussels Sprouthound.

Lucky had been a parting gift from Charlize six months ago, when she had moved to a boarding house on Main Street, a few doors down from the Skunk 'n Donuts. There was no falling out between them, she just wanted to live a simdroid life closer to that of Sherlock Holmes, her hero. She had even petitioned, and won, the right to change the number on the boarding house to 221B, the same as Holmes's abode, but the town would not go along with changing Main Street to Baker Street.

Grave had come up with a name for the dog instantly, the little dog a near spitting image of the Luck Dragon in an old movie Grave particularly enjoyed: "The Neverending Story."

Not that the evening had gone entirely according to plan. He had tried to settle down with a glass of his favorite cheap wine, Duct Tape Chardonnay, *the wine that can fix anything*, but Barry had interrupted him with a phone call from Polk, who launched right into his news.

"Grave? Polk here. We've confirmed that the victim was Wright Orville."

"You're certain?"

"Yes, and I've let Captain Morgan know, so he can notify next of kin."

"Right."

"Well, then."

"Yes, goodbye then."

Polk clicked off and then the doorbell rang, sending Lucky into a barking frenzy. It was who Grave feared it would be: his father, Jacob Grave, and Jacob's fiancé, Ida Notion, who quickly put the evening into a death spiral. Ida had had a vision, it seems, and when Ida has had a vision, everyone must know that Ida has had a vision, in great detail. And she had launched right into it as soon as he had opened the door.

"Simon, call out the guards, release the hounds, there's been a murder, I'm sure of it." She said this while rushing past Grave into the living room, her signature gypsy skirt swirling, not waiting for Jacob to catch up. Her personal drone, Crystal Ball, which actually looked like a flying crystal ball ringed in red fringe at its base, hovered near her, mimicking Ida's every dramatic gesture, or at least as best as a drone can with nothing but fringe for creative expression.

The years were being less and less kind to Grave's father, and Simon thought Ida Notion was the cause. Yes, he had been a slow-moving, cantankerous old man before she came along, but now the needle of decrepitude had swung far right, into a zone that suggested death was long overdue or, in any case, that someone should at least deal with the smell of the man.

As Ida continued her rant in the living room, Grave waited patiently at the front door for his father to make his way up the only two steps to Grave's front porch.

"Hi, dad." He waved him toward the door.

Jacob Grave didn't return the greeting. "She's on a real tear tonight, Simon. Be a good fellow and get me a beer."

A voice from behind them said, "Don't bother, Simon, I'll get him a beer. I hope you have a good stout."

It was Jacob's personal drone, Bubba, which featured the simulated voice of Jacob's long-dead partner, Bubba Grace, who had exited all earthly concerns at the hands of a burglar some twenty years ago.

Grave glanced over at Barry, who was trying his best to hover as inconspicuously as possible. "Barry, give Bubba a hand, won't you."

Barry looked unhappy. "I do not have hands, Simon, but I will be happy to lend a claw or magnetic grappler to the cause."

"Whatever. Bring two beers and a small glass of brandy for Ida."

Barry nodded and buzzed away with Bubba, each racing to be first to the refrigerator-synthesizer.

"Now," said Grave, turning back to Ida. "I'm afraid I missed what you were saying. What's this about a murder?"

Ida was already seated in Grave's rocking chair, working it briskly through its repertoire of moans and creaks. "I'll wait for my brandy, thank you."

Grave nodded silently and sat opposite her in an old, uncomfortable ladder-back chair he kept in the living room for conversations like this, letting discomfort and pain be the guide for the length of the conversation. Lucky had fallen asleep draped around Grave's neck, his snore almost a purr.

Jacob Grave made his way to the couch and plopped down with a sigh that suggested both relief and pain. "Wait till you hear this one, Simon. It's a doozy."

Barry and Bubba quickly returned with the beer and brandy, and then took up watchful positions high in the corner of the room, leaving Crystal Ball to rock in the air by herself at Ida's shoulder.

Ida took a sip of the brandy, and began. "I saw a dog, a dog of massive size, almost impossibly massive, and it was tearing a man to pieces."

"How terrible," said Grave, withholding all he knew.

"Indeed," said Ida.

Jacob Grave jumped in. "Tell him about the music, Ida."

"Oh, yes," she said. "There was the strangest music, like the scream of a banshee being strangled. Eerie. Other-worldly."

"And get this, Simon," said his father, "it was a children's song."

"Let me guess," said Grave. "*The Itsy Bitsy Spider*."

Ida stopped rocking, eyes popping. "You know about it!"

"Yes, Barry and I have just come from the murder scene. But tell me, did you see anything else?"

Ida frowned. "Not much. There was a swirl of people. Let's see. A couple of dark figures, more wraiths than men. And a woman. A young woman."

"Quite a crowd," said Grave.

"Oh, no," said Ida. "They came and left, each in turn. The woman was there, and then the dog, I think, and then perhaps the wraiths. Or maybe the wraiths came first. I'm not sure. The image faded quickly."

Grave pressed her. "But you *saw* the murder?"

Ida shuddered. "The beginning, yes, but it was so violent, I had to shut it down for my own safety. These images can overwhelm someone like me."

"Let me press you a little further, Ida. Was there a car nearby, or anything really?"

Ida closed her eyes. "I didn't see a car, but there was a blanket. And a marsh. I could see the reeds and rushes and grasses swirling in the moonlight." She suddenly started, her eyes opening wide. "Oh, my god, I forgot the man in the sky."

"What?" said Grave.

"A man, big as the killer dog. He was in the sky, and he was *laughing*."

9

The ride to the station had taken longer than expected. Traffic on Main Street had been shut down for the town's parade of the day, a marketing device dreamt up by the mayor's daughter. The goal was to attract tourists from the major throughways headed to the Atlantic beaches, as well as the new Mars Terminal, but the only benefit to the town seemed to fall to the local theater group, the Crab Cove Players, who were paid handsomely for dressing up like crabs, salty crabbers, wooden mallets, and Old Bay tins, and marching in feigned jubilation down Main Street. The effect reminded Grave of one of those old commercials played at movie theaters more than a century ago, featuring cartoon characters trying to coax cinema goers to buy candy and popcorn: *Let's all go to the lobby, let's all go to the lobby.*

Sometimes, but not today, the parade would end with a V-formation of hovercycles driven by members of a "motorcycle" club known as the Sons of Irony. Grave wasn't sure what the irony was all about; perhaps it was just the fact that they didn't ride traditional, long-gone motorcycles. And, to be honest, he wasn't exactly sure what irony meant. Still, he remained suspicious of the club. They were up to no good, he was sure of that, but just what they were up to remained a mystery. He thought their participation in the parades was just a cover for some hidden, nefarious activities. And he was just as sure that he would have to face off against them in the weeks and months ahead.

The delay also gave Grave time to think of other things as well, including the laughing man in the sky. His first thought was that the man must surely be Lachlan McLachlan. Ida's visions were never very precise, so a man in the sky could easily be a man standing high upon a bluff. But the more Grave thought about it, the harder it became for him to imagine that McLachlan had a laugh in him, let alone a laugh appropriate for a murderer.

"I just don't see him and a bwa-ha-ha laugh together," he said out loud.

Barry, who had been going through his morning programming adjustments, stopped in mid-whir. "You mean McLachlan?"

Grave was startled. "I see you were paying attention last night."

"Yes, sir. Bubba is not much of a conversationalist, as you know, and Crystal Ball is a bit standoffish, so I was free to follow the conversation."

"And you think McLachlan may be our laughing man in the sky?"

"All but the laughing part, sir. He seemed on the whole quite humorless on our first meeting."

"Yes, yes, I had the same impression."

"So, if I were a detective, which I am assuredly not, I would say a man standing, or in this case laughing, on the top of a bluff would create an appropriate image in the mind of one Ida Notion."

"Or it could be someone else."

"Of course. Crab Cove of late has seen more than its share of jet-packers from the mainland, as well as flying cars."

"So it could be someone else entirely."

"Yes, although jet-packing after dark would be a clear traffic violation."

Grave chuckled. "I don't think that would worry a murderer."

"No, sir."

They both fell silent as the car lurched forward, the last strains of a tuba's oom-pah-pah fading away as they crossed Main Street and continued toward the station.

Grave suddenly sat bolt upright and screamed at the driver of the driverless car. "Faster, faster, to the station!"

Barry beeped in confusion. "Sir?"

"Don't you see, Barry, we've forgotten a known known."

Barry groaned. "Please, sir, the known knowns and known unknowns and what all are just, just—"

"Confusing. Yes, I know, but here's the thing. I've been sitting here focusing on a flying man when we've forgotten the most basic flying object."

Barry would have thrown up his hands to indicate he was perplexed by Grave's remarks, but not having hands, he just emitted a curt sound somewhere between a moan and a fog horn.

"Don't you see," said Grave. "We have a murder victim, but *where* is his personal drone?"

"Oh," said Barry, who then wobbled in a way that suggested a second thought. "Of course, he had no personal effects, so maybe the murderer took the drone as well."

Grave puffed out his cheeks and sighed. "Yes, yes, perhaps you're right."

Barry sensed Grave's disappointment at an easily thwarted *ah-hah* moment. "Of course, you could be right, sir."

Grave said nothing. The car sped on.

10

The Massey-Ross Behemoth Gigantix 6000, commonly referred to as the MRBG 6000 by technicians and simply as "Mr. Big" by the detectives who relied on it, would have been a wonderful addition to the investigation tools available to the Crab Cove Police Department. Its crime-solving prowess was legendary, ringing up success rates approaching 98 percent and solution times of an unheard-of average of three days, regardless of the crime.

Unfortunately, the Crab Cove Police Department didn't have an MRBG 6000; it had an MRBG 3000, which was accurately dubbed the "Mr. Bug." Its success rates were fifty-two percent and 312 days, respectively, not much better than a coin toss. Even so, Captain Morgan relished its one advantage: it had been free, a hand-me-down from the Baltimore Police Force, gladly accepted.

Unlike Mr. Big, which despite its moniker was no bigger than a man's overstuffed wallet, Mr. Bug weighed in at a relatively humongous 512 pounds, with dimensions approximating a four-drawer filing cabinet. Despite its size, Captain Morgan had insisted it be placed in his already cramped office, so he would have immediate access to its analyses, perorations, and prognostications. Morgan liked the way its dull gray exterior matched his equally dull gray desk. And besides, the top of Mr. Bug provided more than 400 additional square inches of display space for his Captain Morgan Rum collectibles, or as it did today, a suitable landing pad for Rum, his personal drone, who looked the part: trimmed in red and gold, a tiny sword attached to its side, a black beard outlining a face with eye decals, all topped with a red tricorn hat that sat neatly between its rotors. Rum didn't have the swash and buckle of the man on the label of Captain Morgan Rum or the rum for that matter, but he had a certain panache, at least in the eyes of his owner.

A significant downside to Mr. Bug, however, was that it restricted Captain Morgan's signature pacing. Where once he could take several strides, turn, and stride again, now he could only turn and turn again, giving him the appearance of a dysfunctional figurine on a Swiss cuckoo clock.

Morgan turned and turned again. "We'll give Grave a couple more minutes. No sense doing this twice."

He sat back down behind his desk and looked pensively at his fingernails, looking up every few seconds to make sure everyone was still in the room. Each time he saw the same two officers, Detective Amanda Snoot, whose personal drone Goth hovered just above her head, and Sergeant Barry Blunt. But as always, Blunt was no more than a suggestion of a sitting man, his entire being cloaked by trenchant nondescriptitude. If Blunt's personal drone, Object, hadn't been hovering nearby, the captain would have been hard-pressed to say anyone was sitting in the chair opposite him.

Detective Snoot was another matter entirely. If Blunt was nearly invisible, Amanda Snoot was almost too much there. Thin as a rail, with an oversized head, she was what Grave called "a walking doorknob," albeit a doorknob with an explosion of close-cropped, rust-colored hair that dominated her clothes, which were universally black, from shirt to slacks to shoes. Such was her dour beauty that coming upon her unawares would invariably make a person startle and jump back. So, too, was her drone, Goth, a fist-sized rotorless drone that hovered wraith-like near her shoulder, shimmering like patent leather. In the two years Snoot had been on the force, she had gained the respect of everyone, including Grave, at least to a point. He was sure she was the one who snagged the chocolate donut every morning.

Morgan caught sight of Detective Grave heading their way by the same circuitous route he always took, eschewing a straight-line approach in favor of a quick turn to the left to get a cup of coffee and a chocolate donut. As always, he had arrived to find an empty coffee pot and a donut box equally empty except for a few smears of icing.

Morgan waved at him, and Grave responded with a nod and headed to Morgan's office, trailed by his drone, Barry.

"Grave, about time," said Morgan. "Take a seat and let's get to it."

Grave glanced around. "Where's Charlize and Smithers?"

"Not on the case, at least not yet," said Morgan.

Grave smiled. "Still hasn't found the cat, eh?"

"Oh, no," said Morgan, "she found the cat, all right. She's with Tilda in the briefing room, doing a case dump and review."

Grave frowned. He'd have to do the same thing if he couldn't figure out a way to escape Tilda's clutches.

"Good," said Grave, "good, good."

"All right, then," said Morgan. "You'll be working the case with Blunt, as usual, with help from Detective Snoot."

Grave tried his best to force out a smile in Snoot's direction, but his lips and jaw muscles only managed a polite grimace, which was returned with double effect by Snoot, who was no fan of Grave's.

"I'm thrilled, too," she said, folding her arms and looking away from Grave.

"Well, peachy," said Morgan. "Let's at least play nice on the case, shall we?" He raised his eyebrows, kept them there, and turned to face each of them, so they could see that his eyebrows were dead serious about what he had just said and that they better damn well comply and indicate so with a nod of the head.

They each nodded in turn.

Morgan looked back and forth at them one last time to make sure his eyebrows had done their work, and finally, let them drop back into his sad face. "Good. Charlize and Smithers will be joining the case as soon as they're finished, probably later today. Now, let's get on with it. We've input all the data from all sources: Polk, the CSI team, crime scene drones, and the information you streamed last night, Grave, about our friend on the bluff, Lachlan McLachlan. So, we've got the known knowns and so on. Now, let's see what the MRBG 3000 can tell us."

He walked over to Mr. Bug and punched three buttons labeled one, two, and three, a helpful aid in case someone couldn't figure out the sequence.

Mr. Bug flickered to life with the help of an array of nonfunctional but nevertheless impressive green lights, a sure sign that Morgan had indeed pressed the one-two-three buttons in the proper sequence. The lights, which continued to flash and blink, were followed by a series of clicks, which were followed by a hum, which was followed by a tiny bell, which was followed by a burning smell, which was followed finally by a message on its small message screen.

The message was: *Processing. This may take two minutes or perhaps longer.*

Below the message, on a separate screen, a new message began to appear a letter at a time. This, as they had all learned on their first day with the machine, was the while-you're-waiting message, which was typically a famous quotation designed to be thoughtful while time-consuming.

That message said: *"A really good detective never gets married."* (Raymond Chandler)

Grave puffed out a sigh, Blunt grunted in a negative but measured way, and Snoot rolled her eyes.

"What is this thing," said Snoot, "a frickin' Magic 8-Ball?"

Morgan frowned back at her. "It is the future, detective—the *future.*"

"So," said Grave, "shall we discuss the case while we're waiting for Mr. Bug here?"

Morgan pointed a finger, a messenger of his anger, at Grave. "Don't call him that. He's the MRBG 3000."

"Well, he's more like a Mr. Bug if you ask me," said Blunt, in a rare show of emotion, albeit emotion coming from a nearly invisible man-shaped area across the room.

The sniping back and forth ended abruptly as Mr. Bug, who was designed with drama in mind, issued his I'm-Done gong, which over the years had lost its ring of authority. It sounded more like a cymbal dropped on a carpet. A new message began appearing on the second screen, replacing the Raymond Chandler quotation.

The new message read: *Ask again later.*

Snoot threw up her hands. "Frickety frickin' Magic 8-Ball!"

Morgan reflexively slapped the top of Mr. Bug hard, hoping that blunt force trauma would coax a solution from the machine, which had hummed and clicked its way to silence, its screens now blank. All he managed to do was startle Rum, who sped away to the far corner of the office.

Morgan tried to recover. "All right, *all right,* it's a bit early for a solution. I think we can all understand that."

No one said anything.

"So, let's to the tasks at hand."

Grave interrupted. "Sir, if I may?"

Morgan squinted at him. "Yes?"

"I have two additional bits of information. First, when I was driving in this morning, a thought came to me: where's the victim's drone?"

Morgan seemed startled at first, then smiled. "Yes, his drone. Of course, maybe the murderer took it."

Grave could hear Barry stifling a told-you-so buzz. "Yes, and there's more. I had a conversation with Ida Notion last night, and—"

Morgan threw up his hands. "Stop right there, Grave. We're not going the psychic route on this one. It's all just *nonsense*."

Grave held up a single finger. "I know how you feel about this, sir, but what she said was uncanny, almost a verbatim account of what we saw and what Charlize deduced, or abduced, or reduced, or *whatever*— with one additional clue."

Morgan was both intrigued and wary. "A clue? Well, come on, then, let me have it."

"She said she saw a man in the sky. That could be the victim's drone, or someone with a jet pack, or even someone in a flying car."

"Or just her vivid imagination," said Morgan, rocking back in his chair. "Let's stick to the facts. The known knowns."

"Yes, sir," said Grave. "Here's what I'd suggest."

Morgan began nodding as Grave spoke, his plan more than reasonable.

11

The team dispersed, each focused on their marching orders. Blunt would accompany Grave to interview the widow. This case seemed to have domestic roots, so starting with her seemed the right way to begin. The investigation could then branch out from there. One of those branches would be tackled immediately by Detective Snoot, who would visit the victim's company to see if anything business-related might be in play. Captain Morgan, for his part, would do his usual part, which meant sitting behind his desk and waiting.

The thing about dispersal, however, is that it is best done quickly. Detective Snoot seemed to sense that and was through the squad room and out the front door before Grave had managed to find and collect Sergeant Blunt. Lack of speed meant that he was grabbed by the arm by Retective Tilda Must as soon as he walked out of Captain Morgan's office.

"Grave, a word," she said, tightening her grip and pulling him toward the briefing room. "Sergeant, you can wait at your desk," she said, directing Blunt with a jabbing motion that Blunt interpreted as decisive.

"But I'm on a case now," said Grave, struggling to break free, with not a smidgeon of success. Simdroids had the grip strength of a hungry eagle.

"First things first. Now get in there." She released her grip with a shove high on the scale of *shovingness*, sending him flailing into the briefing room.

Charlize and Smithers were on their way out.

"Grave, I found the cat," said Charlize.

"Good for you," said Grave. "I don't suppose you can find me an exit."

"Oh, Grave, just cooperate. It's entirely painless—and necessary."

She signaled to Smithers. "Come on, we need to talk to Captain Morgan about this man-on-the-marsh case."

Grave groaned. He wanted this case to himself, and he certainly didn't want someone coming along and naming the case for him. "Don't you have other cats to find?"

"If she did," said Tilda, glaring at him, "she would do it by the book, according to police procedure, with speed and efficacy, and unlike a certain detective I could name."

Grave noted that she had trouble pronouncing efficacy, which through some programming error, came out *efficasuhsuhcy*, a polysyllabic infarction of sorts.

Tilda pointed at the chair. "Take a seat, and let's begin."

Grave sighed and sat. "Very well."

Tilda sat opposite him, the empty table between them.

Grave sighed again.

"Nervous, are we?"

Simdroids are incapable of real emotions, but the latest models, including Tilda, could simulate even the most nuanced facial expressions, as she did now, a look of evil joy or joyful evil on her face.

Grave felt like a frog about to be dissected, but he steeled himself in silence, not a single *ribbit* escaping his lips.

"So," she began, "once upon a time, in a town called Crab Cove, there was a murder most foul..."

12

Detective Snoot was happy to be out of the station. Despite her affection for the color black, she was a sun-worshipping surfer on her days off, known throughout the small surfer community as "Twiggy," which she had been told was a reference to a thin model of the previous century. To her, it just meant another reference to her preternatural thinness.

Her assigned hovercruiser awaited, but it was such a warm and pleasant day, she decided on a different mode of transportation.

"Let's take the hoverboard, Goth."

Goth, nodded in a way to suggest acknowledgment and apprehension.

"Don't worry, I won't get too far ahead."

Snoot popped the trunk, slipped the board out of its protective case, and hit the activation button. The board hummed and vibrated loudly before settling down to a purr in her hands.

"Greetings," said the board. It was a police hoverboard, so like other police drones and simdroids, his voice was that of late actor Morgan Freeman, and like all the others, his name was Larry. "Please select a program."

Snoot punched in the code for freestyle boarding.

"Excellent choice," said Larry. "Do you have the requisite certifications for this mode? If so, please enter your cert code now."

Snoot punched in the code.

"Wonderful to have you onboard again, Detective Snoot. And do let me say how much I love your footwork."

"Good to be aboard, Larry," she said.

"Will Goth be coming?"

"Yes."

"I'll try not to go too fast, then."

"Don't worry about Goth."

"As you wish. So, do we have a destination or are you just going to wing it?"

"A destination. I'll enter it now." She fumbled with the piece of paper that contained the address of C3 Corporation, and entered it into Larry's system.

Larry buzzed and clicked as she entered the data, then resumed his normal hum. "The trip will take seven to twenty minutes, depending on your route selection. Do you wish the fast, straight route or the slow, scenic route?"

Snoot smiled. "Let's do the *fast*, scenic route."

"As you wish," said Larry as brightly as he was programmed to do. "Shall I include fence vaulting in the mix?"

"Yes, and house jumping as well," said Snoot, positioning the board and climbing on.

"Zoom-zoom," said Larry, and they were off.

13

Grave tapped his fingers on the table, waiting for Retective Must to launch into her interrogation. She called it a debriefing, but it was an interrogation, all right.

"So," she began, "the topic at hand is the Hawthorne Mansion Murders."

Grave was incredulous. "What? That was years ago."

"It's just our starting point, one illustrative of a theme that runs through each of your criminal investigations."

"Oh?" Try as he might, the one-syllable question came out more like a threat.

"I know you disagree with retection in all its forms, detective, but the rules are the rules, and here we are, and here we must proceed."

"Get on with it then. What is this so-called *theme* of mine?"

"We'll get to that. First, a question."

Grave crossed his arms. "Go on, then."

"Would you agree, detective, that if we use as our starting point, the endpoint in a murder investigation, namely the conviction and sentencing of the perpetrator, and then work our way backwards to the actual commission of the crime, along the way we will be presented with evidence and the detection of that evidence in a logical, coherent way, albeit in reverse order?"

Grave looked bewildered. "I have no idea what you just said."

"Come now, detective."

"I don't, I really don't."

Retective Must let out a mechanical sigh. "Okay, let me simplify it for you. Would you agree that the collection and evaluation of evidence in a proper, logical way, leads to the apprehension of a criminal."

Grave was about to shrug his shoulders and offer an alternative view when Captain Morgan, eyes in full bug, burst into the room.

"Grave," he shouted. "Come quick."

Must was incensed. "Captain, I must *insist*."

"Later Tilda, there's been another murder."

He turned back to Grave. "Lachlan McLachlan, the bagpiper on the bluff."

Grave was already out of his seat and running for the door.

14

Grave tried his best to get comfortable in Sergeant Blunt's new hovercruiser, but it was one of the new old driverless ones they'd inherited from the Baltimore police, who had moved on to flying cars. Not even the amusing graffiti left by unattended miscreants on the inside panels of the passenger compartment had stemmed Grave's fear of a sudden collision and death in which he would no doubt have to part ways with several of his limbs.

"What are we, Blunt, the hand-me-down capital of criminal investigation?"

Blunt startled. "What?"

"Nothing."

They grew silent again, which was not unusual when they were on a case, and things needed sorting out. They had two murders now, or at least two killings, and the only person who'd been interviewed was the second victim. Grave wondered what manner of man or machine was capable of taking down the mountain of a man that was Lachlan McLachlan.

"So," said Blunt, "I'm a beat behind you on this case, what with my problems with Rip."

Grave nodded. "Not much to catch up on, really. How is Rip?"

Blunt's curt chuckle was more sardonic than he had intended. "Oh, Rip is fine. She's always fine, but her mischief..." He let the words hang there.

"I hear that's to be expected. Don't they call it the terrible twos?"

"Indeed, they do, sir, and let me tell you, it's way more terrible when the two in question is invisible."

"So what did she do this time?"

"I'd rather not get into it, sir. Can we just focus on the problem at hand?"

Grave shrugged. "You sure?"

"Yes, it's pretty embarrassing, sir."

"All right, then, let me tell you about Mr. McLachlan, who was in my estimation, the worst bagpipe player I have ever encountered."

The hovercruiser sped on. Grave, with help from Barry, filled Blunt to the brim.

15

A typical crime scene is a place of order, the area secured, each movement controlled, each procedure fully considered, each action intentional. The crime scene that greeted Grave and Blunt, however, was one of pure chaos. Simdroid officers named Larry were running this way and that as police drone Larrys dived and weaved and wobbled and darted about, seemingly without reason.

Grave could see Polk and his CSI team huddled behind their van, peering over its hood to watch the action, along with Captain Morgan, Charlize, Smithers, and Snoot. Polk's drone, Simon, his name no doubt a poke at Grave, hovered nearby, along with Rum and Goth, all wise enough to stay out of the action.

Snoot? thought Grave. *What's she doing here? She should be at C3.* He filed the thought away for future consideration and turned back to the problem at hand.

Grave knew that shouting *Larry* in the midst of a crime scene was a bad thing to do, but he was about to do just that when he caught sight of the reason for all the chaos.

Haggis, McLachlan's personal drone, in full watchdog mode, was lashing out at anyone and anything who came near him. He was hovering over the body of McLachlan, who even sprawled on the ground was a mass to be reckoned with.

Grave raced toward him, arms raised, trying to think of the shutoff command, the code word McLachlan had used to turn Haggis into a compliant drone. He knew it was an F-word, but not that F-word, not the F-bomb.

"Flim-flam," he shouted.

Haggis continued in full rage mode.

"Fiddle-faddle!"

Nothing.

Grave went on to try feathers, fecundity, fedora, falafel, falderal, even fenestration, to no effect. Then it came to him.

"Fiddle-de-dee!"

Haggis stopped in his tracks.

Grave approached him cautiously. "Guard mode off, phone mode on, hover, and follow."

Haggis wagged his mechanical tail and hovered at Grave's side.

Grave turned to the others, who were making their way toward him, not sure if their safety was a thing of certainty.

"It's all right," said Grave. "He's okay." He looked down at Haggis. "Albeit a bit bloody." He looked down again. "And missing his head." *How was that possible?*

Polk was the first to get close to the body. "Bite marks. A lot of them."

Charlize and Smithers came next. "What about slashes. Was a knife involved?"

"Yes," said Polk. "But no, this is definitely not a Clinker. Not his signature at all."

The news was not what Charlize wanted to hear. She wanted to be on this case, but a connection to serial killer Chester Clink would have been even better. She would have much preferred to be chasing him, without Grave or the others. She knelt down and touched what remained of Lachlan McLachlan. "Time of death, 8:37 p.m., give or take a minute." She stood back up and took a step back from the body, reluctantly making way for Grave.

Grave peered down at Haggis. "So Haggis here is the killer?"

Polk gave him an odd look. "Are you serious?"

Grave shrugged. "Of course."

"Well, look again. You might notice that both the victim and this mechanical flying dog here are missing their heads."

Grave looked down at McLachlan and then back at Haggis. "Oh. Oh." He grew silent for some seconds, trying to parse out the possibilities, which seemed to have gone rogue in his head and disappeared.

"Wait," he said at last. "What about all the blood on Haggis?"

Polk and Charlize pulled out their DNA scanners.

"Not human," said Polk.

"Actually, dog's blood," said Charlize.

"Yes," said Polk. "A mix of mastiff and bloodhound."

Grave frowned. "Two dogs?"

"No," said Charlize, "the dog was a mutt, a blend of mastiff and bloodhound."

Grave nodded. "What would you call that? A masthound? A bloodtiff?"

"Well," said Polk, "I'd call it strange, because the blood on McLachlan here is all his own, and only a few of the bite wounds have traces of the masthound's blood."

"Odd," said Charlize. "You know, it reminds me of Sherlock's famous cases, *The Hound of the Baskervilles*."

"Because of the dog?" said Grave.

"Because of the dog's DNA." She closed her eyes and then began reciting a line from the story, using the voice of Basil Rathbone. *"It was not a pure bloodhound, and it was not a pure mastiff; but it appeared to be a combination of the two—gaunt, savage, and as large as a small lioness."*

"Interesting," said Grave. "McLachlan here, when he had a head, talked about a demon hound trying to mate with one of his mastiffs, and—" Grave suddenly stopped and spun around, scanning the scene. "Where's Fred?"

Captain Morgan, who had been trying to follow the details with some difficulty, suddenly chirped: "Who's Fred?"

"His dog," said Grave. "A pure-bred mastiff, and huge."

Morgan took off his hat and ran his hand over his bald head. "Damn. So we're looking for a dog, a drone dog's head, and the victim's head."

"And the murderer, of course," said Blunt, who had finally found his voice.

"Wait," said Morgan. "Let's start at the beginning." He turned to Detective Snoot. "Snoot, you were first on the scene. What did you see?"

"No, wait," said Grave. "Why are you even here? I thought you were going to C3 Corporation."

"I was," said Snoot, "but the hoverboard had a mind of its own. Halfway there, it suddenly changed direction, and despite my protests, brought me here."

"Standard procedure," said Morgan. "The call went out, and it had to respond."

Charlize stepped forward, gently nudging the captain aside. "Did you see more than we've seen?"

Snoot shook her head. "The scene was just as you see it, except for one thing. Haggis here was hovered over the body, protecting it. When CSI arrived, of course, all hell broke loose." She gave Polk an admonishing look.

"We were just trying to do our job," said Polk.

"And Haggis was headless?" said Charlize.

"Yes," said Snoot. "It's mystifying. How could he even move without a head?"

Sergeant Blunt appeared, or rather almost appeared, beside them. "It's a new-new thing in drone technology. June was telling me about it just the other day. Ramrod Robotics is also working on it. They call it Distributed Intelligence, or DI."

"Dis-what?" said Morgan.

"Distributed Intelligence, sir," said Blunt. "It's a project for the military. Think about it. If an enemy shoots the drone's head, no more drone. But if the drone's intelligence is spread throughout its limbs, rotors, and systems, it will stay in the fight until the last bolt."

"Whoa," said Morgan.

"Indeed," said Blunt.

Morgan turned back to Polk. "Anything more from the scene?"

Polk smiled. "Oh, yes. Although I haven't had a chance to look at it."

"At what?" said Morgan.

"That," said Polk, pointing at the body.

Morgan looked confused, so Polk tried again. "That folder, sir. He's lying on a folder."

Charlize beat Grave to the body and pulled out the folder, giving the contents a cursory look. "Diagrams. Formulas. Specs for what appears to be a Haggis on steroids."

"Let me see that," said Morgan.

Charlize reluctantly handed him the folder. Morgan rifled through it and then handed it to Grave. "Here, Grave, it's your case, it's your evidence."

Charlize groaned. "But sir, I want to be on this case. That folder could have clues, and as you well know sir, it has always been an axiom of Sherlock's that the little things are infinitely the most important."

Morgan didn't like her tone, and couldn't remember what an axiom was, so he growled back at her. "Who said you *weren't* on this case? Listen, we've got two dead bodies, a missing dog, and two missing heads, not to mention one or more murderers. It's every man on deck for this one, you and Smithers included. But I want Grave in charge. Do you have a problem with that?"

She did, but she still said, "No."

"Fine, then. Grave, get this thing started—and finished—as quickly as you can. I'll expect a report from you in the morning."

Morgan turned and headed for his hovercruiser, Rum breaking away from the other drones and following at Morgan's shoulder.

"Yes, sir," said Grave.

Morgan stopped and turned back. "And Polk, any chance we can have more information by tomorrow morning?"

Polk nodded. "I'll do my best."

Morgan nodded back, strode to his car, and drove away.

Grave waited until the car crested a hill and disappeared. "Well, then, here's what we're going to do."

16

Every advance in technology comes with at least one unintended consequence. In the case of drones, the victors over cellphones, what followed was SDAD, or Seasonal Drone Affective Disorder, a syndrome that blossomed in the summer season, when tourists and drones stormed into town. It afflicted many people, particularly in Crab Cove, a town where change was something best whispered, and only in the right company.

A perfect example was the woman sitting across from Grave, one Prissy Orville, widow of Wright Orville. There was simply no way to describe her without starting with her SDAD affliction, which came with sound-elimination earphones to protect her from the buzz and whir and other "hideous" sounds that drones make, as well as go-blind goggles that prevented her from seeing anything, including drones, heaven forefend.

There was not much to say about her face, except that it was mostly unavailable. You couldn't see her eyes, and the goggles were so large, there was not much of a nose to see, either. Still, she had long, silky blond hair and a shapely chin, which went nicely with her shapely body, which Siwas on near full display in a shimmering black unitard so popular with the neo-yoga set, an exercise regimen and mind-body experience performed entirely while hanging from one ankle over a tank of water.

Grave had for some minutes been trying to explain his presence at her mansion, which was surprisingly close to the old Hawthorne

Mansion, where he had first met Smithers. Her inability to hear or see, however, had been an obstacle, particularly in gaining entrance. It had required the help of her simdroid gardener, Lesley, who looked like someone who should be famous, although neither Grave nor Blunt could figure out just who that might be. His voice was pleasant enough, though, and he was very apologetic about the situation.

He had let them in—all except Barry and Object, of course—and then escorted them to Prissy, who was midway through a neo-yoga pose involving extreme contortion and the flexing of the muscles in her derriere, a position she referred to as Rumpus One.

Lesley had managed to get her down from her shackle and change the settings on her earphones and goggles to permit at least a vague awareness of sights and sounds, but even so, conversation was painfully long, with many stops and restarts for clarification.

His latest question had puzzled her at first, but Grave had quickly clarified.

"Yes, yes," she finally said with a chuckle. "I thought you said *enemas*. But yes, he did indeed have enemies, many enemies."

She went on to list them. First and foremost was his top competitor, Chance Fortuna, CEO of DroneOn Corporation. "I've never actually seen or heard the man, of course, but I met him at a cocktail party once. Very short, given the direction of his voice, and oh, his smell. Like boiled gym socks."

Next on her list was the entire staff of Wright Orville's company, C3 Corporation. "He was universally hated. I think that goes with brilliance sometimes, don't you? People are just jealous. Still, Wright could be a right bastard. In fact, he was most of the time. Even his simdroids hated him."

And then there were the family members, most notably Wright's brother, Frank, who served as C3's COO. "They just didn't get along. I could see Frank killing him, just to get his hands on the company."

And Frank's wife, Wanda. "A classic gold-digger. I'm not sure how she would benefit from Wright's death, but she's a schemer, that one. She could find a way."

And Wright's father, Irving Orville, the retired founder of the company, affectionately known as Irv-Orv. "I call him Daddy-O, and he's a real piece of work, let me tell you. Hates retirement and would like nothing more than to be CEO again, on *his* terms."

And Prissy's and Wright's son, Right. "He may as well be part of a video game. You know, those horrific ones. Blood and guts. Shoot 'em ups. I know he's my son, but there's something odd about him. And naming him Right was wrong, dead wrong. He's only twelve, but I could see him killing Wright—or *me*—for that alone."

And Prissy herself. "I won't lie to you, detective. He was not my first choice in a husband, and he's proved to be the last person on earth anyone would want to marry. Of course, with this affliction of mine, this SDAD business, I'd be hard-pressed to see or hear him well enough to strike a blow. Have I mentioned that he was a bastard?"

Grave assured her that she had, and was about to wrap up the interview when Sergeant Blunt came back into the room. Because of Prissy's sensory limitations, Grave had quietly instructed Blunt to have a look-see around the house. From the way Blunt was shrugging, or seemed to be shrugging—it was hard to be sure what this cloud of a man was ever doing—Grave was confident Blunt had found nothing of importance.

He turned back to Prissy. "Thank you for your time, Ms. Orville. I'll let myself out."

He stood and motioned Blunt toward the door.

"What did you say?" said Prissy.

"I said I'm going," said Grave.

"Snowing? In *summer?*"

Grave started to clarify but stopped. The back and forth could have gone on indefinitely. Instead, he motioned for Blunt to follow him out of the house.

"Well, at least everyone liked him," said Blunt once they were outside.

"Indeed."

"What next, sir?"

There were so many directions to go. Too damned many directions. "Listen, I think we need to split up now. Take the folder and show those plans to June. See if she or Ramrod Robotics knows anything about, you know, what-did-you-call-it?"

"Distributed Intelligence."

"Yes, and what McLachlan may have been up to. I'll head over to C3 Corporation. Talk to Orville's brother. Get a sense of the company— and the man."

Blunt seemed to be nodding. "Very well, sir. Why don't you and Barry take the hovercruiser? I'll give June a call, and she can just pick me and Object up. I'm sure she'll want to sort this out at Ramrod's lab, and we're already halfway there."

"Okay," said Grave. "And speaking of calling, where are those silly drones of ours?"

Blunt whistled, then shouted, "Object!"

His drone appeared first from behind the house, followed almost immediately by Barry.

There was something about the way they hovered close to one another, almost conspiratorially, that gave Grave pause. Sometimes technology had a mind of its own, and who knew what it was thinking or where it was headed?

17

Charlize had heard that two heads were better than one, but in the case of missing heads, she doubted the old saying applied.

Grave had run off to talk to the widow, leaving her and Smithers and Snoot behind at the scene. Snoot was keen to explore the system of caves beneath the bluff.

"I used to play in them as a child. The entrance is right at the water's edge, and they'd make as good a place as any to hide something. And a fine home for that so-called demon dog everyone's talking about."

Charlize was not so sure the search would lead to anything, but she was happy to have the crime scene to herself. She wanted a closer look at McLachlan's kennels and house. "Okay, but keep Goth's channel open so I can monitor your progress. And look carefully. Remember what Sherlock always says: *the world is full of obvious things which nobody by any chance observes.*"

Snoot didn't like Charlize's arrogance, the way she always took command, or even her damned quotations, but the precaution was warranted. "Right."

Snoot motioned to her drone. "Come on, Goth. Set to open channel. Scanner on. Recorder on."

"Open, on, on," said Goth.

Charlize watched them go, then turned to Smithers. "Keep your channel open as well, so we can keep track of her."

"Of course," said Smithers.

"Well, then, let's have a look at those kennels."

"What are we looking for?"

"I have no idea, but remember, *it is a capital mistake to theorize before one has data.*"

Smithers knew the rest well. *"Insensibly one begins to twist facts to suit theories, instead of theories to suit facts."*

"Indeed, Watson, indeed."

They moved away from the immediate crime scene, being careful not to disturb anything, and made their way up the hill to McLachlan's home and kennels. As they climbed, Charlize scanned both sides of the path, hoping to find a clue that might unravel the crime or at least help reveal the chain of events that led to the murder.

What had led McLachlan down the hill? Why was he carrying that folder? Was he meeting someone? Running from someone?

As they crested the hill, McLachlan's white clapboard house came into sight, beside it, the large fenced-in kennels, where half a dozen mastiffs began their barking appeal for food.

"Watson, put a call in to animal control."

"Yes, sir." He was long past the point of caring whether she called him Watson or Smithers or Smithers-Watson. He now answered to any name at all, and when she was on the hunt, he knew it was best that he not challenge her. He stepped to the side and talked briefly into his hand.

Charlize continued with her instructions. "I don't want them taken away. Just get someone who knows dogs to watch over them for the next few days. My god, they're *huge.*"

Smithers nodded and talked into his hand again before turning back to her. "They're sending a vet's assistant. Should be here in half an hour or so."

"Good. All right, then, let's have a look in the house."

They moved to the closest door, which was wide open.

"He must have left in a hurry. He wasn't headed for a meeting with anyone, Smithers. He was running."

The door led to the kitchen, which could have been an exemplar for the bachelor life. Everything was such a jumble, it was hard to figure out what part of the mess was made recently.

"Wow," she said. "Neatness was not one of his talents."

Smithers was about to agree, but a scream came out of him instead. It wasn't his scream. It was the scream of Detective Snoot coming across the open channel.

Neither Charlize nor Smithers had the capacity for fear, but they knew it when they saw it. Or heard it.

They raced out of the house.

18

The ride to the headquarters of C3 Corporation, a near illusion of glass and steel that stretched the limits of the word *building* and any concept of geometry, was thankfully swift. Grave and Barry barely had time to send off his data recordings to Mr. Bug, who he knew would be delighted with the possibilities presented by Prissy Orville. He could see Mr. Bug's message screen lighting up now: *Everyone is guilty!*

After some confusion on the location of the entrance to the C3 building and a rather long wait at reception, a drone had appeared to guide him and Barry to the office of Frank Orville, brother of the deceased, and its company's chief operations officer. Along the way, the drone Dolores, a state-of-the-art rotorless drone of recent manufacture, droned on about the history of the company. Grave could tell that Barry was in awe of her, this shimmering, rotorless vision in chrome. So much so that the old-fashioned, four-rotor drone remained strangely quiet throughout her spiel.

"From its roots as Crab Cove Corporation, maker of fine robotic vacuums, to its emergence as Crab Cove Cellular, a serious player in the cellphone industry, to its unparalleled preeminence in the brave new world of rotorless drones, C3 has one goal, and one goal only, in mind."

Grave's first thought was *money*, but Dolores finished her thought with, "*Service*. From our quality products to our quality helpline, to our quality 24/7/365 technical support, our goal is to provide the absolute *best* in drone technology to serve our customers. Yes, *service* is our goal, and better and better service is what drives us in our relentless quest to serve."

Grave thought she was finished, but she added, "Service, service, service—that's us. Ah, here we are, Detective Grave, the office of my master."

Dolores issued a series of clicks and the office door, a thick piece of glass with "Frank Orville, COO" etched in glass, in a type font named Profundity, rose straight up into the ceiling and disappeared.

Dolores led him and Barry into the office, which was even more confusing than the exterior of the building. After some moments, he caught sight of his quarry, Frank Orville, sitting behind a hunk of glass geometry that set new standards for the word *desk*.

Unlike his tall, muscular brother, Frank Orville was short and nearly as thin as Detective Snoot. Like Snoot's, his head was overly large, giving it the appearance of a balloon on a string. Wide-set eyes—one blue, one brown—a vertical slice of a nose, and a matching horizontal slice of a mouth completed the balloon face. Grave couldn't imagine him performing any act of physical effort, let alone physical violence.

"Frank, may I introduce Detective Simon Grave of the Crab Cove Police Department, Detective Badge 667, who is here to ask you questions about your brother, now sadly deceased."

Frank Orville sighed and stretched his hand across the lump of glass to shake Grave's hand. "Howdy."

Grave took the man's hand in his and dialed up a handshake in the three-out-of-ten firmness range, which he found to be a polite grasp in most cases. *Howdy, indeed*, he thought. For some reason, the man was dressed up like a cowboy, ten-gallon hat and all—*even chaps!*—and Grave's obvious surprise wasn't lost on him.

"Ah, the outfit," Orville said. "It's Casual Cowboy Day, something we do here from time to time, usually when the boys have a gig in town."

"The boys?" said Grave, looking around for a chair and finding none.

"Yes, my foreman and his team are re-creation simdroids, and damned good."

"Re-creation? Of what?"

"Ah," said Orville with a sly smile. "Let's keep that a surprise, shall we? I'll introduce you when we take the tour."

"The tour?"

Orville spread his arms wide. "Of this, the company, our manufacturing floor—what we do here, detective. Surely, you want as much background as possible, correct?"

Grave nodded. "Yes, a tour would be fine, but first I have a few questions, if I may." He looked around again for a chair. "I don't suppose you have a guest chair."

Orville chuckled. "Of course."

A chair, also of strangely shaped glass, suddenly rose from the floor.

"Isn't that amazing?" said Orville. "I never get tired of it. Oh, if you could have seen the look on your face. No chair. Chair. *Priceless.*"

19

When the engineers at Ramrod Robotics designed and built Charlize, they gave her the beauty of actress Charlize Theron, the strength of a bull, the eyes of an eagle, the speed of a cheetah, and the grace of a gazelle. Thus equipped with this menagerie of traits and skills, she was standing beside Snoot by the time the detective's scream had changed to an uproarious giggle, the abrupt change in mood prompted by the same stimulus: a dog of immense size, now rolling around the floor of the cave with her.

"Isn't he marvelous?" Snoot said between paroxysms.

Charlize nodded, but it was an analytical nod, not a nod of affirmation or appreciation. "A bloodhound-mastiff mix smeared with phosphorescent clay to simulate the demon dog in *The Hound of the Baskervilles*."

"Funny you should say that. That's what his tag says. *Baskerville*. His name's Baskerville."

Charlize nodded again, taking in the information. Someone, it seemed, appreciated Sir Arthur Conan Doyle as much as she did.

She turned back to the situation at hand. "What was that scream about?"

"He surprised me. Came at me howling, teeth bared. I thought I was a goner."

"And why aren't you?"

"He wasn't after me. He was after Goth, my drone." Snoot pointed to a pile of metal parts along the wall of the cave. "And he got him."

"That's more than one drone."

"Yes, quite a pile. I suspect we might even find the personal drone of Mr. Orville, or what's left of it."

"Good. We'll take it with us. Get someone to sort it out. There could be data, images, sound perhaps." She looked back toward the cave entrance. "Where is Smithers?"

As if on cue, Smithers suddenly appeared in silhouette as he raced into the cave, coming to an abrupt halt beside them but still trying to catch up on all he now saw. "Oh, my, you are fast. Whose dog is this? What's all that junk over there? Where's the emergency?"

Charlize quickly brought him up to speed, then instructed him to collect the remains of Goth and the other drones for further analysis.

Smithers opened his doctor's bag and shoved the pieces in, filling the bag to overflowing. "That should do it. I say, I don't suppose you've seen the head of McLachlan's drone, or perhaps McLachlan's head?"

Snoot shook her head. "No, just Baskerville and the other unfortunate drones, and of course Baskerville's water bowl and feeding bowl over there."

"So he's not a wild dog?"

Charlize and Snoot were about to answer, but a male voice suddenly boomed from the darkness of an adjoining cave. "No, he's not."

Charlize recognized the voice immediately. She had listened to recordings of it over and over again in her investigation of serial killer Chester Clink. There was no doubt it was him.

Charlize pulled out her stun gun and moved in the direction of the voice. As she did so, a bright light came on in the adjoining cave. Clink was sitting at a table, the head of McLachlan in front of him, partially dissected, the brain fully visible.

Clink was the kind of man you'd pass on the street without even noticing him. Neither short nor tall, fat nor thin, he was the epitome of average. His hair, a blend of blond and gray, was cropped short, but not in any dramatic way that would make him stand out in a crowd. In fact, of all his features, only one stood out: his eyes. If there were eyes paler than ice blue, Clink possessed them, and they had the effect of fixing you in place when they were aimed in your direction, as they were now at Charlize.

"Come in, why don't you, and have a seat. I was just having a look-see at Mr. McLachlan's brain. I'm sure I'll find he had no musical ability whatsoever."

Charlize inched forward, her gun aimed directly at Clink's head. "You killed him?"

Clink shook his head and gave her an odd smirk. "No, someone beat me to it, but I still get to have my way with the man, as you can plainly see."

"If not you, who?"

"I think you mean *whom*, Charlize, but no, I won't reveal that. Honor among killers, you see."

"You know my name?"

Clink smiled up at her. "Oh, Charlize, of course I do. I make it my business to know the smart ones, the ones who could do me harm. What is it your friend Mr. Holmes always said?"

Charlize knew immediately. *"Mediocrity knows nothing higher than itself, but talent instantly recognizes genius."*

"Indeed, but don't jump to the wrong conclusion, Charlize. You're the *talent*, not me."

Charlize couldn't help smiling. For all his evil, this man was fascinating, as fascinating to her as Moriarty was to Holmes. "A bold comment for a psychopath."

"Psychopath? Oh, no, no, no, Charlize. What is it you're Holmes always says? Ah, yes, *I'm not a psychopath, I'm a high-functioning sociopath.*"

Charlize gave him a nuanced smirk, then got back to the matter at hand. "So, back to our friend, McLachlan. If you didn't kill him, why take his head?

Clink shrugged. "Any trophy in a storm, eh, Charlize?"

"Trophy? But it wasn't your trophy to have."

Clink shook his head. "Ah, but I *earned* it, Charlize."

"How do you figure?"

"Oh, I know, it wasn't my signature style now, was it? Well, Charlize, when a man like me is presented with certain sounds, his usual methods go out the window."

Charlize guessed. "Like the sound of bagpipes?"

"Oh, how perceptive of you, Charlize. Yes, *poorly played* bagpipes. I must admit, I went into quite a frenzy. *Atypical behavior*, your profilers would call it."

"Why not just break the bagpipes?"

"Oh, Charlize, what's the fun in that?"

"But there weren't any bagpipes at the scene."

"You will find them in the bay, underwater."

"I see."

"Do you, Charlize? Do you?"

"Oh, I see many things, and none more clearly than when you say my name. *Charlize*. It's how Hannibal Lecter would say it, isn't it? So you wanted the brain to see what it tasted like. Is that it? Is he *your* hero?"

He grinned back at her and made a *tch-tch-tch* sound. "Oh, Charlize, I thought you were smarter than that." And then he disappeared, along with the image of the table, leaving an empty cave.

Charlize lowered the stun gun and turned back to Snoot and Smithers in frustration. "Dammit, a *hologram.*"

"So it seems," said Snoot, "but we have his dog."

Charlize cocked her head. "We do. Perhaps we can use that to our advantage."

"And we've at least solved the mystery of the demon dog," said Smithers.

Snoot frowned. "But what was Clink doing here? Why this cave? Why the charade of the demon dog?"

"Good point, detective," said Charlize. "Perhaps this has been Clink's secret lair all along, and the demon dog was meant to protect it. At any rate, let's have a look around. Snoot, how far does this cave system extend, anyway?"

"Oh, it goes on for several miles. Caves connected to passages connected to more caves. It's a labyrinth."

Charlize looked at Baskerville. "But perhaps your new friend here can show us the way."

"Good idea." Snoot turned to the dog. "Baskerville, let's go home."

Baskerville bounded away, disappearing into the darkness of a nearby passageway, Charlize, Smithers, and Snoot in pursuit.

20

Sergeant Barry Blunt's wife, June Thursday, the nearly invisible spokesperson for Ramrod Robotics, pushed the folder back across the desk toward her equally elusive husband. She started to speak, but felt uncomfortable in the presence of their drones.

"Friday, Object, would you mind leaving the room for a moment?"

The drones buzzed and whirred and politely wobbled out of the room without a word.

Barry watched them go, then turned back to June. "What? Why was that necessary?"

June sighed and tapped a finger on the folder. Even though they'd only been married a few years, Barry instantly recognized that she had selected her middle finger, The Finger of Great Importance, to do the tapping. "What you have here is a game-changer."

"Oh, in what way?"

"In a big, *big* way, Barry. Imagine a world without drones, and you'd be well on your way to what's contained in this folder."

Barry looked down at the folder, which continued to receive a drumming from June. "So, what's the big deal?"

June slumped back in her chair. "I'm not sure I know how to describe it, but our engineers, who don't know *how* it could work or even *why* it would work, but assure me that it *will* work, call it a *neural node.*"

Barry threw up his hands. "June, *English.*"

"Simply put, or at least *simplerly* put, if that's a word, it's a device that could perform all the functions of a drone without the need for a drone."

Barry frowned. "Wait, so it would be like earphones or something?"

June tapped The Finger of Great Importance on her right temple. "No, it would be an *implant*. Instead of sending, receiving, storing, and processing information and data through your drone, you'd do it with the help of a neural node implanted in your brain."

Barry shook his head in disbelief. "Why on earth would anyone do that?"

"Barry, think about it. Did you actually choose to buy your first cellphone? Or your first drone? No, technology forced it on you, made you think you couldn't possibly live without it. You and everyone else will get in line for this implant, you just wait."

"But there's no need for it. Drones are fine."

June rolled her eyes. "Oh, come on, Barry. You can't go anywhere now without a gazillion drones buzzing around you. It's getting crazy out there. And if the Simdroid Suffrage movement has its way, simdroids *and* drones will have the right to have their own drones soon. Drones with *drones*, Barry. Maybe even drones with drones with drones. It's madness."

"But they're like our pets. I don't know what I'd do without my Object."

"Barry, you could get your own beer from the refrigerator."

"He does more than that. He's like a buddy."

June shook her head. "Look, you know I've always said thank god for Friday, but seriously, when it comes right down to it, I could easily do without her, at least the flying and buzzing part. And just think of the number of people affected by Seasonal Drone Affective Disorder. It was horrible here last summer, and this summer we'll have more than twice as many drones in the air, what with this new Mars Terminal."

Barry nodded, then shook his head. "Well, I *still* can't see having someone implant a cellphone in my head. I'd rather just go back to cellphones."

If June's eyes were capable of rolling harder, she would have chosen that response. Instead, she puffed out her cheeks in pure exasperation. "You don't get it. The neural node would be more than a cellphone. It would be a separate persona. A separate you, but connected to you. Yes, it would be your phone service, but it would also be like our drones, with all their capabilities, except flying."

"So what you're saying is that instead of a world with drones flying around us like gnats, we'd have a world where everyone walks around talking to themselves?"

June crossed her arms. "Barry, you're impossible sometimes."

"Well, isn't that what you're saying?"

"No, it definitely is *not* what I'm saying. What I'm saying is that the neural node is, in effect, a separate brain, doubling our problem-solving capacity and letting us tap into that."

"So I'd be more intelligent?"

"No, but you'd have two brains that could work on the same problem or *different problems* simultaneously."

Barry laughed. "Ha, why stop there? Why not implant multiple nodes?"

June leaned across the desk, looking Barry right in the eye. "Exactly."

"And who would even want that?"

The answer came to him quickly, as if a second brain had suddenly kicked in. *The military.*

June read the look on his face. "Exactly, the military, but more to the point, who would want to *stop* this?"

"Anyone who has a stake in the success of drones."

"Yep, and who would murder to stop this?"

"Someone at C3 Corporation or maybe even DroneOn, their chief competitor."

June smiled at him, egging him on. "And what does that mean, Barry?"

He smiled back at her. "It means the Wright murder and the McLachlan murder are probably connected. Someone wanted those plans."

"Or wanted to stop them."

"Right, right, I have to let Grave know." He stood up, grabbed the folder, and raced to the doorway. "Object, I need you!"

Blunt's Object came, and they went, leaving June to deal with the curious looks Friday was giving her. She slid her hands off the desk to give The Finger of Great Importance the cover it needed. "So, Friday, what say we head off to Crab Cove Daycare and see what damage my invisible daughter has done today?"

Friday was not capable of true laughter but could simulate, through changes in pitch and a series of rapid beeps, a chuckle roughly approximating a chuckle. "No calls from the headmistress or the police or the fire department, so I think we'll find all is well."

June pushed back from the desk. "If only."

21

Grave wondered how long it would take a person to grow comfortable in a solid glass chair, and the word *never* came to mind as total numbness came to his nether regions.

The call from Blunt through Object through Barry had been a welcome relief, allowing him to step out in the hall with Barry to listen to the message. As he listened, he kept his eyes on Frank Orville, who had seemed anything but nervous during Grave's preliminary questions.

Of course he had a reason to kill his brother: he would take over the company, be even wealthier. And yes, he had hated everything about his brother, particularly the way he bullied everyone, including him. But he was his *brother*, after all, so he would never kill him. And yes, he had an alibi. He was at home, playing chess with Dolores, a fact that Dolores presented to Grave in the form of a hologram, which conveniently—perhaps too conveniently—showed Orville making an ill-advised move, a nearby clock clearly indicating the approximate time and date of his brother's murder. Why a man would be up at 1:11 a.m., playing chess with his drone, Grave didn't know, but the time stamp didn't lie.

When the message ended, Grave smiled up at Barry. "A game-changer, eh? Well, let's get back to it."

He walked back into Orville's office, and reluctantly sacrificed his hind parts once more. "So, Mr. Orville, do you know a Lachlan McLachlan?"

Orville noticeably blinked. "No."

"A rather large man with a thick Scottish accent?"

Orville blinked again. "No."

"Runs a kennel up on a bluff out near the marsh?"

Orville blinked and threw in a shrug. "No, should I?"

"He was murdered not ten feet from where your brother was murdered."

Blinks, shrugs, and a complete loss of facial color followed in the wake of Grave's question, but Orville persisted. "How awful, but no, I don't know any such man."

Grave glanced up at Dolores, wondering what other holograms she had in her repertoire. "And where were you last night, Mr. Orville, between seven and ten?"

When a blink is your go-to response, why change? Orville blinked, hard. "Why, let me see. Yes, yes, I was with my wife, Wanda. We were at the Crab Cove Cinema 16, watching that new remake of *The Magnificent Seven*."

Grave rolled his eyes. "On the first evening after your brother was brutally murdered?"

Orville shrugged. "No love lost, you see. And besides, we'd both been looking forward to seeing the movie. A distraction, if you will, from the news."

Grave smirked. "A distraction? Of course." He made a mental note to talk to Wanda Orville, soon.

He pressed on. "Seems Mr. McLachlan was quite the inventor."

Orville's whole body seemed to tighten and contract. Even his head seemed to have lost air. "Really?"

"Oh, yes. Have you ever heard of distributed intelligence?"

Orville blinked yet again. "Yes, of course. Purely theoretical. A pipedream of the military."

"So, you don't use that here at C3?"

Orville actually managed a chuckle. "I would love to. The military would be all over that. Money for the taking."

"Interesting," said Grave. "Now, one last question and then I'd like to take that tour you mentioned."

Orville seemed relieved. "Shoot."

"What do you know about neural nodes?"

Orville tried his best to screw up his face into a question mark, to lend credibility to an answer Grave instantly knew was false, but his eyelids were blinking and fluttering like an urgent message in semaphore. "No, what's that?"

Dolores, who had no ability to screw up anything, issued a series of rapid clicks that were as telling as the look on Orville's face.

Grave smiled at them both in turn, then stood. "Oh, nothing, really. Shall we have that tour, then?"

22

Sergeant Blunt, folder in hand, pushed into the fishbowl office of Captain Morgan, trailed by Object, who immediately buzzed over to join Rum on top of Mr. Bug. The captain had his back turned to the door and was busily rearranging his Captain Morgan Rum tchotchkes on his credenza: figurines, clocks, badges, pins, ribbons, and bottles of the rum itself, ranging in size from a bottle no bigger than a thumbnail to a bottle the size of a serious fire extinguisher. It was not an exercise that the captain did out of concern for neatness or boredom; it was just one of his myriad ways of thinking about a problem. The feeling around the station was that if you strapped him down in a chair, his brain would shut down completely. The man just had to be fiddling with something to have even a single thought.

Morgan turned and squinted at the door at the sound of its closing, and knew that Sergeant Blunt must be within hailing distance. "Is that you, Blunt?"

A voice came from a chair across from Morgan's desk. "Yes, sir, Grave said I should get this information to you as soon as possible."

Morgan looked down at the folder that had appeared on his desk. "Ah, yes, the folder. What did you and June find?"

"It seems to be plans for something called a neural node, a device designed to replace drones."

Blunt expected him to screw up his face at *neural node,* but Morgan just laughed. "Replace drones? Well, that'll be the day."

"No, seriously, June and the engineers think it will work, although the plans seem a bit confusing and incomplete."

Morgan gave his tchotchke collection one last appreciative look, and sat down behind the desk, groaning with the effort. He really did need to retire. "So, what is a kennel owner and crappy bagpipe player doing with plans like that?"

"Exactly, sir, and more important, who would kill to get those plans or destroy them?"

Morgan's eyebrows shot up. "I see what you mean."

"And with Wright Orville in the drone business himself, perhaps the murders are related."

Morgan nodded and looked over at Object. "Can he download the folder information and June's analysis into the MRBG 3000?"

Object spoke up. "Downloading now, sir. Should only be another 30.7 seconds or so."

Morgan turned back to Blunt, or at least where he thought Blunt was. "Fine. Any word from Grave?"

"He's at C3 Corp, interviewing Frank Orville and scoping out the company."

Morgan nodded. "And Charlize and Smithers?"

"They should still be at the crime scene, looking for additional clues."

Object beeped loudly. "Ready, sir. All data input."

"Excellent," said Morgan. "Would you kindly press the buttons? No, not that one. Start with the one marked one and then on to two and so on. Yes, that's it."

Object pushed the buttons with his extended probe, and Mr. Bug whirred to life, the sound of crunching data almost audible as the lights flickered and flashed.

A message appeared on the screen, indicating that processing would take exactly five minutes, twenty seconds.

Morgan sighed. *Five minutes, twenty seconds with Blunt?*

"So," Morgan began, "how is that little girl of yours?"

Blunt returned the sigh, wondering where to begin. He knew June was on her way to pick up Rippley. He just hoped the little girl hadn't burned down the childcare center or disappeared on one of her "adventures in invisibility."

"Well," he began.

23

Detective Snoot was right: the cave system went on for miles, and for every small cave, there were four or five tunnels leading to or away from it. The odds of a human finding anything were astronomical, but Charlize and Smithers were simdroids. And as simdroids, they were adept at solving even the most labyrinthine problems. Still, Snoot, on childhood memories alone, was not only holding her own but leading the way.

"Jimmy Forester tried to kiss me here," she said, pointing to a small indentation in the wall that as indentations go, was really no more than an indentation.

Charlize gave her an acknowledging grunt. She was growing tired of these little discoveries. "Yes, fine, but which way now do you think?"

Snoot looked at each of the available tunnels in turn and then pointed to the smallest. "That one. A little tight for us grownups, but when I was a child—"

"Yes," said Smithers, also annoyed. "Yes, you were smaller then."

"Exactly," said Snoot. "You'll have to crouch down a bit, but I'm sure it leads to a large cave."

Charlize aimed her flashlight into the darkness. "Are you sure? It seems to narrow even further."

"Yes, of course," said Snoot. "That's the cave where my friend Emma—"

"Never *mind*," said Charlize louder than she realized. "Let's go."

They crept slowly through the tunnel, which thankfully opened into a large cave after less than a minute of crouch-walking.

Smithers was the first through and swung his flashlight in wide arcs to take in the expanse of the cave, finally settling on a wall switch, which he flicked on, near blinding Snoot with the light from a hundred bulbs in a crystal chandelier hanging at the center of the cave.

"Wow," said Snoot. "I don't remember anything like this."

"I think they call this a man cave," said Charlize. "A room totally devoted to the interests and tastes of a single man."

Shelves lined the walls. A large-screen television took up most of one end of the cave, faced by a brown leather couch that sat on a round oriental carpet that nearly covered the entire cave floor. Books on every topic sat in stacks at either end of the couch.

Smithers picked up a handful of the books. "He reads a lot for a serial killer, don't you think?"

"Not at all," said Charlize. "Most psychological profilers would give serial killers great latitude in their hobbies. Besides, they have to do *something* between killings."

Smithers began reading off the titles, dropping each book on the floor as he read. "*One Hundred Years of Solitude, Clover Doves, The Blue Rat, The Complete History of Red Hair, The Leadership Secrets of Squirrels.* Pretty eclectic."

"Look at this," said Snoot, drawing their attention back to the empty shelves. "He's fled."

Charlize looked at the dust patterns on the shelves. "Not for books. See here, it's more like Captain Morgan's tchotchke display."

Smithers leaned in for a look. "Trophies?"

"Precisely," said Charlize. "The dust has revealed in absence the lost presence of evidence."

Snoot and Smithers spoke as one. "What?"

"The dust has outlined everything that occupied these shelves. Just look." She pointed at several spots in turn. "A comb, a key, a lipstick, a driver's license, or other identity card."

Snoot and Smithers nodded as one.

"And from the looks of things, our work here is about done. I'm sure one of these passages leads down to the waterline, where he must have had a boat, perhaps even a small submarine. We won't be finding him today, and I doubt he'll ever return."

"But all these wonderful books," said Snoot. "Surely he'd come back for them."

"No," said Charlize. "If he valued the books, they would have been on the shelves, not in jumbled stacks around the couch. No, reading was a means to an end for him."

Smithers pointed at the wall. "What about the television, then?"

Charlize shook her head. "No, none of this matters to him, really. Not the books, not the television, not the chandelier or any of these trappings. No, he's all about the killings and his little trophies. Normal life is just a hobby to him, something he plays at, but not seriously. You know, something to pass the time between killings."

"Well, then," offered Smithers, not sure what to suggest next.

"Well, indeed," said Charlize. "Yes, let's go. Snoot, which tunnel?"

Snoot pointed at the tunnel under the television. "That's the one. I remember, because—"

"Yes, yes," said Charlize. "Lead on."

Smithers was already leading the way, his flashlight outlining the tunnel, the sound of waves growing louder as they descended.

Somewhere up ahead a dog barked.

24

Grave and Barry were following Orville and Dolores through what appeared to be caves, in this case, caves of glass at the crystalline headquarters of C3 Corporation.

As they proceeded down the corridor, Frank Orville pointed out office after office, most of which were empty. "Marketing director, PR director, graphic design team. They must be in the conference room, planning our next launch."

They stopped in front of another office, where a burly and balding older man in a three-piece black suit could clearly be seen hunched over his desk. Behind him were financial charts showing curves that seemed to frown instead of smile. "That's Brad Dingle, our chief financial officer. His drone there is called Malcolm, one of our hybrid drones."

"Hybrid?"

"Yes, it's really for people just like Brad. People who need technology but just can't seem to keep up with it. Malcolm gives him basic phone service, minimal apps, and a functionality even he can understand. Frankly, I think a monkey would want something more, but that's Brad. I mean, he's still using Excel spreadsheets, if you can believe that."

Grave had no idea what Excel was, and he wasn't about to ask. "He looks worried."

Almost as if he had heard them, Dingle turned to look at them, then quickly looked away.

"Worried is right," said Orville. "The boom in drones is pretty much over. Unless we come up with the next new-new thing, I'm afraid our growth is pretty much at a standstill. Maybe that's what the marketing team is up to. Anyway, our stopgap is improved efficiency and cost-cutting, and a focus on the sizzle of our drones, but even that has its limits."

"Yes, of course," said Grave, not following a word. Money and its various intrigues had always been a mystery to him. "Um, shall we move on?"

Orville led him down a side hallway to an office that, judging by its opaque door, was a place of some secrecy. "This is where the magic happens, the lab of our chief designer, James Phizz. His friends call him Sloe Jim. You know, *Sloe Jim Phizz?* Get it?"

Grave managed a smile back. "Yes, how droll. Do you suppose we could stop in and chat with him a bit?"

Orville looked troubled. "Well, there's still a lot more to see."

"It might be important."

"Very well." Orville punched in a code on a small panel, and the door to Phizz's office and laboratory slid silently to the left.

Orville took one step in and called out, "Jim."

A tall, strikingly handsome man in a white lab coat stepped out from behind a line of equipment and robotic devices, trailed by a drone the likes of which Grave had never seen, which for a drone, was equally handsome. The two of them seemed out of place. The man and his drone looked more like Hollywood actors hired for the day to promote the company. Even Barry seemed to be taken aback, emitting a soft, appreciative whistle.

The man came toward them, adjusting his lab coat. "Yes, Mr. Orville, how may I help you?"

Orville nodded toward Grave. "I'd like to introduce you to Detective Grave, of the Crab Cove Police. He's handling the, um, *investigation.*"

Phizz held out his hand. "Ah, yes, I've been expecting you."

Grave could not disguise his surprised look. "You have?"

Phizz lifted his hands palms up. "Of course. We've *all* been expecting you. Terrible business. *Terrible.*"

"Yes," said Grave. The man seemed nervous. "So, this is where the magic happens."

Phizz laughed. "Well, that's the idea."

Grave looked around the lab. "May I ask what you're working on?"

Phizz pointed to his drone. "Fast Eddy here. Drones are so commonplace now that it's hard for any drone, even a new drone, to stand out and capture market share."

"So," said Grave. "Fast Eddy is supposed to do that? How?"

"First off, eye appeal," said Phizz. "Admit it, you were immediately drawn to him, weren't you? I could see it in your eyes."

"Well, he is rather unique."

Phizz rose to the subject. "And sleek. And elegant. And stylish. And fast as all get out."

"But expensive as hell to produce," said Orville.

Phizz frowned. "Yes, that's the problem." He turned to Orville. "But we'll get there, boss."

Grave decided now was the time for his real questions. "So, Mr. Phizz, what can you tell me about distributed intelligence or neural nodes?"

Phizz's eyes grew wide. "Well, I . . ."

A soft sneeze, one quite feminine, one more like the chirp of a bird than anything nasal, interrupted them.

Orville seemed to recognize it. "Wanda, is that you?"

A young woman, so beautiful she could have been a new species, stepped from behind a piece of lab equipment. "Yes, dear."

Orville glared at her and then Phizz, then turned to Grave, his voice quavering with suppressed anger. "Detective Grave, my wife, *Wanda*."

Grave couldn't help noticing that her sweater was buttoned out of sequence and that there was a certain blush around her neck. "My pleasure," said Grave, taking her hand, which seemed to glow from the inner heat of an even warmer moment, now past—but present.

25

Five minutes is not long, but five minutes *and twenty seconds* can be an eternity when you're trying to explain the trouble a two-year-old girl can get into, let alone one that's invisible. Hiding quietly in corners. Leaving the daycare center entirely. Pulling down little boys' pants. Ruffling playmates' hair. Not answering when called upon.

"Of course, they won't let her play Hide-and-Seek," said Blunt.

"No, I guess not," said Captain Morgan, who was growing tired of listening. Still, he had to admire the little girl. She was a pistol.

Mr. Bug began to whir and beep as Blunt was about to mention Rippley's bathroom escapades.

"Wait," said Morgan. "I think we have something."

Across town, at Crab Cove Daycare, June began her sentence with exactly the same urgency. "Wait," she said, "she did *what?*"

"Appeared," said the headmistress, a woman of girth and grouch, with a voice that suggested sand and rocks shaken in a can. "I had no idea she was so, so cute."

June was stunned and thrilled at the same time. "You saw her? Really *saw* her?"

The headmistress could not have smiled more broadly. Every silver-capped tooth gleamed back at June. "Yes, yes, and oh, how beautiful she is. Those eyes, those rosy cheeks, that shock of red hair. Oh, oh."

June stopped her at the second oh, afraid the poor woman might explode. "Wait, do you mean you could see her *completely?*"

"Oh, yes, right down to her freckles."

"Not like me, then?"

"No, not cloudlike at all. Totally visible, completely solid, if only for a few seconds. Would you like me to describe her in greater detail?"

June waved her off. "No, no, but that's wonderful!"

"Yes, yes, it is," said the headmistress. And then her smile turned upside down. "And then she did something, well, *horrific.*"

June wiped away a little premature tear of joy from her eye and braced herself for what might come next. She really didn't care what Rippley had done. *Her little girl could make herself appear to the world!*

"So," the headmistress began, privately congratulating herself for her spoonful-of-sugar approach to the current problem.

At about the same time, way back across town at Crab Cove Police Headquarters, Captain Morgan was working on a similar opening line. "So," he said, looking down at Mr. Bug's screen, "what have we here?"

What we had here was a blur of words, coming across the screen in such quantity and with such speed that Captain Morgan couldn't keep up with it. "What the—" he began, slapping the top of Mr. Bug, hard.

The message, if anything, accelerated until the screen was a uniform gray and every light on Mr. Bug was blinking insanely. And then it suddenly stopped, the screen going blank, the lights slowing to a steady throb.

A few seconds later, the screen brightened, and a brief message appeared: *Processing Interrupted. Now Accepting New Data. Please Stand by.*

Morgan slapped Mr. Bug again, but without any serious force. "New data?"

"Must be from Grave or Charlize or Snoot."

Morgan glanced up at his Captain Morgan Rum Cuckoo Clock, whose gleaming golden sabers indicated one minute before the hour. Any second now, a little figurine of Captain Morgan, lord of rum, would come ambling out in mock swash and buckle, and announce that the hour had reached late afternoon-*ish.*

Captain Morgan sighed. "Well, I guess that's to be expected. They've all been gone for quite some time without reporting in."

"Yes, sir," said Sergeant Blunt, happy that the rest of the team had come up with new data, new clues, perhaps even a solution to the case. "Maybe we have our murderer."

Morgan nodded happily, but then Mr. Bug began beeping, drawing them both in for a new message: *Processing time 37 minutes, 14 seconds.*

Barry groaned. He had reached the point in his storytelling where Rippley's exploits would surely take a turn for the worse.

26

The tunnel opened on a large, water-filled cave brightly lit by a score or more of LED lanterns that had clicked on the moment they had stepped onto the small wooden pier at the water's edge. The reflections of the lapping water on the walls and ceiling of the cave, and on them, gave the scene an otherworldly feel.

"Just as I thought," said Charlize, leaning down to pick up a small comb. "One of his trophies. Ah, and look here."

She bent down again, brushed aside a seagull feather, and picked up a clump of hair. "I doubt I even have to scan this for DNA. It's hair from Baskerville. Seems we've lost them both, and they've left in quite a hurry."

"And obviously by submarine," said Smithers.

"Well, yeah," said Snoot. "This cave used to lead down another twenty feet or so to a tunnel that led to the beach. That's where we used to enter."

Charlize tucked the comb into an evidence bag and put it in her pocket. "It appears we've flushed him from his lair. The question now is where he'll turn up next."

"I'll have Goth alert the Coast Guard," said Snoot, who immediately realized her mistake. "I mean . . ."

Charlize tried to console her. "Goth would have been happy to do that, and would have done it well, I'm sure."

27

Grave tried his best to ignore the obvious beauty of Wanda Orville, but there she was, wasn't she, a wonder to behold, each feature more delightful than the next. Why, she even sneezed beautifully.

So, as he approached the problem of what to say to this vision before him, he couldn't decide whether to hem or haw and so he had done both, which had only led to confusion on the part of one Wanda Orville.

"Detective?" she said with concern.

My god, even her frown is beautiful, thought Grave. *And the way she knits her brow. Why, it could knit the best sweater ever created! And that voice. Like a songbird!*

Frank Orville's voice woke him from his reverie. "Detective, are you all right?"

Grave was suddenly aware that everyone was staring at him, or rather, glowering at him. "Oh, yes, of course. I was just thinking about my next question for you, Mr. Phizz."

"Yes?" said Phizz, eager for any distraction that would take the conversation, and particularly Frank Orville's suspicions, away from his tabloid-interruptus exploits with Wanda just minutes ago.

"Oh, um," began Grave, regaining his composure somewhat. "We were talking about distributed intelligence and neural nodes, I believe."

Wanda rolled her eyes, which Grave noted were an unremarkable blue but nevertheless had the effect of tractor beams on his attention.

"Oh, dear," she said, "this conversation is way beyond my paygrade. If you'll excuse me, gentlemen?" She started moving to the door.

"Of course," said Grave, tipping an imaginary hat at her as she walked by—*that walk, that perfume!*

When she reached the door, he quickly recovered and called after her, adding, "Of course, I'd like to talk to you further about the death of your brother-in-law."

She looked back with a smile that Grave would have needed pages to describe. "Of course. Just make the arrangements with Frank." And she was gone.

Grave turned back to Frank and Phizz. "Now, where were we? Oh, yes, distributed intelligence and neural nodes."

"Yes," said Phizz, "you mentioned that. Frankly, both concepts are pipedreams. Distributed intelligence has its backers, of course, the military being just one, but its practicality is suspect, and its cost would be astronomical."

"I see," said Grave. "And neural nodes?"

Phizz chuckled and turned to Frank Orville to encourage him to chuckle, but Frank was in no mood for chuckling. Phizz quickly turned back to Grave. "Once again, let me be frank."

Grave thought briefly about pointing at Frank and blurting, "No, he's Frank," but restrained himself. "Please."

"Neural nodes are impossible. There are just too many problems making the links between metal and flesh. Limb replacements? No problem. Organ replacement devices? Yes, but with difficulty. But fiddling inside the brain? No, that just wouldn't work. In fact, it's ridiculous."

"Really? Isn't it just one step beyond what we're doing now with paraplegics and quadriplegics? I mean, we have them up and walking within days."

Phizz had been shaking his head and smirking the whole time Grave had been talking. "Completely different ballgame. Neural nodes would mean linking a machine brain with a human brain, and somehow having them work together in the way data is handled, stored, and processed. Nope. Not gonna happen, at least in our lifetimes."

"I see," said Grave. "But humor me, and this is a question for both of you." He looked back and forth at them, estimating their willingness to humor him, and they replied with nods.

"So," he continued. "Imagine, if you will, that both concepts were possible, even economical. What would you do, what would any drone company do to acquire that knowledge and bring it to market? Or, for that matter, what would you do to stop it from coming to market?"

If synchronized blinking were an Olympic event, Frank Orville and Jim Phizz were unquestionably going for gold.

28

Sergeant Blunt was halfway through another story about the exploits of his young daughter, Rippley, when Object suddenly started beeping. A call was coming in.

Blunt leapt at the opportunity. "That could be Grave, sir. I'd better take it."

Captain Morgan, who had only been half-listening to Blunt's stories, grunted in a positive way and turned his attention back to Mr. Bug, whose lights seemed to be flashing in a more purposeful way. Perhaps the machine was approaching a conclusion.

Blunt motioned Object out of the captain's office, and the two of them made their way through the crowded squad room and then outside, where reception was always better.

"It's June, sir," said Object.

And then June's voice came on. "Barry, the most wonderful thing has happened."

Barry had a bucket list of wonderful things, but he couldn't imagine any of them being of interest to June, so the best reply he could manage was, "Oh?"

"Rippley can make herself *visible*, at will." She paused between each word to make him understand the import of her news, which was not lost on Barry.

"Oh, wow, that is wonderful news. So she can appear anytime she wants?"

June laughed. "Yes, visible or invisible, it's her choice now."

"Incredible, and does she know how she does it?"

"Yes, she thinks so. It involves a way of breathing and mental focus. I don't know, it's complicated, but listen. I'd like to take her out to Chuck E. Crab tonight. A celebration seems in order."

Barry hated Chuck E. Crab, but he knew Rippley adored it. "Okay, let's do that."

"So when do you think you can break away? If we get there by five or so, there will be fewer kids, and it will be much quieter."

Barry remembered their last time at Chuck E. Crab and the way the children had run free, at high volume. "I'll see what I can do, but it could be touch and go here, what with these murders."

He could hear her sigh. "Do your best, then. Rippley will so enjoy herself, and she deserves this."

"Don't worry, I will. Bye then." He waved at Object, who nodded and terminated the call.

Rippley visible? Barry wondered if his child could teach him how to be invisible or visible at will, and not permanently stuck in this midway nightmare of near invisibility.

He laughed to himself. *No one would recognize me.*

He motioned for Object to follow him back into the station, but Object was looking at the parking lot. Charlize, Smithers, and Detective Snoot were climbing out of Charlize's sleek Duesenberg.

Object began wobbling nervously. "Sir, something's wrong."

Barry looked at his colleagues, then around the parking lot. Everything seemed normal. "What do you mean?"

"Sir, where's Goth?"

Barry looked back toward the car. No Goth. "Oh, no."

Charlize had measured Object's reaction and concern from the moment they had stepped out of the Duesenberg and was the first to speak.

"Goth didn't make it," she said.

"A real fighter, that one," said Smithers.

Snoot held back her tears. "He put up a good fight, but he was no match for Baskerville."

Barry frowned. "Baskerville?"

"All shall be revealed, Sergeant," said Charlize. "Come on, we need to input data into Mr. Bug and bring the captain up to speed. It's been a very interesting day, to say the least."

She pushed past him and walked up the steps and into the station, followed by the others, leaving Barry and Object in the parking lot.

"Come on, Object, let's find out what happened to your friend."

Object said nothing but slowly whirred away toward the station.

29

Grave had waited patiently as Frank Orville and Jim Phizz had gone through their synchronized blinking routine, each landing a perfect mystified shrug at the end.

Grave rolled his eyes in frustration. "So, you wouldn't do *anything?*"

"Oh, all right," said Frank. "If I thought distributed intelligence or neural nodes were even remotely possible—and let me be clear, I don't—then I would do anything and everything to get my hands on anything that would keep me in the game."

"But it's still ridiculous," said Phizz, expressing his own frustration. "Are we through here? I have actual work to do on *real* concepts."

Grave shook his head. "You're right, I'm sure, but one last question. Again, let's assume the concepts are possible, and you've suddenly realized that your competitors are well ahead of you, ready to supplant your *real* concepts. Who are those competitors?"

Frank chuckled. "Finally, something I can answer. We have competition from companies all over the world, of course—everyone's making drones. But first and foremost, here in Crab Cove, we compete directly with Ramrod Robotics and their simdroid empire, and with DroneOn, a small but up-and-coming company you may or may not know is backed by a Russian oligarch and his crime syndicate."

Now it was time for Grave to blink. He had expected Ramrod Robotics to be in the mix; they had already established a foothold, or rather a crabhold, on the market with their rent-a-drone program. Tourists in Crab Cove for a day or a week could exchange their personal drones for drones more suited to a summer vacation environment, which to Ramrod meant drones that simulated the voices and facial features of beach-movie actors and crab-based cartoon characters, including Crabula, Clawman, Crabantula, Crab House Charlie, Crabface, and Crab Cove's signature superhero, Danger Crab.

DroneOn was something else entirely. They had come out of the box fast, but with products that lacked the technological bells and whistles of C3 or Ramrod products. Their drones tended to be lumbering, noisy, old-fashioned rotor models of poor quality. *Clunky* was a word that came to mind, and *cheap*. If distributed intelligence and neural nodes were real or at least theoretically possible—and the engineers at Ramrod had assured June they were—then DroneOn would stand the most to gain. And with the backing of a Russian syndicate, they would be the one company most apt to invoke extreme measures. Still, the blinking duo of Frank and Jim were certainly not off the hook.

"I see," said Grave. "Well, then, Mr. Phizz, I think you can resume work on your next great invention." Grave turned to Frank. "Shall we continue our tour?"

"Of course," said Frank, who then turned to Phizz. "I'll talk with you later."

Frank escorted Grave and Barry down another long hallway of glass to another opaque door controlled by a coded entry device.

"Our production floor. Any secrets we have—and we do have some *real* secrets—are guarded here on the production floor. Also, there's a lot of heavy equipment, so keep your hands at your sides. Wouldn't want you drawn and quartered in here." Frank smiled at him in a way that suggested otherwise.

Grave dutifully slapped his hands to his sides. "Let's go in, then."

When Frank opened the door, Grave's eyes went wide, and Barry whistled. The entire production floor was filled with simdroids dressed as cowboys, Mexican peasants, and banditos. He looked around and started checking off names: Yul Brynner, Steve McQueen, Horst Buckholz, Charles Bronson, Robert Vaughn, Brad Dexter, and James Coburn.

The Magnificent Seven!

30

Captain Morgan and Sergeant Blunt were spellbound by the story being recounted by Charlize, Smithers, and Snoot, as were Object and Rum, who seemed to visibly wobble in anguish when Snoot described Goth's death at the jaws of Baskerville.

Throughout the story, Morgan kept interrupting, sure that he had heard enough to determine who McLachlan's killer was.

"It must be that drone Haggis!"

Charlize had shaken her head. "No."

"Wait, what about his real dog, Fred?"

Charlize had shaken her head once more. "Wounds don't indicate that's possible."

"So, it's Clink after all!"

Charlize rolled her eyes. "No, it just doesn't fit."

Finally, he had just thrown up his hands in frustration. "Well then, *who?*"

Charlize had smiled. "There are still a number of possibilities, but before I tell you my theory, let's hear from Mr. Bug. Smithers, have you input all we know?"

"Yes," said Smithers, "except whatever Grave's found."

Charlize smirked. "I'm sure he'll have something *interesting* to add, no doubt, but let's see where we stand, shall we? Captain, would you like to do the honors."

Morgan grunted, lifted himself from his chair, and walked over to Mr. Bug to push the start buttons. "Let's hope we get something more than last time."

"Oh," said Charlize. "What did it say?"

"It said, *Ask again later.*"

"You see," said Snoot. "We might as well rely on a Magic 8-Ball."

Captain Morgan gave Snoot a sharp glance, then hit the start buttons. Mr. Bug came to life once more with a satisfying array of flashing lights and simulated-thinking sounds. Its little screen announced that processing would take no more than six minutes.

"Hmm," said Blunt. "It's getting faster. Maybe we'll get an answer this time."

Snoot was less confident. "Yeah, right."

Morgan looked up at the clock. "Where in hell is Grave? Sometimes I wonder about that man."

Everyone nodded, including the drones, but said nothing as Mr. Bug continued its relentless, if so far unsuccessful, pursuit of truth, justice, and the Crab Cove way.

Captain Morgan walked slowly back to his chair and plopped down, wincing as bottom met chair. "Where in the hell *is* he?"

His question went unanswered as Mr. Bug went into a paroxysm of processing and began vibrating to the point that it began walking across the floor like an out-of-balance washing machine. A large green light on its top began to pulse with some purpose, something it had never done in the entire time it had been part of the Crab Cove Police Department.

Captain Morgan was out of his seat in a flash, or as flashy as a preretirement captain can manage. "Come on, Blunt, give me a hand here. Hold it down!"

He and Blunt began wrestling Mr. Bug back to its normal position.

"No, wait," said Charlize. "It's slowing down."

Captain Morgan eased his grip on Mr. Bug, but could still feel the vibrations running up and down his arm.

And then Mr. Bug stopped with the finality of a rock actually hitting rock bottom. No lights. No sounds. No vibrations. Just a hunk of overheated metal.

"Wow," said Blunt.

The assembled team looked back and forth at each other for some seconds before Snoot offered her analysis. "Well, it's at least more entertaining than a Magic 8-Ball."

"Wait, look here," said Smithers. He pointed at Mr. Bug's screen. "Is that a message?"

Say what you will about Captain Morgan's death embrace on the aging process, he was still a competitor. He pushed the others aside, bent down to look at the screen, and then, without giving care to what he had actually read, shouted for everyone to hear. "We have our killer! It's *The Magnificent Seven!*"

Everyone blinked, but none more than Captain Morgan, whose brain began to catch up with his words, parsing them, ruminating on them, even rearranging them—*we seven have our magnificent killer, seven magnificent killers we have*—in an attempt to make sense of them.

Finally, his brain locked in on the only possible explanation. "Grave!"

He turned back to Mr. Bug and gave him a good kick in the processors.

31

Grave sat quietly in the Crab Cab he'd taken from C3 Corporation, and wondered whether the data he and Barry had transmitted to Mr. Bug would yield any useful results.

It had certainly been interesting data, particularly the part about Yul Brynner, the shop foreman, a simdroid that by day played the part of Chris Larabee Adams in *The Magnificent Seven*, albeit in a contrived scenario related to drone production, and by night worked his way through the entire Yul Brynner catalog in various little-theater performances around Crab Cove. Not surprisingly, he was most proud of his performance as "the gunslinger" in *Futureworld*.

"It's my most nuanced performance," Yul had said. "A human playing a simdroid is one thing, but a simdroid playing a human playing a simdroid is something else. More layers than your proverbial onion."

Like Grave, the only way that Frank Orville could have possibly known about the original Magnificent Seven was from someone older, and Grave had guessed correctly.

"Yes, my father," Orville had said. "Irving Orville, the founder of C3 back in the day. He's retired now. Lives with me and Wanda. I can't tell you how many times he forced me to watch *The Magnificent Seven*."

As the two of them reminisced about the movie and their fathers, Grave noted that each of the six other "magnificents" had approached Yul to whisper in his aural port. Something was up, but Grave wasn't sure whether it had anything to do with the murders or his presence. The whispering could have been nothing more than a desire not to interrupt Grave's conversation with their boss. Still, the conspiratorial looks, and especially the way James Coburn had tapped his hand on his sheathed knife, had given Grave pause. *Could they possibly be involved in the murders?*

As the reminiscences reached that awkward ending stage, when neither party could think of a single other reminiscence, Orville had agreed to meet with Grave at his home the next morning, which would also give Grave the opportunity to talk to both Wanda and Orville's father.

Grave had thanked him for his time and the tour and had followed him quietly back through the glass maze to the front door and his waiting Crab Cab, where he sat now, thinking, Barry buzzing away on the seat next to him, transmitting data to Mr. Bug. Grave wondered what the machine would make of his seven magnificents.

The robocab interrupted his thoughts for the third time. "Destination?"

The voice was sultry, a compilation by an actress whose name Grave couldn't remember.

The cab persisted, trying a new tack. "This is Crab Cab number thirty-six. My pressure indicators indicate that someone is sitting in the passenger compartment. If this is the case, please state your destination at the sound of the beep."

The cab beeped.

Grave started to say Crab Cove Police Headquarters, but he wasn't ready for the chaos of the station, let alone the continued harassment by Retective Tilda Must. So instead, he said, "Crab Cove Cinema Cemetery, please."

It was not a choice made on a whim. He wanted to pay his respects to Reverend Bendigo Bottoms, whose gospel hour on local radio had kept him company and offered him sound advice as he pursued life and criminals. He also had a crime-related reason in mind. He wanted to talk to Victoria Skunkford, a little girl who had helped him solve more than a few cases. Although she had been thoroughly dead since the eighteenth century, she was definitely up to the minute on the comings and goings of new arrivals at the cemetery. If the spirits of Wright Orville or Lachlan McLachlan had arrived, she would know all about it and might be able to help him solve their murders.

The cab acknowledged the destination and then launched into a preprogrammed commercial and video about the cemetery.

"Thank you for selecting Crab Cove Cinema Cemetery as your destination of choice. Whether you're seeking a final resting place for yourself or a loved one, you can't go wrong with Crab Cove Cinema Cemetery, the first best place to think of when the last worst thing has happened. Located on three hundred acres of rolling hills with bay views, we not only offer funeral and burial services but a vast array of video opportunities to share your life and your achievements with those who survive you. Choose a theme, and we will place you in a section with other like-minded guests. Whether you're a fireman or a food truck vendor, we have a section for you.

"When you arrive, please stop by the office for details about our new Youth in Asia section, as well as our discount packages and other themed sections. Now, sit back and relax, and enjoy a few of our most popular at-grave videos, and remember, death may not be your first choice, but here at Crab Cove Cinema Cemetery, our services are second to none."

Grave had seen the commercial before, so he just closed his eyes and tried not to think about the fact that he was in a driverless cab hurtling down the coast highway at ninety miles an hour. He was only mildly comforted that, whatever might happen, he was headed for the right place.

32

Sergeant Blunt was the first to break the silence that had followed Captain Morgan's shouted report of Mr. Bug's findings. "I don't get it. What does *The Magnificent Seven* even mean?"

Captain Morgan, who had been staring into space behind his desk, came back to life. "You're too young to remember. Hell, *I'm* too young to remember, but my grandfather forced me to watch it several times. It's an old movie starring Yul Brynner. Based on another, even older movie called *The Seven Samurai*."

Snoot was intrigued. "A movie?"

"Yeah, a put-upon Mexican village hires seven gunslingers to help them fend off a bandito who's terrorizing their town."

Snoot laughed. "And Mr. Bug thinks we're looking for seven gunslingers? I'm sorry, I'd rather go with a Magic 8-Ball."

Charlize, who had been puffing on her Sherlock Holmes pipe, which thankfully came without the smell of burnt vegetable matter, suddenly dropped the pipe to her side. "Mr. Bug's pronouncement should not be taken literally."

Captain Morgan's eyebrows shot up. "Oh?"

"Indeed, sir. I think we will find—in fact, I'm certain of it—that the data that resulted in Mr. Bug's conclusion is based on input from Detective Grave, who as we know, is at C3 Corporation, maker of drones."

"So?"

"So, I have it on good authority that C3 has replaced all its human workers with no fewer than seven simdroids."

"You don't say."

"I do say, and I say further that, given the age and inclinations of its founder, one Irving Orville, now retired, it would not be unreasonable to assume, nay postulate, that said simdroids would be designed to resemble the aforementioned magnificent seven, and might somehow be involved in the murders of Wright Orville and Lachlan McLachlan."

Captain Morgan started to say something, but Charlize held up a hand. She was on a roll. "I know further of a simdroid actor who bears a remarkable likeness to Yul Brynner, who played the lead magnificent, one Chris Larabee Adams. I know this because I recently sat through a performance of *Crabelot*, our town's droll adaptation of *Camelot*, in which said Yul Brynner simdroid plays King Arthur, or rather King Crab. The role is not part of Brynner's oeuvre, but his performance was compelling nonetheless."

Snoot shrugged. "So, are we looking for the gunslingers, the bandito, or the Samurais?"

"Perhaps none of the above," said Charlize.

Captain Morgan, who had little tolerance for the inscrutable, screwed up his face. "What?"

"Not just what," said Snoot, "but who? Who's the damned killer?"

"Ah," Charlize said, finger pointed to the heavens with a finality that suggested she was ready to reveal the killer. "That, my friends, is unknown. What is known is that the data that led to this conclusion by our robotic analyzer here was input by our Detective Simon Grave."

Captain Morgan screwed up his face still further. "So?"

"So," said Charlize, "considering the source, *The Magnificent Seven* may mean nothing at all."

33

At ninety miles an hour, no destination was too far in Crab Cove, so it took just a matter of minutes to reach Crab Cove Cinema Cemetery, which had become so popular, some people brightly referred to it as the nexus of death.

For a fee, you could memorialize your life in full-color videos, played nonstop on a monitor affixed to the top of your gravestone or obelisk. And, if money was an object, you could always agree to host commercials on your video, which would help defer your costs, maybe even make your family some money as you moldered away.

Grave thought the whole prospect was ridiculous, but his father thought otherwise and was already working with the design and creative teams at the cemetery on what his father called an "action thriller" of his life as a detective. The video's production seemed to be the only thing his father talked about these days, other than the Crab Claws, the town's minor league baseball team, which three weeks into the season had yet to score a run, let alone win a game. His father blamed the problem on a lack of hitting and pitching and laid blame at the feet of the team's manager, Corky Cooley.

Barry broke him away from his thoughts. "The data has been transmitted, sir. May I ask why we're here?"

Grave had a number of reasons but only shared one with Barry. "To talk with Victoria."

Barry wobbled in the air the way he always did when Grave mentioned what Barry thought was an imaginary friend. It worried him that Grave could carry on lengthy one-sided conversations with this girl, which Grave insisted was a girl of ten years old, who had lived and died in the eighteenth century.

"Sir, shouldn't we be heading back to the station. I'm sure it won't take Mr. Bug long to process the information, and—"

"No," said Grave, interrupting him. "I have business with her. Business that could help solve these murders."

Barry buzzed softly. "Yes, sir. Do you mind if I wander about? I hear they have a not-to-be-missed new section called Youth in Asia."

"Not at all, but meet me up the hill in fifteen minutes. This shouldn't take too long."

Barry offered a hum and a nod and sped away up the main path. Grave tracked him until the drone disappeared over a hill, and then walked up the side path that led to the bench frequented by Victoria.

He was in luck. Little, redheaded Victoria Skunkford, forever ten years old, was sitting on her bench, wearing the same outdated gingham dress she always wore. Those who could see her, which was a small number, thought she was a tour guide or a docent, like many real staff members who dressed up in period costumes to underscore the history of the cemetery.

He called out to her, and she responded with that disarming smile of hers. Grave would have been proud to call her daughter if he had been proud enough to call anyone his wife, but prospects of marriage seemed remote at the moment. There was no Mrs. Grave on the horizon.

"Detective Grave, I've been expecting you."

Grave walked up and sat down next to her. "Good to see you again. Has the cemetery been keeping you busy?"

"You think?" she said with a laugh. "So many new arrivals I've lost count. It's that new Youth in Asia section. People are just opting out of life left and right now."

"Not me," said Grave. "They'll have to drag me here kicking and screaming. Not that it won't be nice to spend more time with you."

"Don't be silly. I have it on good authority that you'll be a grouchy old geezer before you end up here."

Grave's eyes widened. "You know that?"

Victoria frowned, which Grave found just as charming as her smile. "Oh, I've said too much."

"So, this mortal coil that unwinds for us is just fate?"

She crossed her arms. "Detective, I can say no more. Now, what brings you here today?"

Grave could tell by her demeanor that any further attempts to learn more about fate or any other topic related to death was simply off the table. "Two murders. Perhaps you've heard about them."

"Ah," said Victoria, warming to the subject. "You must be talking about Wright Orville and Lachlan McLachlan."

Grave was delighted. "So, they're here?"

Victoria shook her head, then laughed. "Not completely."

"What?"

"McLachlan doesn't have his head, for one thing, but mostly, I was referring to an incomplete process. They've both just completed their orientation, and are now in stasis isolation."

"Stasis what?"

"Isolation. It's for the best. For everyone. We've found that the newly oriented tend to have a never-ending stream of questions. And, to be Frank, they can be very annoying."

"So you keep them locked up?"

"No, isolation. Stasis Isolation."

"Sounds like they're locked up to me."

Victoria looked away. "Anyway, there's nothing much else that happens now until their bodies arrive from the morgue. Do you know when that will be?"

The frowning face of Jeremy Polk, the medical examiner, suddenly appeared in his head. "I would think a week or so, perhaps sooner. Our medical examiner is quite thorough."

"I see. I'll tell them a couple of weeks, then. No sense in giving them false hope of a quick outcome. Hope is not much of a commodity here. Anyway, I've dealt with your Jeremy Polk before. You call him thorough. I call him snail slow."

Grave chuckled. "That's true, but listen, before they went into this stasis thingy, did either of them mention their murders?"

Victoria smiled. "I thought that's what you'd like to know, so I asked them. McLachlan, of course, doesn't have a head, so he didn't say a thing."

"We're still looking for it. If we can reunite it with his body, will he be able to say anything?"

"Oh, of course. Now, as to your Mr. Orville, let me just say that I have never met such a mean-spirited man. He just won't accept that as life goes, he's pretty much out of options. Rails on and on about the unfairness of it all. Everyone was so relieved when he went into stasis."

"I've heard he was a difficult man in life."

"Well, he continues as such in death. He is such a bother."

"So, what did he say? Did he mention his murder?"

Victoria sighed. "He did, but I doubt that it will be of much help. He remembers running and that he was terrified of something, a dog he thinks. And two sounds, one from the sky, the other a woman's scream."

"A woman?"

"Yes, but he doesn't remember who. And he certainly doesn't remember why he was there."

"I see. How long will his spirit be here?" Grave remembered discussing this with Victoria a couple of cases ago. The cemetery, she said, was like a waystation, with multiple final destinations. Where people ended up, she would never say. All she would offer was that ultimate destinations, which numbered in the thousands, were based on a complex algorithm known only to a few people up the chain of command.

"He seems determined, so if I had to guess, I'd say he's going to be here forever, either at the cemetery or, more likely, out near the marsh where you found him. People who don't let go, just never go."

Grave nodded. "Good. That means we have time."

"Shall I press him further? Sometimes they remember more details, and I'm sure he'd be happy about a brief break from stasis."

"Yes, please."

"Well, then," she said, standing. "I'd best see to that. Will you come again tomorrow?"

"Yes, of course." He stood and shook her hand. "Always a pleasure, Victoria. Now, before you go, could you point me in the direction of the Reverend Bendigo Bottoms?"

"Ah," she said. "What a wonderful funeral that was, and what a wonderful man. The gospel choir was magnificent. Now, if you'll just go back to the main path and turn right, you'll find your friend's grave about a hundred yards further on. Just follow the sound of the gospel choir. Adding them to his video was just brilliant."

Before Grave could respond, she was gone.

34

Captain Morgan announced what everyone already knew, just from the smell coming from Mr. Bug, the distinct odor of burnt wires and melted solder. "He's gone."

Charlize shrugged. "Just as well. He's not been very helpful of late."

"No," said Detective Snoot. "A Magic 8-Ball he's not."

"No, he certainly wasn't," said Blunt, his voice seemingly coming from a different location in the room every time he spoke.

"Still," said Smithers, "he gave it his all. I wonder, captain, would you mind letting me tinker with Mr. Bug a bit? In off-duty hours, of course. Perhaps there's a way to restore him to his old self."

"An old self isn't going to help," said Snoot. "We need a new self around here."

Captain Morgan's head bobbled from side to side as he weighed his options. "Okay, Smithers, go ahead and see what you can do. In the meantime, I'll contact the Baltimore Police and see if they have any newer analyzers available. Maybe we can get an even better one."

"That would be great," said Snoot.

"Now," Morgan continued, "for whatever reason, Detective Grave has seen fit to go incommunicado on us. Blunt, do you have any idea where he might be?"

"Well," said Blunt, "I assume he's still at C3, but if he's not there, my guess would be the cemetery."

"The cemetery?"

"Yes, sir. He mentioned something about paying his respects to the Reverend Bottoms."

"Look, I don't care if he's in Timbuktu, I want you to find him, and find him fast. We need him here, not wandering off in the middle of a double homicide investigation."

Blunt put all thoughts of sharing the evening with his family aside. "Very well. Object, with me."

Everyone watched as Object weaved his way out of the room, presumably following his near-invisible master.

Snoot watched in amazement. "How does he do that?"

Charlize shrugged. "Object is equipped with radar and heat-seeking upgrades. If you want to know where Blunt is, just keep your eyes on Object."

"Whatever," said Morgan. "Now, where does that leave us?"

Charlize was quick to jump in. "That leaves us, captain, at the nexus of vast possibilities, in a veritable bouillabaisse of evidence, clues, and leads. That place where professionalism and persistence come together to turn the unthinkable into the probable and the probable into a certainty we can all embrace."

The captain raised his eyebrows. "Wow, did Sherlock Holmes say that?"

Charlize beamed. "No, captain, that one's all mine."

Captain Morgan summed up everyone's reaction. "Oh."

35

Grave was embracing the certainty of death, as he always did when he came to the cemetery, but he only had time for a light embrace because the Reverend Bendigo Bottoms' gravesite was closer than he thought.

Victoria had been right. All he had to do was follow the sound of the gospel choir. And now that he saw them in living color, on a ninety-inch screen, with the reverend out front, clapping and dancing in rhythm, they were a revelation. He had always listened to them on the radio but had never imagined how wonderfully they moved to the music.

A voice startled him. "Pretty fine, huh?"

It was the late reverend himself, though not in the flesh. He was there, but not there, much like Sergeant Blunt, but if anything, more visible.

Grave stammered to get anything out, but all he could manage was a series of false starts. The reverend, who was never at a loss for words, had no trouble filling the gap. "Miss Victoria said you'd be here, but I never expected you to come."

Grave finally managed speech. "Well, no, I mean yes, I was planning to come, but work, well, you know how that goes."

The reverend shook his head and smiled. "Lord knows work was always a distraction for me and mine. But it continues here." He pointed at the video screen. "And it's a wonderful thing to see how my sermons are actually received by the people who visit or just pass by. I never had that with radio."

"They definitely had an impact on me, reverend."

The reverend nodded. "I know. I could sense that when we had our little talk about life a couple of years ago. I must say it was the strangest conversation I'd ever had in a Skunk 'n Donuts."

Grave smiled at the memory. He had missed the punchline in a sermon the reverend had given about life being like a tuna fish sandwich, and when he had seen him in the donut shop, he couldn't resist asking just why that was so. He and the reverend had talked about it for over an hour until Grave was thoroughly convinced that life really was like a tuna fish sandwich. "That was quite a talk you gave me."

The reverend chuckled. "Indeed it was. So, are you still listening to my radio program?"

Grave frowned. "Um, no, you're no longer on the air. Your death and all."

The reverend was astonished and angry. "Not on? *Not on?* But my contract says—*clearly says*—taped recordings would be rebroadcast *in perpetuity* even after my death. What don't they understand about *in perpetuity?*"

The reverend's image began to flicker, and then he was gone. Grave looked around, hoping the reverend would reappear, but a minute came and went with no such happening.

"Come on, reverend, I have some questions for you. Important questions. Talk to me."

But the voice he expected to hear was not the voice he actually heard, a completely different voice coming from behind him. "Who are you talking to, sir?"

It was Blunt, no doubt come to retrieve him.

"No one, Blunt, just thinking out loud."

"Well, there's plenty of that going on at the station, sir."

"Don't tell me. Morgan wants me back there posthaste."

"If not faster, sir."

Grave gave the reverend's video one last glance, then turned and headed back to the parking lot. "Did you bring a car?"

"Of course, sir, if you can call it that."

"Oh, what's wrong with it?"

"It's one of the older models. I'll actually have to drive it."

Grave smiled. "Then, yes, we can call it a car."

Now all he had to fear was Blunt's driving skills.

36

When Grave and Blunt arrived back at the station, they walked right into a lively discussion of a topic near and dear to everyone in the force, particularly Grave, namely, the identity of the officer responsible for the missing chocolate donut each morning. Two theories had developed, each with spirited backers, the first that Corporal Higgins, who invariably arrived early for the morning watch, was the culprit, and the second that the real culprit was that kid at Skunk 'n Donuts who filled the order every morning. Higgins and the kid were known fanciers of chocolate donuts, and both had means, motive, and opportunity to carry out their dastardly plot.

Grave, a man of deep suspicions, was more generous in his analysis. "I blame everyone."

"Well, of course you do," said Charlize, "but the real question is not *who* did the deed but *why* we order just one chocolate donut in the first place."

That comment seemed to take the wind out of the arguments on both sides. Officers stopped in mid-sentence, huffed or sighed, and wandered back to their desks one by one, leaving Grave, Blunt, and Charlize standing there with Retective Tilda Must.

Must! thought Grave, but before he had a second thought, Must had him by the elbow, dragging him toward the interrogation room. "Come with me, *now.*"

There were few voices in the world Grave disliked more, but at this particular moment, the booming voice of Captain Morgan was music to his ears.

"Grave, get in my office. You there, Must, let him go!"

Must opened her mouth to protest, but seeing Morgan's fast approach and the look he was giving her, said nothing and immediately released her grip on Grave.

"You can have him in half an hour, retective."

Must nodded. "So long as I get to talk to him today. My report is already past due."

Morgan grunted at her, first because grunting was his go-to response to myriad situations, second because he wanted to acknowledge what she had said, third because he wanted to dismiss the importance of what she had said, and fourth because he knew a well-formulated, nuanced grunt was more powerful than any word in any language.

Must, fearing that the grunt was preamble to physical violence, backed away without another word.

Grave's elbow, which had been enjoying its freedom, now found itself locked in the grip of Captain Morgan, who was waving his other arm over his head.

"Homicide squad, in my office, *now*," he boomed.

General scurrying ensued, each person keen on reaching Morgan's office so they could claim their favorite spots. "Favorite" being a euphemism for a place they felt safe. "Safe" being a euphemism for freedom from bodily harm. "Freedom" being a euphemism for trapped in Morgan's office, subject to his will and every whim, and there was just no euphemism capable of easing the pain, anguish, and fear that came with that.

Amidst the scurrying, no one noticed that the medical examiner, Jeremy Polk, a man small enough to elude scurrying, had not just arrived, but had taken up his usual space to the right of Captain Morgan, whose eyes seemed to be telekinetically moving each of the other team members into place, like pieces on a chessboard.

When he was satisfied that men, women, and drones were in position, he cleared his throat, issued a grunt of absolute authority, and began. "I want to review where we are on both cases. I know we don't have much yet, but the mayor wants an update, and I'm afraid our Mr.

Bug has given up the ghost. It's up to us now and all our investigative skills." He turned to Polk. "Jeremy, let's start with you. Any results?"

Jeremy blinked three times, his signature blinkathon when called upon to reveal his findings. "Let's start with Wright Orville, shall we?"

He scanned the assembled team, and seeing and hearing no objection, moved on. "He was found on the marsh with wounds of two types, one indicating rather severe dog bites, the other lacerations from sharp instruments."

"Let me stop you there, Polk," said Morgan. "We have three possibilities when it comes to dogs: McLachlan's drone dog, Haggis, a mysterious demon hound reported by McLachlan to be in the area, and McLachlan's real dog, Fred."

Charlize raised her hand. "Sir, if I may."

"Go on."

"The demon dog, as you call him, is actually the pet of Chester Clink, a dog part mastiff and part bloodhound named Baskerville, in homage to a Sherlock Holmes fictional dog of similar breeding."

Morgan seemed annoyed. "Yes, yes, I was going to mention that. We input that into Mr. Bug." He suddenly stopped and looked at the deceased Mr. Bug. "Not that that will do us any good." He turned back to Charlize. "Okay, is that all?"

Charlize offered her own electromechanical blink, which usually indicated she had encountered someone immune to logic and reasoned thought. "Well, of course, sir, there's the third dog, Fred."

"Exactly," said Morgan.

Detective Snoot stepped forward, her signature move for gaining attention. She could have just raised her hand, but she preferred to insert herself into a situation, which she found gained her immediate attention and, she thought, an advantage in any argument. "Sir, you're absolutely right. On the other hand, Fred has gone missing."

Morgan was incredulous. "Missing?" He looked around the room. "Does no one *really* not know where that dog is?"

What followed among the team could best be described as synchronous looks of chagrin, followed by headshakes and general looking down at the floor.

"I see," said Morgan. "Well, then, Smithers, be a good fellow and write this down on the board: *Where's Fred?*"

Smithers moved to the board without comment and wrote down the captain's question.

"Wait," said Grave. "Let's add *What's Fred?* too."

Morgan grumbled. "Grave, we know he's a dog."

There was mischief in Grave's smile. "Do we? Sir, Fred was the so-called pet of an accomplished inventor, someone apparently on the cusp, or perhaps even over the cusp, of startling, far-reaching discoveries that have or might or could change our world in incomprehensible ways that—"

Morgan had had enough. "Get to the point!"

Grave did. "Fred could be a simdog, perhaps one trained to kill."

Charlize chimed in. "He has a point, sir. We really didn't get a good look at him."

"Okay," said Morgan. "Let's add *What's Fred?* to the board. Does that mean we have to add *What's Baskerville?* as well?"

"No," said Snoot. "Baskerville is one hundred percent real dog. And if I may, sir, while we're on the subject of missing things, where's the car?"

Morgan seemed startled. "What? Has no one followed up on that?"

"Well, yes, and no," said Grave. "I've confirmed with his wife, Prissy, that it was not Orville's car. The man never drove."

"A chauffeur, then," said Morgan.

"No, sir, he didn't have one. He was pretty much a cheapskate. According to his wife, he usually bummed rides from his employees—another reason people hated him."

Morgan threw up his hands. "Okay, then. Smithers, add *Who's Car?* and *Where's the Car?* to the board."

Smithers did so without comment.

Morgan turned to Polk. "Didn't your team take molds of the tire tracks? Isn't that what you're supposed to do?"

Polk, who had been huffing and puffing throughout the exchange about dogs and cars, impatient to move on, cleared his throat in a way that no one in the room could ignore. "Captain, we may as well ask if there were a hundred cars at the scene. The place is a known point of liaison for lovers. There were tracks galore, meaning the situation was worse than having no tracks at all. Plus, if it was a hovercar or a flying car, there'd be no tracks."

He leveled his gaze at Morgan and waited for any response. Hearing none, he continued. "Now, if I may continue. The dogs have some importance, true, and we can come back to them, but can I, um, proceed with my findings?"

Morgan nodded.

"Very well. Now, as to the lacerations, they were long and deep and quite precise."

Charlize raised her hand. "Could they be from a Bowie knife?"

Polk nodded. "Yes, that's possible, but as you pointed out at the scene, they do not indicate any involvement of our notorious Chester Clink."

Morgan chimed in. "Even so, let's add *Where's Clink?* to the board. I can't help thinking he's connected somehow."

"But," said Polk. "*But*, it is not likely. The wounds indicate a Clink-like precision, yes, but neither his preferred locations nor depth."

"Yes," said Charlize. "I think we'll find that Clink's involvement was accidental, a coincidence. He would never strike so close to his hideout. It's just not his M.O."

"Even so," said Morgan, pointing at Smithers, "keep *Where's Clink?* on the board. He's a tricky bastard." He turned to Charlize. "Keep me up to speed on the Coast Guard's search."

Charlize nodded, and Morgan turned back to Polk. "Please continue, Jeremy."

"Wait," said Grave. "Could any of the wounds possibly have been made by a smaller blade, say a switchblade of the size and type used by James Coburn in *The Magnificent Seven?*"

Polk, a man of many blinks, outdid himself before replying. "Um, yes, that's possible, too."

Captain Morgan was having none of it. "Grave, what is this ridiculous fascination of yours with that movie? Whatever you input into Mr. Bug flat out killed him."

"Ah," said Grave. "It is unusual, I admit, but one of our suspects employs seven additional suspects in the form of simdroids designed to duplicate the actors in that movie. I have talked to them, and let me assure you, they were anything but friendly."

"All right," said Morgan. "I know I'll regret this, Smithers, but put *The Magnificent Seven* on the board."

Morgan looked around the room to make sure no one else was about to interrupt, then turned to Polk. "Jeremy, if you please."

Polk was quick to continue. "So, as you all know, my gut instinct at the scene was that Wright Orville died from fright, and I was correct. He clearly died of a heart attack."

"So the wounds were postmortem," said Grave.

"Indeed," said Polk, rolling his eyes at Grave's statement of the obvious. "Just not enough blood to think otherwise."

Captain Morgan threw up his hands. "So where does that leave us?"

"One possibility," said Grave, "is that the killer and his dog inflicted their wounds not knowing that Orville was already dead. They could have caught him even as he was falling down."

"That's possible," said Charlize, "but it is also possible that we are dealing with a second killer."

Jeremy Polk cleared his throat with an *ahem* of biblical proportions, immediately quieting Charlize. "Please let me finish *my* analysis."

He looked back and forth at the members of the team until he was satisfied he had their attention. "The lacerations could have been from a Bowie knife, yes, and they were done with almost Clink-like precision, yes, but unless I am completely wrong, we have at least two different types of blades and at least *three* wielders of those blades." He gave Grave a quick look. "Yes, even a James Coburn blade."

Some blinked, some gasped, some raised their eyebrows to attention at the word *three*, but it was Grave who was first to speak. "Well, no one has accused Orville of being popular."

A titter, a form of laughter not usually associated with a team of professionals, erupted from the team but evaporated quickly as Captain Morgan leveled his gaze on them. "Let's keep to the facts, please. Jeremy, go on."

Polk blinked hard—and slow—as if he were resetting his brain. "Charlize was also correct about the wine and the perfume. I found traces of a red wine, a piquant, somewhat fruity Pinot Noir with hints of clay that suggests a California origin, specifically a 2048 Chateau Plateau, a wine that according to its marketing slogan is *always on the level*."

He stopped and looked around the room, expecting some level of appreciation for his analysis, but found none.

"Good," said Morgan. "We should be able to track that down at local outlets. Smithers, add *Red Wine* to the board. Jeremy, please continue."

Polk shrugged. "So, we have the wine, and we also have traces of perfume on the victim's clothing and the beach towel, suggesting extended intimate contact with the wearer of said perfume."

"Yes, the woman," said Morgan. "Go on."

"The perfume is extremely floral, so floral in fact that it can only be one brand, Day-Z-Dew, a perfume that despite its rather mundane name is extremely expensive. So our woman is either very rich or knows someone very rich like Wright Orville."

Grave interrupted. "Sir, I've interviewed Wright Orville's wife, Prissy, and had a brief encounter with Frank Orville's wife, Wanda. I could be mistaken, but I think both were wearing floral perfumes."

Charlize raised her hand. "Captain, if I may. If Polk can provide me with the chemical analysis of Day-Z-Dew, my programming should be able to detect it on anyone."

"Good," said Captain Morgan, turning to Polk. "Let's do that, shall we. Grave, take Charlize and Smithers along with you for any follow-ups with the women suspects in this case."

Polk and Grave nodded, although Grave's nod suggested mixed feelings involving too many detectives in the same kitchen.

"Okay, then," said Morgan. "Smithers, add *Perfume* to the board. Oh, and *Who's the Woman?* With *Prissy Orville?* and *Wanda Orville?* under that." He looked around the room. "So, shall we move on to the McLachlan murder?"

"Not quite yet," said Grave. "We are forgetting there were reports of something in the sky that night, so what was it?"

Morgan sighed. "Okay, okay, let's add that to the board, too, Smithers."

As Smithers looked for space on the board, Captain Morgan's drone, Rum, began to make incoming-call noises.

Morgan looked at his watch. "That'll be the mayor. I'd better take this. Let's take a ten-minute break."

The team worked its way to the door in a way that suggested headlong flight.

37

Ten minutes of freedom is ten minutes of freedom, and everyone on the team had their own idea about how to spend that freedom. Snoot had gone immediately to her computer to start researching the latest drone models and dog breeds. Charlize and Smithers had huddled in a far corner of the squad room to discuss the case further. Jeremy Polk had hovered around the coffee machine, clearly wanting coffee but unsure about how to operate the machine. Blunt had rushed outside to call June with the possible bad news—at the current pace, going to Chuck E. Crab seemed impossible. The drones Object and Barry had hovered in another corner of the room, making beeping sounds approximating laughter, the possible result of a particularly appropriate drone joke. Detective Grave, wary of a run-in with Retective Must, had raced for the bathroom and its nearest stall, where he could be reasonably sure of privacy, although there was always the risk of a drone straying from an adjoining stall.

The ten minutes came and went with alarming speed, the sound of Captain Morgan's booming voice marking its end and the beginning of the re-scurrying process.

Morgan looked particularly annoyed. "Seems the mayor wants me to hold a news conference as soon as possible. I've managed to push that off to late tomorrow afternoon, but that only gives us twenty-four hours to make progress on these cases."

He turned and looked at the board. "We have some leads, some things to follow up on, and more people to interview. Anything else on the Orville murder before we move on to McLachlan?"

Snoot stepped forward. "It occurs to me that there may be a lot to learn from drone activity in the marsh area during the time of the murder. I know a lot of the newer drones have location-blocking technology, but most don't. We should be able to identify them and their owners and go from there."

"Excellent idea, Snoot," said Morgan. "Smithers, if you would."

Smithers moved to the board and began writing.

"Snoot," said Morgan, "take the lead on that, would you?"

"Yes, sir."

Morgan scanned the room. "Anything else?"

Grave raised his hand. "It may be premature, but perhaps we should list suspects on the board as well."

Captain Morgan, a man noted for jumping to conclusions, surprised everyone. "Yes, I think that would be premature. Hold your suspicions until we meet again tomorrow. In fact, let's fix that in time, shall we? The next meeting will be tomorrow at 3:00 p.m. sharp. That will give us time to identify suspects based on more evidence, and for me to prepare for the news conference."

He looked around the room to make sure everyone agreed and then continued. "Okay, then, let's discuss the McLachlan case. Who wants to start?"

38

Discussion of the McLachlan murder had proceeded swiftly, perhaps too swiftly. Polk identified similar, but not exact, lacerations of the upper body, but couldn't say whether the decapitation was the coup de grace or as Captain Morgan incorrectly put it, "the Coup de Ville," a reference to a long-defunct automobile. Neither could Polk claim with any certainty that McLachlan's head, now presumably in the hands of Chester Clink, was a post-mortem act of the killer or killers.

Once again, Chester Clink's name was bandied about as the possible killer, but Charlize and Smithers felt certain that Clink's involvement was coincidental, Clink in their view seizing the opportunity for a trophy. Charlize's comment about Clink's impersonation of Hannibal Lecter only drew a brief grunt from Morgan, who didn't even ask Smithers to put that on the board.

Detective Grave then put forth his theory that everything centered on distributed intelligence, neural nodes, and related industrial espionage, which received enough support that Morgan directed Grave to follow up with C3, DroneOn, and even Ramrod Robotics to determine whether this line of inquiry had any validity.

Detective Snoot didn't support the espionage theory, pointing out that if espionage were involved, surely the killer or killers would have taken the folder found near the body, the folder with McLachlan's plans and drawings. Her alternative theory was that McLachlan was just a witness to the Orville murder, and needed to be eliminated.

Morgan, who liked simple solutions and was a staunch supporter of Occam's Razor (simpler solutions are more probable than complex ones), applauded Snoot's theory. Charlize and Smithers pointed out, however, that at least one other simple solution—a botched robbery—was possible, at least for Orville, although neither supported something so simple and commonplace.

Discussion had then turned to Fred, McLachlan's missing dog, and whether it was a real dog or a simdog. Finding a real dog would have little impact on the case, but if Fred were a simdog, that would be a whole different kettle of canines. A simdog would have possibly recorded all that had happened. Morgan asked Snoot to form a team of simdroid officers and lead that search as well.

With assignments and next steps now clear, Morgan adjourned the meeting and sent them on their way, leaving him alone in his office with Rum.

"Any thoughts, Rum?"

Rum buzzed and hovered near the board, now covered with Smither's scribblings, and extended a probe to point at the last item.

"What's this one mean, sir?"

Morgan squinted at the item, which seemed to have been written in a different hand.

Where's the chocolate donut?

39

It seemed an odd thing to do, but odd things done was part of Detective Grave's milieu, so the odd thing had him trying to hide behind his near-invisible partner, Sergeant Blunt, as they raced for Blunt's squad car with their drones Object and Barry trailing. Retective Must wasn't fooled at all and was on them in a flash.

There was more than a little simulated anger in her voice. "Stop right there, detective. The jig, as you say, is up."

Grave was about to say something distracting about the Elizabethan origins of the phrase and its offshoots, including dancing, trickery, and racial slurs, but Blunt was on her in a shot, another phrase he was about to think about, but deferred to Blunt, who was now looming over Must, which made Grave think of women and fabric, not to mention warp and woof, which made him think of dogs.

Fortunately, Blunt interrupted his thinking, which was about to mention simdogs. "Yes, it is," Blunt said. "As you know, Article 17, Paragraph 6, Subparagraph C of the Uniform Code of Retection states, and I quote: *Post-investigatory interviews shall be conducted at a time and place acceptable to the detective being interviewed.*"

Must was about to respond, but Blunt held up his hand and waved it in front of her face so she could at least see a determined blur. He then turned to Grave. "Detective, is this a time and place of your choosing?"

Grave could only smile. "No, it is not."

As Must stood there, stunned, Blunt motioned Grave into the car, and they were gone in a shot, a phrase much slower than their actual movement.

Blunt pushed the old hovercar to its limits, only slowing down after the image of an angry Must disappeared entirely.

"Whew," said Grave. "That was a close one. I had no idea you knew about the uniform code."

Blunt chuckled. "No one does, sir. I made it up."

"What?"

"Yes, sir, it was just mumbo jumbo, and did you see the look on her face? It threw her completely."

Grave thought briefly about the phrase *mumbo jumbo* and its 18th-century origins, a dismissive reference to an African god, but decided laughter was more appropriate. "Blunt, Blunt, I had no idea you could get up to such mischief."

"Well, I wouldn't normally, of course, but I'm in a hurry. A night of celebration with June and Rippley."

"Ah, a birthday?"

"No, sir. I've been meaning to tell you this because it is so fantastic. Get this: Rippley can make herself visible and invisible *at will*."

The news was jaw-dropping, so Grave's jaw dutifully followed the news. "You're kidding."

"No, it happened at daycare. Completely floored the headmistress."

"That's wonderful. Here, pull over and let me out. I can get a taxi. You need to get home."

The car slowed to a stop in front of a house that looked familiar. "No need for that, sir, you're home."

Grave had to admit that he was, even though he would have preferred to see a house with an empty front porch, and not one fully occupied by his father and his father's fiancé, Ida Notion, plus his dog, Lucky, and several drones.

"Well, then, thanks for everything, and please bring Rippley by the station. I'm sure everyone would like to see what that little imp looks like."

"Oh, I will, sir. I think she'll make a wonderful spy one day."

"Or magician," said Grave, stepping out of the car. "I'll see you tomorrow, first thing. We need to head out to Frank Orville's place."

Blunt nodded and sped away, leaving Grave to consider phrases appropriate to describe the looks on the faces of his guests.

40

Ida Notion couldn't wait for Grave to make it to the front porch, so she danced down the steps and raced to him, her red-fringed wonder drone, Crystal Ball, in servile pursuit.

"Simon, the most wonderful thing. I've had another vision."

"Oh?" said Simon, walking past her and heading for the porch. "What was it this time?"

Ida chased after him. "Simon, Simon, slow down, I need to talk to you."

"On the porch, Ida. It's been a long day. Could we at least sit down?"

"Of course, Simon."

Grave climbed the steps, picked up Lucky, and sat down next to his father, who shrugged and gave Simon an oh-it's-just-Ida-being-Ida look.

"How are you, dad?" *He looks like hell*, thought Grave.

"Fine, Simon, fine." *I feel like hell*, thought Jacob.

Ida was apparently too excited to sit down, so she loomed over them. "Simon, listen—*listen.*"

Grave sighed heavily and gave Lucky a scritch under the chin. "Oh, I'm listening, Ida." *I could actually use a glass of wine.*

Ida pursed her lips. "This is serious, Simon. Serious *business.*"

"I know that, Ida. So what's the excitement all about?" *A glass of wine, and maybe some peanuts.*

Ida grabbed a nearby chair, pulled it over close to Grave's, and sat down, their knees nearly touching. "Simon, I've had another vision."

"You already said that." *Do I even have wine?*

She waved her hands to shush him. "Yes, yes, but here's the thing. It's about the laughing man in the sky."

"Yes, we're looking for him. We're thinking a flying car or maybe someone in a jetpack." *Yes, I remember putting a bottle in the refrigerator-synthesizer just this morning. My god, that seems like a lifetime ago.*

Ida shook her head. "No, but yes, all that's possible, but what I mean to say is the man was wearing a *sombrero.*"

She sat back in her chair and giggled, which for Ida was an annoying, high-pitched chitter not unlike Woody Woodpecker.

A chill ran through Grave. "A sombrero?"

Ida slapped her thighs with both hands. "Yes, can you imagine? And the man looked just like that old-timey actor, whatshisname from that movie whatzit." She turned to Grave's father. "What's his name again, Jacob?"

Jacob grinned at Simon. "Eli Wallach, Simon, the actor who played Calvera the bandito in *The Magnificent Seven.*"

Grave started to say something, but then stopped and motioned to Barry, who was hovering nearby. "Wine, Beer, Brandy."

Barry nodded and flew away, followed by Crystal Ball. Bubba, who seemed to be taking on the persona of Grave's father, hovered lazily at Jacob's shoulder.

Grave turned back to Ida. "Ida, this is amazing."

Ida clapped her hands together. "Oh, Simon, I just *knew* you'd love it."

"Yes, Ida, but now let's go over it again, shall we? From the top, and don't leave out a single detail."

41

Parents who took their children to Chuck E. Crab could reasonably expect to encounter four things: singing, dancing animatronic crabs, a noise level approaching a fusillade of cannon fire, and the general mayhem of a hundred or more children set free from there playaday lives.

To most parents, this meant hours of agony at great expense, but for Barry and June, it meant pure joy. Their daughter, Rippley, could not just make her presence felt, but seen. *At will.*

One minute she was there, and the next second she was gone, lost to complete invisibility, only to pop up again seconds later, somewhere else. So Barry and June had spent the evening laughing and clapping their hands with delight. Barry had hoped to discuss Rippley's "new normal" with June, but the noise level prohibited any meaningful conversation.

It wasn't until they had left Chuck E. Crab, their ears still ringing, and had settled a sleepy Rippley into the back seat, that they could share their wonderment.

"It's amazing," said Barry, climbing behind the wheel and starting up their old hovercar, a 2034 Toyota Flo-Spinner that had hovered through the years well beyond any expectations.

"It is," said June, "and we'll have to be extra careful now. She was a pistol before, but now—oh, my goodness."

"I know, I know, but she's so beautiful. I had a feeling that she would be, of course, but seeing her now. It's just wow. She looks just like you."

June gently punched him in the arm. "Come on, she's prettier than that. And that red hair, those freckles. She's like a little doll."

She was indeed doll-like but in a tall, gangly doll way. At just over two, or as Rippley put it, *celebrating her 750th Day Birthday*, she stood as tall as any over-achieving four-year-old, with the vocabulary and gift for gab of a motor-mouthed teenager. Her red hair, which June could now see needed a good trimming, was curly to the point of Little Orphan Annie. She had the tiniest of noses and eyes so blue they took your breath away. All that with skin approaching alabaster liberally sprinkled with freckles of cinnamon and paprika.

Barry laughed at the sight of her. "She's a doll, all right, but she's still a handful."

"I know," said June, now more serious. "Barry, do you think she'll be all right? I mean, in the life ahead."

Barry reached over and squeezed her hand. "Of course. In fact, I think she'll be brilliant."

"Oh, you. Of course you'd say that."

"I mean it. Listen, I want to share her with the world, starting tomorrow morning at the station. Grave specifically asked to see her, and I know everyone else would love to see our beautiful little girl."

"I don't know. It might be a bit much. I mean, it's so soon, and she's just had one hell of a night."

A voice came from behind them. "Me ready for my reveal, mom."

June couldn't help laughing. "Your *reveal*?"

Rippley began giggling. It was a disarming giggle that could only come from a small child as precocious as Rippley.

"Yesh, it's like dad always says. Time to put up or shut down."

Now it was Barry's turn to laugh. "Shut *up*, not shut down."

Rippley broke into full-out laughter as Barry and June shook their heads in wonder.

"Well," said June. "I do have to give a presentation at work tomorrow, but what the heck—the station it is."

Barry turned back and looked at Rippley. "For your reveal."

Rippley let out a whoop, and just as quickly settled back down in the backseat and went to sleep.

Tomorrow would be a big day, perhaps bigger than June and Barry—or even Rippley—could ever have imagined.

42

Ida and Jacob had stayed for hours, Jacob for the beer and Ida to detail her visions with a tongue let loose by more than one brandy. Grave, for his part, had consumed enough Duct Tape Chardonnay to make Ida's giggle seem cute and endearing.

They had talked about her visions first. The night was moonlit, with long shadows cast by the bulrushes in the marsh and the man running for his life. And there were other shadows, six in all, some racing toward the man, others seemingly running backward toward him, which Ida explained as shadows of different sizes and shapes closing in on the man from the direction of the car.

As the murder began, Ida had shut down, unable to watch, so the sequence of events and any view of the knife wielders was lost. When she dared look again, all was quiet. The man was down. The shadows were gone. And the car was missing.

As little as Ida was able to add to Grave's understanding, there was at least one stunning piece of information he'd have to discuss with the team: *six shadows*. One was Orville, one was certainly a dog, one had to be the woman, but what about the others? Who or what could they be? From the description, they seemed to be working in concert, closing in on him from different directions, but was that really the case? Grave knew from previous experience with Ida and her visions that she tended to compress events into a continuous stream when in reality, events were often spaced apart by seconds, minutes, or even hours. Still, three knife wielders seemed to fit Polk's analysis of the wounds, and inexplicably, one of them could have been James Coburn, and one could have been Eli Wallach. He'd have to go back to C3 for another look at *The Magnificent Seven*.

Grave had tried to sort all this out in the moment, but by the second glass of wine, he knew it was futile. His last thought about her vision was that she was often wrong, missing important pieces of information, or worse, combining multiple visions and assuming they were the same vision. So Grave's confidence level, particularly where it concerned James Coburn and Eli Wallach, was low.

Conversation had then turned to Ida's skills as a psychic, which then turned to Grave's admission that he saw dead people, but only certain dead people.

"There's this little girl in the cemetery I talk to from time to time about various cases."

That admission had Jacob calling his son a "looney," and cautioning him not to mention it at the station, which Grave then admitted he'd already done. His father had buried his face in his hands and proclaimed him an "idiot."

Ida seemed jealous of his ability and pressed him for details, calling his description of Victoria "remarkable."

She said she knew of other people with similar skills, and asked whether he saw all dead people or just this one girl.

"If you're seeing every dead person you come across, that would be one thing, but if you're just seeing this girl, it's probably not *your* skill at all, but hers. She wants you to see *her*."

Grave had then admitted he had seen and talked to the spirit of the Reverend Bendigo Bottoms, which had made Ida's eyes go wide.

"You may be a late bloomer."

Grave wasn't sure that was a good thing but went on to describe his conversation in great detail, including the reverend's anger at learning his program had been taken off the air.

Ida had burst out laughing. "Well, he must have scared management to death, because his show was on when we drove over here tonight."

All Grave could think of then was his 1965 Austin Healy Sprite and its radio, which was stuck on the reverend's station at full volume. It had been sitting idle ever since the reverend's death and the station's turn to loud static.

Perhaps it was the third (or maybe the fourth) glass of wine that had him running off the porch, pulling off the car's protective cover, and jumping inside. Ida and Jacob had to cover their ears when Grave started up the car, not from the sound of the engine, which was now a very quiet electric motor, swapped out by Charlize when she had served as his companion and sometime mechanic, but from the noise of the gospel music that had erupted from the car's speakers.

The sound had brought his sleeping street to life, porch light after porch light coming on to witness the auditory event, as gospel music gave way to the booming voice of a man now moldering in his grave.

And no doubt smiling, thought Grave.

43

Grave couldn't be sure whether the buzzing noise was coming from his wine-addled head or some new fault in the radio of the Sprite, but it was definitely interfering with his enjoyment of the drive to the palatial home of Frank Orville and his wife, Wanda. Not surprisingly, the gospel music had brought everyone out on the mansion's front porch, although Grave was certain there must be another name for the size and expanse of it and the eight Corinthian columns that defined it and seemed to hold up the whole dwelling, which seemed to stretch on to the horizon in both directions.

There was something antebellum south about the scene, except instead of slaves moving about with silver trays of tea and toast and marmalade, there was a team of simdroids, and it didn't take Grave two seconds to figure out that the simdroids were the magnificent seven, led by Yul Brynner as the butler. No sign of Eli Wallach, however.

Charlize, Smithers, and the familiar blur of Sergeant Blunt were already in animated conversation with the Orvilles, including Frank, Wanda, and the patriarch of the family, Irving Orville. Grave parked the Sprite next to Blunt's police hovercruiser and made his way quickly up the marble steps, trailed by Barry, who was already busy recording a video of the scene.

Charlize met him halfway and pulled him aside. "Grave, a word."

Grave dutifully stopped and let her lead him to a spot out of earshot of the others, who seemed to be remarking on the joys of silence.

"We've only just arrived," she said, "but I'm already suspicious of these simdroids, particularly Yul Brynner, who's insufferably polite and arrogant."

"Well, he would be, wouldn't he? I mean, he's Yul Brynner. All those roles of his seemed to require it."

Charlize nodded. "Maybe, but my sensors and programming suggest a game's afoot, a game he's holding close."

"All right, let's keep that in mind, then. Tell me, do we have a room set aside for interviews?"

"Yes, they're giving us the main dining room. There's a table, enough chairs for all of us, and complete privacy."

"Good. Where do you think we should start?"

"I'm curious about the father, Irving Orville. I think it would be good to get his perspective before we interview Frank and Wanda. And I'd suggest saving Yul for last. I really think we'll need a full background on the others before we can figure out what he's up to."

"Okay, that works for me. Any word from Captain Morgan this morning?"

"Nothing really. I called in to let him know we'd arrived. You'll be interested to know that Tilda Must is at his elbow. I could hear her strident voice when he took the call from Rum."

Grave winced. "Ouch."

Charlize smiled. "Don't worry. You'll do fine when the time comes."

"May that be in some glorious future, centuries hence. But speaking of time, let's get this show on the road."

Charlize stepped to one side. "After you, sir. I'll follow your lead."

They walked back up the steps, faced by what looked like a curious choir, or maybe a firing squad, of silence.

44

Amanda Snoot was a competent detective, more competent in fact than she was often given credit for. Perhaps it was her diminutive size or a workaday grim expression she hid behind on most days, but for whatever reason, people underestimated her. Still, she had to admit that she was making headway.

Why else would Captain Morgan entrust her with two important lines of inquiry, the missing dog and air traffic over the crime scene? Yes, some might say this was all grunt work, the absolute dregs of an investigation, but statistics suggested otherwise. It was always something mundane that turned the tide and led to the apprehension and conviction of the perpetrator.

Snoot relished these details, and it was pursuing them that had made her a detective in the first place, so she had set to work with preternatural eagerness.

Air traffic and communications was the easiest part, although it took several hours to sort through the multiple sources required to get a true picture of what was happening at the exact moment Wright Orville's heart had stopped.

Two flying cars had passed by overhead in the minutes before and after the murder. The driver of the first car had been in the middle of an argument with his wife about how a simsteak should be cooked and hadn't noticed anything. The driver of the second car, however, had reported nearly colliding with a large drone near the scene, a drone that appeared to be diving toward the ground.

Snoot had searched and searched for further evidence of the mystery drone, but had found nothing. Perhaps it had been using cloaking.

Phone logs were also problematic. There was evidence that sixteen calls had been made by various drones within a five-mile area of the crime scene, but none close enough to be of interest and all cloaked or blocked to prevent detection of the owner.

Snoot decided to move on to the dog, Fred. Animal Control had found nothing so far, but was continuing its search. Frustrated by their slow progress, Snoot decided to head out for a search of her own. After a brief stop at the Skunk 'n Donuts on Main Street, which was once again out of chocolate donuts, she had driven to the crime scene and the McLachlan kennels, which were still draped in an overabundance of crime scene tape fluttering in the wind.

Despite instructions not to do so, Animal Control had emptied out the kennels, transporting all the other dogs to their shelter on the south side of town, near the crabbing docks. Nothing remained at the kennels but half-empty bowls and a lingering smell of dogs and urine.

McLachlan's house smelled of dog as well, but there was no sign of Fred, so she had decided to look around outside, which also turned up nothing at all. Her next thought was to explore the nearby caves again, but the thought of the darkness and cold, and the potential of running into a possibly returning Chester Clink gave her pause.

She decided instead to sit down on McLachlan's bench overlooking the bay and watch the freighters glide by as she considered next steps. What was she missing? Had she done everything she could do? Were there other possibilities for sniffing out this missing dog?

Sometimes answers can be sniffed out by the sniffing—in this case, a rather large dog sniffing at the back of Snoot's neck.

Fred!

45

The Orville Mansion was nothing to sniff at. From its expansive porch to its echo-producing foyer, to its grand staircase, which seemed to swirl into the heavens, the mansion was magnificent. Grave now realized that the Hawthorne Mansion, the only other mansion he'd ever been in, was no more than a caretaker's cottage compared to the Orville Mansion.

After a few minutes of gawking in the foyer, which was lined top to bottom with ornate, gold-framed paintings of old men in berets, Frank Orville directed Yul to show Grave and his team into the dining room, where the interviews would take place. Yul's acting skills were extraordinary. A gunslinger most days, he could, when asked, be every bit the officious butler that Smithers had been in his former life, and more. If anything, he took butlering to a new level.

So it was with practiced panache that he slid back the large oak pocket doors that separated the foyer from the dining room, and led them in.

"I do hope this will suffice," he said.

Grave's first thought was that the room would not only suffice but would be the perfect setting for a world summit. A large oak table sat square in the center, surrounded by what must have been at least thirty high-backed chairs, each filigreed with gold.

The table itself was a work of art. Grave didn't know quite what to think of its ornamentation, which portrayed hunting scenes using a technique like, but unlike, cloisonné.

Yul noticed Grave's interest. "Beautiful, isn't it?"

Grave nodded. "Yes, remarkable."

"From what I understand, it was made from a single tree. Just imagine how large it must have been."

"It's a wonder, no doubt."

Yul looked at the assembled team. "Now, before I bring in our patriarch, Irving Orville, a word about the accommodations. The table is evident, clearly, but let me draw your attention to the buffet, where you will find coffee, tea, bottled water, and a selection of the Orville's favorite Basque dishes."

"Basque?" said Blunt.

"Yes," said Yul. "The family is of Basque descent, people originally from a region in the Pyrenees that straddles the border between France and Spain. The Orvilles, who emigrated to America in the late nineteenth century, were originally named Orzabal, but that name was changed to Orville by the immigration officials."

"Interesting," said Charlize. "I guess that explains all the berets in the paintings."

"Indeed," said Yul. "Now, as I was saying, there are several Basque delicacies here for your enjoyment."

He led them down the length of the far wall, pointing out dish after dish on the long, room-length sideboard. "This is Basque cake, originally from Cambo and made from flour, sugar, and butter. It is said to be quite wonderful when topped with black cherries or pastry cream. Frank Orville thinks there's nothing better after a brisk walk along the shore."

He took a few steps down. "Now this, this is Bayonne ham, which is salted and dried according to Basque tradition. We have it flown in directly from Bayonne."

He continued. "This is a stew called Marmitako, which is made from tuna, a traditional favorite of Basque fishermen."

On he went. "I'd use some caution here. These are Espelette peppers, quite strong, named for the village where they were originally grown and dried. You might pair them with the next dish here, which is called Ardi-gasna, or ewe cheese. Then again, most people prefer to have Ardi-gasna topped with black cherry jam or quince jelly, which we've provided, as you can see."

He moved further down the line, past large pots containing coffee and hot water for tea. "Then again, if you find the Basque food too exotic for your personal tastes, I have taken the liberty of laying in a supply of chocolate donuts, two dozen in all, for your further enjoyment."

He did a quick bow. "So, I wish you luck with your interviews. If you'll excuse me, I'll go get Mr. Orville."

Without another word, he left the room, closing the doors behind him with a flourish.

"He makes a wonderful butler, don't you think?" said Smithers. "Better than I ever was."

"I wouldn't say that," said Grave. "You were a wonder to behold at the Hawthorne Mansion."

"Still, I much prefer my new role now. A country doctor, companion to an amazing detective, suits me just fine."

Grave nodded. "I guess it does. Now, who's for some food?"

Charlize and Smithers, being simdroids, shrugged at the array of food and moved away to find seats at the table. Grave wasn't sure which Basque dish Blunt had decided to try, because he was focused on the greatest delicacy of them all.

Chocolate donuts!

46

There was little doubt where Fred had been hiding. His coat was covered in the red clay characteristic of the nearby caves. Snoot remembered well how her mother had raged at her when little "Snooter" had come home after a day of playing in the caves with friends. Her clothes would have to be washed and washed again.

Snoot laughed at the memory, and then her eyes went wide. Two thoughts had popped up and intertwined in a way that sent chills down her spine: the clay, the caves.

The clay was phosphorescent. Kids would intentionally roll in it and then race outside into the light to wait for the sun to set. Then they'd play Chase the Glow until their parents called them in. Clink's dog, Baskerville, or even Fred, would have presented a frightening image in the dark, and since both were so friendly, they would have surely chased after Wright Orville. Of course, it didn't explain the ferocity of the dog bites, but it was a clue nonetheless.

And then there were the caves. They were cold, which meant they were an ideal place to avoid thermal detection, even by the latest technology of the EverEye Satellite, which was sensitive enough to detect mice.

The *ah-hah* moments kept coming. Clink must have selected his cave hideout *because* of the cold; he knew he couldn't be detected there. And that meant he would probably be seeking a new cave or some other thermal free zone, and there were only so many of those within range.

Clink always had a Plan B, so the cave would probably be close enough to minimize his time under the watchful eye of the EveryEye.

And the next *ah-hah* was a head slapper. They'd failed to get EverEye imagery of the night of the murder. That imagery would surely show who did what to whom—they could re-create the entire sequence of events.

Clink was within their grasp if they acted quickly, and they could learn a lot from the EverEye imagery. Delighted with her discoveries, Snoot shouted out for Goth, so she could call Captain Morgan and the Coast Guard with the news.

Just as quickly, she realized that Goth was no more, and the only way to notify anyone was in person. She raced for her old hovercruiser and its dead radio, Fred bounding along beside her.

47

Interviewing suspects is the most basic, and yet most advanced, skill of any detective; it is both a requirement and a challenge. Done correctly, in the hands of an experienced detective, it approaches an art form. Come at a suspect too softly, and you get nothing. Come too hard, and you get the same result: nothing. Come with chocolate smeared on your lips and chin from the quick consumption of three chocolate donuts, and you get what Detective Simon Grave was getting right now: a laugh erupting from the suspect somewhere between a chuckle and a chortle, with hints of a barely suppressed guffaw.

Fortunately for Grave, Charlize was quick to jump in with the first question, distracting Irving Orville long enough for Grave to find a napkin and wipe the chocolate from his mouth, with the help of Smithers, who pointed from spot to spot until Grave's lips and chin were chocolate free.

"Mr. Irving Orville," she began, "we are here this morning with the hope of acquiring enough knowledge about you, your family, the C3 Corporation, and your unfortunate son, Wright, to apprehend, charge, and convict his murderer or murderers forthwith."

Irving Orville shrugged his shoulders and rolled his eyes in just the way you'd expect from a family patriarch and retired CEO—with arrogance, annoyance, and a healthy dose of entitled impunity. "Understood, and call me Irv, or Irv-Orv, everybody does."

He was tall, even sitting down, with shoulders broad but hunched from time. The datasheet said he was eighty, but he looked younger, his face largely unwrinkled but for mildly drooping bags under his pale, rheumy blue eyes. His nose was large, almost weapon-like, resembling the blade of a small hatchet. A pencil-thin gray moustache danced over thin lips as he spoke, his voice low, suggesting deep caverns. He was dressed for comfort and leisure—old jeans, a yellow sweater to fight the morning chill, and never-run running shoes. A black beret, or Txapel as he called it, sat atop his bald head, raked at a jaunty, yet almost imperious, angle.

Grave watched the way Orville's eyes were playing over Charlize, trying to get her measure, as he awaited her question. He hoped Charlize wouldn't fall into a trap commonly used by suspects to turn the tables: familiarity. Befriend the detectives. Make them empathetic toward you. And delay, delay, delay.

She didn't. *"Mr. Orville,"* she continued with some emphasis on the formality of the interview, "where were you on the night of the murder?"

Orville clearly winced. "What? For the love of god, you can't think I would kill my son. I mean, yes, he was a piece of shit and was running my company into the ground, but no, absolutely not, I wouldn't do that."

Charlize persisted. "You haven't answered my question."

Irv-Orv glowered at her. "I think I have. But here's a question for you. Perhaps one of you can tell me why I'm being grilled by a simdroid of a fading actress, all got up in a Sherlock Holmes costume? And who's this other one got up like Doctor Watson? He looks just like Peter O'Toole."

Grave, chocolate-free, was about to intervene, but Charlize fixed a steely look on him and then turned back to Irv-Orv, leveling the same steel on him. "Perhaps one day, I'd be happy to answer your questions, sir, but today is for *my* questions. You can answer them here, in the comfort of your home, or we can take you down to the station. One way or another, you will answer our questions. Now, as to the night of your son's murder, where were you?"

Irv-Orv glanced back and forth between Charlize and Grave. "This really is quite preposterous."

Grave tried to match Charlize's steel. "Answer the question."

Irv-Orv slumped back in his chair. "Very well. Doesn't matter, really. I was with an *escort.*"

Charlize gave him an appraising look. "I see. And by *escort,* may I assume you are referring to a woman or simdroid who specializes in sexual services?"

Irv-Orv nodded and looked away. "Yes, a simdroid. Since my wife died, you see . . ." His voice trailed off.

"Understood," said Charlize. "Now, are we talking about a freelance sexbot or one from an established release center?"

Irv-Orv frowned. "What a terrible name for it, but yes, the *release center* on Main Street."

"And the name of the service provider?"

"I don't know her real name, of course, but she goes by Stella Tunella. Her slogan is *Stella Tunella, Good for a Fella,* if you can believe it. I'm sure she'll be able to corroborate our, um, *appointment.*"

"Of course she will," said Charlize, turning to Grave. "Sir, would you like to continue?"

Grave nodded. "Yes, thank you. Now, Mr. Orville, you mentioned one aspect of interest to us, namely Wright's being a bit of fecal matter generally hated by everyone."

Irv-Orv nodded. "He was a *dick.* Offended everyone. Disliked everyone. Cheated everyone. You name it, he screwed you over."

"Yes, we know," said Grave. "Now, as to the second thing, the fact that he was, as you say, running the company into the ground. Could you expand on that?"

"I'd be happy to, now that the company has reverted back to me."

"To you? I thought the company would go to his brother, Frank, what with your retirement?"

Irv-Orv looked incredulous. "Frank? No, Frank's an imbecile. He's the last person I'd want running the company. His title is purely for show. I mean, see here, if you want a look at the paperwork on this, my lawyers would be happy to provide it. The fact is the company reverts to me in the event of Wright's death."

"I see. Okay, tell me about the financial state of the company."

Irv-Orv took a deep breath. "Our CFO, Brad Dingle, can fill you in on the details, but it all pretty much started when I retired. We were a cellphone company then and had been for many years. A stable, *profitable* company with a bright future. Again, talk to Brad. He can show you the numbers and related filings."

"Okay, we will," said Grave. "So, then Apple did its thing, is that right?"

"Yes, and its *thing*, as you put it, with the backing of corrupt politicians, made cellphones obsolete almost overnight. It was beautifully devious. Alert Congress to a new health hazard—an *imaginary* health hazard—and then point out the obvious solution, your new invention, or rather an old invention with new and *completely healthy* abilities."

Irv-Orv slumped back in his chair, shaking his head, which continued for some seconds until Grave continued.

"So, what happened then?"

Irv-Orv laughed derisively. "Then, the shit hit the fan. We had to retool, and Wright just wasn't up to the task and all the changes required to turn a battleship like C3 around. Bad decision after bad decision. Instead of focusing on a limited, high-quality line of drones, he kept introducing new models that were, in a word, shit. No offense to our designer, Jim Phizz. Wright never gave the man time to refine his designs. It was always new, new, new. Stop this one, start that one. Just ask Jim. Anyway, customers dropped away, and the expenses started piling up. I really think we're close to bankruptcy if you want to know the truth. The bastard ruined us."

Grave thought he could actually see tears forming in Irving Orville's eyes. "Is it really that bad?"

Irv-Orv nodded. "Just ask Brad. I mean, we're doing all we can. Trying to get a loan that will see us through. Changing our manufacturing approach. Downsizing the workforce—mostly simdroids now. And we're also cutting back on the number of products. I think we can make it, but it's going to be a challenge."

"You've done all that in the last few days, since Wright's death?"

"Oh, no. Say what you will about Wright, he wasn't stupid. He could see the handwriting on the wall and had started making the necessary changes—with my help, of course. He at least had the good sense to come to me."

Grave made a note to talk with Brad Dingle and Jim Phizz, to see if they agreed. "Now, before I move on from the business side of things, one last question."

Irv-Orv crossed his arms and leaned back in his chair. "Shoot."

"Your simdroids. I see they're doing double duty. How did you come by them, and why choose the magnificent seven?"

Irv-Orv uncrossed his arms and leaned toward Grave. "*Magnificent,* aren't they?"

"Well, yes, but why them?"

"Ah, well, that goes back to my father and grandfather, who were both big fans of the original movie. When C3 was doing well, I thought the seven simdroids would make a wonderful gift to my father, who was suffering from Alzheimer's at that point."

"But wasn't that cured years ago?"

Irv-Orv frowned and shook his head. "The vaccine, yes, but it came too late for my father. I mean, this was twenty years ago. They just couldn't reverse what was going on. Anyway, my dad was spending his days watching that movie. So I thought, if he had the magnificent seven right there with him, they could get him out of his chair—exercise and all, you see—and in effect, make him feel like he was actually in the movie."

"Like he was an eighth magnificent."

"Exactly," said Irv-Orv, looking and smiling at each of them in turn for signs of approval of his wonderful idea. "And it worked, beautifully. He called himself The Basque Kid. We got him a cowboy costume and everything, even revolvers that shot blanks. You know, movie props. And the simdroids followed my instructions perfectly. My dad, before he died, was the happiest man on this planet, and was certain he'd catch and kill the bandito."

"You mean the Eli Wallach character?"

"Yes, the bandito Calvera."

"Did you have such a simdroid?"

Irv-Orv shook his head. "We discussed having a Calvera simdroid but decided it was better, more suspenseful, really, to have him out there somewhere on the arroyo. You know, an unseen threat."

"I see. So, after your father's death—"

"We used them as servants at first. But then, when the company started to struggle, we began using them to replace workers on the manufacturing floor. Simdroids just don't make mistakes, so with a little programming, they were actually increasing our output and our efficiency, for no cost at all.

"And the workers you replaced. Any negative feedback? You know, threats?"

"Ah, I see where you're going there, detective. Disgruntled employee kills company executive in revenge for firing. No, no, nothing like that. If anything, they were more than happy to leave."

"Oh, why is that?"

"I mean, Wright was a dick, treated them like shit. And besides, they knew they could get better pay at DroneOn, our competitor. They were stealing our employees left and right even before we started to struggle financially."

"I see, I see," said Grave. "Nevertheless, we'd like a list of former employees and contact information."

Irv-Orv nodded. "I'll see that you get it. Now, are we done here?"

"Almost, sir. I think we've got the business end covered. Now to the personal side."

"The *personal* side?"

"Yes, what he was like—other than being, you know . . ."

"A dick?"

"Yes, his relationships at home and at work."

Irv-Orv looked crestfallen. "Look, I have things to do, people to call. Can we at least take a ten-minute break?" He glanced at his watch. "Have a snack, formulate your questions, and I'll be back before you know it."

Grave looked at Charlize, who nodded, as did Smithers and Blunt, who seemed eager to discuss what they had just heard from Irv-Orv.

"Okay, then, ten minutes."

Irv-Orv pushed back from the table and left the room.

Blunt was the first to speak. "He seems nervous."

"Yes," said Charlize. "We'll have to follow up on everything he's said. Talk to Phizz and Dingle, for one."

"And the magnificent seven, for seven," said Smithers.

Grave nodded. "Yes, a lot to do, in a short time."

"Shall we split up, perhaps?" said Charlize.

Grave sighed. "No, not yet. I want you here for the interview with Wanda Orville."

"The perfume?"

"Yes, but also Frank Orville. I want your opinion of him."

Smithers raised his hand. "What about the magnificents, sir? I'd like to take a crack at them."

"Yes, exactly. I want you and Charlize to stay here to do that. Meanwhile, the stick is clocking on this investigation. Captain Morgan and that damned press conference. We need to move fast once we finish here."

A chuckle was coming from the general direction of Blunt, a barely discernable image across the table from Grave.

"What?" said Grave.

"You said the *stick is clocking*, sir."

"No I didn't."

Smithers joined in. "You did, sir, and might I say that you mangled the spoonerism in doing so."

"The what?"

"Spoonerism, sir, the way you transposed the beginnings of the words, swapping them, if I may say so, to humorous effect. Still, to be faithful to Oxford don and ordained minister William Archibald Spooner's play on words, you should have said the *tick* is clocking, not the stick."

"I see. Well, I guess I'll stick with stick, because if we don't find something, and soon, Morgan will be taking a stick to us. Or should I say staking a tick to us?"

"Point taken," said Smithers.

Grave clapped his hands. "So, moving on, that leaves Dingle, Phizz, and DroneOn. Who wants whom?"

"I'd like to have a look at the people at C3," said Charlize. "Dig into their financial situation, check out what Irving Orville has told us."

Smithers nodded. "I'd like that, too. My new financial crimes software should come in handy."

"Very well," said Grave. "Blunt and I will follow up on the possibility of industrial espionage and bad blood between the two companies."

"Sir," said Blunt, "I'm sure June would have insights into DroneOn, too. Perhaps she can break free and join us."

"Excellent," said Grave. He checked his watch, then looked back and forth at his team. "So, I guess that's it for the moment. Donuts, anyone?"

Grave didn't wait for an answer.

48

Captain Morgan was thrilled by Snoot's news. A fresh lead on serial killer Chester Clink, the capture of Fred, the glow-in-the-dark dog, and as embarrassing as it was, the reminder that they had failed to check EverEye thermal imaging on both murder scenes.

Morgan beamed at Snoot, who was preoccupied with Fred, who had instantly become the darling of the station. A crowd of officers and simdroids had gathered round to pet him and talk baby talk to him. *Good boy, good boy, good boy* seemed to be the theme of the moment.

Of course, Morgan could never hold a beam for long. "All right, break it up," said Morgan. "Snoot, come into my office, and bring the dog."

The officers dispersed, and Snoot and a now-leashed Fred dutifully followed Morgan into his office. A stranger, a woman dressed all in white, save for a scarlet scarf artfully tied around her neck, was sitting in one of the chairs opposite Morgan's desk, one of those new microdrones, also pure white, hovering near her shoulder, its buzz barely audible. Snoot was very curious about her, but Morgan was speaking again.

"Snoot, I'm not one for praise. You know that. But your performance of late, particularly what you've discovered today, has been exceptional. And to be frank, I think you're ready to form your own team, conduct your own independent investigations."

Now it was Snoot's turn to beam. She could barely control her smile or the tears welling in her eyes. "Oh, sir."

"There's a pay increase, of course, and a partner to boot." He waved his hand in the direction of the young woman. "Let me introduce you to Detective Polly Loblolly. She's just transferred in this morning. One of the Delaware detectives caught up in the final drowning of Delaware. I swear, the water will take us all one day. She'll be junior to your senior."

The woman in white gave her a polite smile and stood to shake Snoot's hands. The differences in the two women could not have been more startling. Where Snoot was short and thin, Detective Loblolly was tall and shapely, with legs from here to Boise and back again. Where Snoot's head was disproportionate to her body, Loblolly's seemed to fit nicely, with a long neck that gave her a regal bearing. Snoot's grey eyes could barely keep up with the comparison checklist, which featured mostly opposites. If the two of them had been words, they'd have been near antonyms. Eyes, grey versus sky blue. Noses, pinched versus turned up. Skin, pale versus golden tan. Lips, thin versus pouty. Hair, flame red and cropped short versus honey blond and long. Body, spaghetti thin versus shapely and toned. Breasts, a suggestion versus an abundance.

There's beauty, and there's beauty. Snoot's was an acquired taste; it came to you in subtle changes in mood and expression, the way she tilted her head when she spoke or ran her hands through her red hair. It was a nuanced beauty, one you grew to appreciate, often deeply, over time.

Loblolly's beauty came at you like a train you couldn't avoid. You could only startle, jump back, and wonder at its approach. Not that you'd ever find Loblolly's face on a magazine cover. Hers was a girl-next-door beauty, almost tomboyish, but still powerful and undeniable.

Snoot's hand disappeared into Loblolly's. "Welcome to the team. I see you like white."

Loblolly beamed at her. "Thank you. I see you like black." Her voice was blues singer deep to Snoot's high-pitched parakeet.

Some beginnings are awkward, and Captain Morgan sensed this beginning was about to derail before it even began. But what choice did he have? He couldn't pair Loblolly with Grave. *Oh, god no. Grave would just spend all day gawking at her.*

"Um, look," he said, "I'll leave you two to it. Snoot, I've left Loblolly's personnel folder there on the desk. You can use my office for the next half hour or so to get acquainted and review the necessary details of the McLachlan case. You know, bring her up to speed, because speed is exactly what we need now. And don't forget the team meeting at 3:00."

"Yes, sir," said Snoot.

"All right, then, I'll leave you to it." He nodded at them both and left the office, closing the door behind him.

Snoot moved behind the desk and sat down, motioning Loblolly to sit back down as well. "So," she began, opening the personnel file, "I see you've moved progressively west with the water."

Loblolly smiled back at her with a palms-up shrug. "Glug, glug, glug."

That was all that Snoot needed to hear. They would be a fine team.

49

The second session with Irving Orville had gone well, and quickly. During the break, he had apparently thrown some psychological switch that made him more open and cooperative. That, or he just wanted to get the interview over with.

In addition to being universally disliked, Wright Orville had apparently been a womanizer, a philanderer, and a serial adulterer, all words that rolled off the tongue of Irving Orville with a mix of feigned distaste and fatherly pride. Grave suspected the father had trained the son.

Irv-Orv wasn't very helpful in narrowing the field of women who could have been at the crime scene. His son apparently had wide-ranging tastes when it came to women. Short, tall, thin, fat, ugly, beautiful, old, young, healthy, sick—it just didn't matter to Wright.

The list of potential suspects was equally long. Wright hated everyone, and everyone returned the favor. On the question of competitors, though, Irv-Orv was clear that only DroneOn would think to rise to the level of murder to gain advantage.

"They're organized crime," said Irv-Orv. "I'm sure of it."

When Grave had seemed to run out of questions, Charlize, who had remained silent during the second session, piped up. "Mr. Orville, a follow-up question on your simdroids, if I may."

Irv-Orv nodded. "Of course."

"You mentioned you'd bought them twenty years ago."

"Yes, from Ramrod Robotics. Early models."

155

"Yes, that's what I'm getting at. They seem more skilled than droids of that era."

Irv-Orv beamed back at her. "Yes, exactly. I'm so happy you noticed. So, in the early years, we got the usual software updates from Ramrod, like everyone did back then, but the charges and maintenance fees were astronomical. And, of course, they would be. Ramrod was the only game in town at the time."

"So the new upgrades?"

"Ah, yes. When we needed them to do more than household tasks, we developed our own software in-house. Even some hardware to go with it."

"Interesting. And who did that programming?"

"Why, my chief designer, Jim Phizz. He's a wonder. Our secret weapon. I wish my son had realized that."

"Oh, and why is that?"

"Wright and Jim didn't get along. Not surprising, of course, but Wright seemed to be especially hard on Jim. Rejected design after design and worked the man near to death."

Charlize turned away from Irv-Orv and gave Grave her patented we-need-to-follow-up look, which involved a slight nod of her head and the raising of one eyebrow. Grave nodded back.

"So," said Charlize, turning back to Irv-Orv, "back to the simdroids, your magnificents. How did your son treat them?"

Irv-Orv frowned. "Worse than humans. They were just annoying tools to him. Beasts of burden."

"I see. So how did the magnificents respond to him?"

Irv-Orv seemed confused. "Respond? Well, like machines. I mean, they're just circuits and programming, aren't they? They don't take offense."

Charlize cocked her head, eyebrows at full attention. "You mean like me?"

Irv-Orv was clearly flustered. "Oh, no, not like you. Well, you're more sophisticated, aren't you? If I've offended you, I'm very sorry. No, what I meant to say was that my simdroids, although they've been tweaked a bit, are still twenty-year-old technology. Their only emotions are programmed in, so they can realistically portray the magnificent seven."

Charlize frowned. "I see." She turned to Grave. "I have no further questions, sir."

Grave glanced at his watch. "Very well, then. Thank you, Mr. Orville, for your time. Now, let's take a quick break, and move on to Wanda Orville."

Irv-Orv nodded. "I'll let her know."

"Shall we say ten minutes?"

"Fine, I'll round her up." Irv-Orv nodded at each of them in turn and walked quickly from the room.

"Quite a family," said Charlize.

"Indeed," said Grave, eyeing the chocolate donuts.

50

Snoot gave Loblolly an appraising look. They had spent the better part of an hour reviewing Loblolly's personnel file, the McLachlan murder, Captain Morgan's collection of Captain Morgan Rum memorabilia, the best drones on the market, the care and feeding of Fred, the care and feeding of Captain Morgan, and life at the station and in Crab Cove, such as it was.

"So, what do you think?"

Loblolly shrugged. "I think the crux of the matter is that we don't order enough chocolate donuts."

Snoot snorted. "Oh, you're going to fit in here quite nicely, Polly." She pocketed her smile. "But seriously, what do you think?"

"Two things. First, I'd like to dig into the file found near McLachlan's body. I have some experience with drone technology—I built my first one when I was twelve. Maybe I can spot something others have missed."

"Okay," said Snoot, sliding the file across the desk to her. "Have at it if you want, but I should tell you that Ramrod engineers have already had a shot at it."

"Not a problem. Always good to have fresh eyes on a problem. Now, second, I think in the end we'll find that the two cases are interconnected and that the key to the whole mystery is that woman running from the scene, whoever she may be."

Snoot nodded. "The woman, yes. We're always at the center of things, aren't we?"

"Indeed," said Polly.

"I'll drink to that," said Snoot, raising an invisible glass and just as quickly putting it down. "Oh, speaking of which, if you want anything to drink around here, bring your own bottled water and never expect to find coffee in the coffee pot."

"Oh?"

"Seriously. The tap water is vile, and even so, the coffee disappears."

"Hmm. Are you sure someone is even *making* the coffee?"

"Hmm right back at you. No, it may be that coffee hasn't been made around here for years. Probably the water."

Polly gave Snoot a devious smile. "I have an idea. Why don't we stake out the coffee pot and the donuts? See what's really going on."

Snoot grinned and leaned toward her conspiratorially. "I like your style."

"Okay," said Polly with a giggle. "Here's what we'll do."

A smile grew bigger and bigger on Snoot's face as Polly laid out her plan and Captain's Morgan's frowning face suddenly appeared at the office window, a finger tapping on his watch.

51

Wanda Orville entered the room as if she were born with one purpose and one purpose only in mind: to enter rooms. Most people upon entering would have scanned the room quickly to see who they were dealing with and then headed straight for a chair, where they could quickly end their journey from A to B.

Wanda seemed to be on safari, stalking some unseen beast. Each person in the room seemed to be a curiosity worthy of an extended appraising gaze, her eyes scanning each of them, assessing them, weighing their potential threat to her, or admiration of her. She passed by each of them in turn, offering nuanced smiles and glances as she made her way along the buffet line, passing quickly by the steaming Basque dishes to pick up a cup and serve herself tea. She then turned back to the table, eschewing the chair designated for her and selecting instead the chair at its head, where she sat down with the flourish of a queen.

In fairness, this was only how Grave saw her enter the room. Blunt, who was less in awe of her than Grave, would have said she looked like trouble on two legs, entering the room the way she did with such dismissive arrogance. If Wanda could have seen his face, she would have seen a sneer.

Charlize would have said Wanda entered the room with all the suddenness of a gust of wind, her Day-Z-Dew perfume preceding her in a floral blast that seemed to overwhelm the room and all the Basque aromas rising from the steam tables. She found the woman instantly annoying and fascinating.

Smithers, a former butler by trade, would have said he'd seen and worked for women like her before, women who by dint and entitlement of wealth expected more than their fair share of fawning and deference. To him, it was just another ho-hum day at the office.

Whatever the team thought of her entrance, Wanda seemed to be quite comfortable with it. She settled into her chair, brushed a piece of lint from her sleeve, and—perfection assured—smiled up at them. "Good morning," she said. "Shall we proceed?"

Although Grave had not altogether recovered from her entrance or her beauty, he cleared his throat with some hint of purpose and began. "Thank you for meeting with us, Mrs. Orville."

"*Wanda*," she said. There was something flirtatious about her smile, at least the smile interpreted by Grave to be directed at him alone and suggesting the prospect of future dalliance.

"As you wish," said Grave. "*Wanda.*"

At that moment of supreme awkwardness, as the rest of the team rolled their eyes at the way Grave had said her name, the pocket doors to the dining room slid open, and Yul Brynner walked in. He nodded at the assembled group and then proceeded to the steam tables, checking each dish with butlerly efficiency. Satisfied, he made a circuit of the table and gave Wanda an odd look as he slowly closed the doors and was gone.

The effect of the look had not gone unnoticed by Grave. Wanda's imperial façade had crumbled, and she was struggling to regain her composure.

"Are you all right?" he said.

Wanda took a deep breath. "What? Oh, yes, I'm fine."

Grave wasn't so sure. "Would you like some water?"

"Oh, no," she said, reaching for her cup. "Tea is fine."

The cup rattled against the saucer as she attempted a sip, changed her mind, and set the cup down. "I'm sorry. Yes, it's just that Yul gives me the creeps sometimes."

"In what way?"

Wanda took another deep breath, and the queen was back. "It's nothing. Please proceed."

Grave waited a moment or two to make sure she was indeed ready and then proceeded. "You met the team when we first arrived, so I'll dispense with formal introductions. Now, we have questions—not many, I assure you—all related to the deaths of your brother-in-law, Wright Orville, and a second murder, that of Lachlan McLachlan."

The questioning proceeded apace. No, she had no hard feelings toward Wright, although he had indeed pursued her for sexual favors, which she had repeatedly rebuffed. As to her whereabouts, when Wright Orville was killed, she declared she was sleeping. As to her whereabouts at the time of Lachlan McLachlan's murder, however, she had drawn a complete blank.

Grave, remembering Frank's alibi, was incredulous. "Nothing? We're not talking *weeks* ago."

She had shrugged and replied, "Perhaps in the bath. I like long baths, detective. With oils, so good for the skin. I generally bathe about that time each evening. So that's my best guess."

He didn't like the sly smile she had given him then, but he had moved on, asking about likely killers. On that subject, she was very certain and very specific.

"Certainly not anyone in the family. That's just ridiculous. I mean, not even his sick son, Right. No, I think you'll find that the killings were directed by one Chance Fortuna, CEO of DroneOn. He's been trying to put us out of business for years, and I wouldn't put it past him and his goons to resort to murder. Really, you're wasting your time here. Talk to him."

With that, she had abruptly pushed back her chair and left the room.

"Well," said Charlize, "that went well."

52

Captain Morgan wondered whether things could possibly be going that well as he watched the interplay between Snoot and Loblolly through the windows of his glassed-in, fishbowl office. He had expected a negative, or at best barely businesslike, exchange between the two—I mean, they were so *different*—but the laughter, conspiratorial whispers, and what looked like instant bonding was wholly unexpected. And welcome.

He took one more look at the empty coffee pot and what remained of the last donut in the box, which had been serially sliced into eighths as officer after officer refused to be the culprit who took the last donut. Captain Morgan had no qualms at all, snatching the remaining piece and popping it into his mouth. Cinnamon. Stale. Not his favorite. Texture like sand. But tasty nonetheless.

He checked his watch—it had been nearly an hour—and began waving at Snoot, who apparently didn't see him. Moving closer, he began tapping on his watch with insistence. Still no reaction from Snoot, who seemed totally absorbed by Loblolly. He moved right up to the window and began tapping his watch even more insistently, a frown deepening on his face.

Snoot finally saw him, came to the door, and let him in. "Captain."

"Snoot." He looked back and forth between them. Snoot and Loblolly smiled back, which seemed to confuse him. "Everything okay here? Did I miss a joke?"

"Oh, no sir," said Snoot. "Just bringing her up to speed on life at the station."

Morgan grumbled. "Stick to the murder, detective." He turned to Loblolly. "Any thoughts on that, Loblolly?"

Loblolly wasn't sure whether she should share her thoughts with the captain, but she took Snoot's quick nod as sufficient go-ahead. "Well, sir, *we've* been discussing the folder at the scene. If espionage was involved, why leave it behind? On the other hand, maybe the folder was planted to create the illusion of espionage."

Snoot jumped in. "And, captain, it seems Loblolly is a bit of a technical wizard when it comes to drones."

"Oh, really?" said Morgan.

"Well," said Loblolly, "I try to keep up."

"So," said Snoot. "She thought she'd have a look at the contents of the folder, determine whether it was legit or just something thrown together to get us off the scent."

Morgan nodded. "I see." He gave Loblolly an appraising look. "I don't suppose your expertise includes old data analyzers?"

Loblolly beamed. "Why, yes. I built one as part of my Master in Robotics project in college."

Snoot marveled at Morgan's smile, which she had never seen so broad. "Sir, I don't think—"

"Well, don't then Snoot. This will only take a second, I'm sure. See here, Loblolly, can you do anything with this miserable hunk of metal in the corner?"

Loblolly's eyes went wide. "Oh my, is that an MRBG 3000?"

"Yeah, we call him Mr. Bug around here," said Snoot.

Loblolly chuckled. "I thought all of these had been sold for scrap years ago."

Captain Morgan gave her a sheepish grin. "Well, that's where Mr. Bug was headed before I picked him up for nothing. You know what they say, don't look a gift analyzer in its data port."

Loblolly frowned. "I don't think they actually say that, sir. You see, Mr. Bug, as you call him, particularly the 3000 series, had an inherent flaw that enabled it—no, even encouraged it—to make wild, fantastical leaps in logic."

"Yes, so?" said Morgan.

"So," said Loblolly, tapping the top of Mr. Bug, "this little baby will tell you exactly where not to proceed. If it says look left, look right. If it says up, think down. If it says Suspect A is the murderer, you can pretty much rule that suspect out. I mean, from a statistical perspective, you'd do better with a Magic 8-Ball."

Snoot snorted, which Morgan countered with a Snoot-directed frown.

"So it's pretty much junk?" said Morgan.

"Yeah, but still, it would be fun to tinker with. I mean, with a little work, maybe I could get it to a 6000 level."

Morgan brightened. "Our Detective Smithers, a simdroid, is also thinking of taking a look at it."

"Well, then, I'd be happy to give her a hand."

"It's a him, and I'd appreciate your help. Just don't let it interfere with your investigation."

"No, sir, of course not."

She looked down at Mr. Bug again. "I don't suppose you've tried hitting the reset button."

Morgan started to speak, then stopped. *There's a reset button?*

53

After the interview with Wanda, Grave had felt the need for a reset, and two chocolate donuts had seemed to do the trick. This time, however, he was careful to thoroughly clean his face before proceeding with the interview. Frank Orville had entered the room quietly, as meekly as a mouse, and taken the proper seat opposite Grave and Charlize. The supreme confidence he had shown during the tour of C3 was gone. He seemed nervous, and perhaps for good reason. Wanda had failed to back up his alibi one way or the other.

Grave got right to it. "Mr. Orville, we know you have a rock-solid alibi for your whereabouts on the evening of your brother's murder."

"Yes, playing chess with my drone."

"Exactly, but what about the McLachlan murder. If I remember correctly, you said you were at the movies with your wife, Wanda, when McLachlan was murdered. Is that right?"

Frank Orville took a deep breath. "Yes, that's right."

"To see the new version of *The Magnificent Seven*?"

"Yes, and it was dreadful. We hated it, especially Wanda."

"Really? Would you say it was dreadful enough for someone to remember the date and time they saw it?"

Frank looked confused. "Why, yes."

"Funny," said Grave. "Mrs. Orville doesn't recall exactly *where* she was that day. Says she might have been taking a bath. No mention of a movie or a night out."

Frank looked stunned. "But we were, we went." He looked quickly from person to simdroids to cloud, searching for help. "She was there. With me."

"Do you have any proof of that? Ticket stubs, perhaps?"

Frank shook his head, eyes wide. "No. I mean, I don't know. Perhaps the stubs. I'll have to look."

"Did you make any stops along the way, to or from the movie?"

Frank threw up his hands. "No, we went straight from here to the theater. I suggested a late dinner, but Wanda said she was tired and wanted to come home."

"Think, Mr. Orville. Did you have any conversations about the movie, before or after?"

Frank shrugged. "No."

"What about your drone? Dolores, is it?"

"Yes, but no, I never mentioned it to her, and besides, I never take her along on an evening with my wife. And Wanda wouldn't have had hers, either. One of our date night rules. Besides, I'd be forever bothered by calls from the office or the manufacturing floor."

Grave nodded. "I see." He turned to Charlize. "Any follow-up questions?"

"Yes," said Charlize, "but not for you, sir. However, I should let you know that we do plan to follow up with several people at your office, as well as the simdroids you employ."

Orville seemed relieved. "That's fine. Yes, of course. Do that." He paused and look back and forth at the team. "So, are we done here?"

"Yes," said Grave. "And thank you for your hospitality. I know it's a stressful time for you and your family."

Grave's thanks was received quickly, with a cursory nod, as Frank Orville left the room.

Charlize began tapping her fingers on the table. "I'm not buying it."

"Nor I," said Grave. "Wanda seems to have selective amnesia, and yet Frank seems very insistent about seeing that movie."

"One or both of them is lying," said Blunt. "To protect each other, perhaps."

"Or to incriminate the other, more likely," said Charlize.

Smithers cleared his throat. "We don't have to buy anything. There should be any number of security cameras at the theater, and on the route they would have taken to get there."

Grave blinked. He should have thought of that. "Yes, of course. Let's get someone at the station to follow up on that."

Smithers nodded. "I'll let them know."

"Now," said Grave, "let's get to it. You know your assignments. And remember, the stick is clocking."

Charlize groaned. "One thing, sir."

"Yes?"

"The perfume. She was wearing Day-Z-Dew. No question."

"So you think she was the woman at the scene?"

"Perhaps. I'll know for sure, or at least at a high probability level, once I smell Prissy, Wright's wife."

"Wouldn't that just confuse things if both women use that perfume?"

Charlize began shaking her head long before Grave had finished his question. "No, I took a sample of air at the crime scene, and one here when Wanda entered the room. When I have a sample from Prissy, I can then have the three samples analyzed."

"But what if all three samples are identical?"

"Only two should be identical. Perfume smells different on each woman. A chemical reaction takes place to create a wholly new scent. Think of it as a perfume fingerprint."

"So if there's a match, we'll have our woman at the scene?"

"Yes, exactly."

"Wonderful," said Grave. "Wonderful."

54

Snoot and Loblolly sat opposite each other at their desks, Snoot's a battered gray-metal desk bought at auction from the Baltimore Police with drawers of two minds. The drawers on the left were hard to open, but the drawers on the right were so easy to open that they'd fall out, even with the slightest tug. The key in working at that desk, as Snoot had learned over and over again, was to remember the difference. Unfortunately, she forgot at least once a week. Her forgetfulness had become a running joke at the station. Once, someone had even posted a sign that said, DAYS SINCE SNOOT'S DRAWERS HIT THE FLOOR: 2. The double entendre was not lost on Snoot, who had ripped down the sign and glared at every patrolman, detective, and drone in sight.

Loblolly's desk, on the other hand, was brand new, a slight that Snoot had noticed immediately. *Why should the junior detective get the best desk?* Of course, she knew why. Captain Morgan was insensitive to such things as the rights of seniority. Your desk was your desk, and he assigned it to you, so you should just be happy with it. Period.

Loblolly looked up from the folder she'd been studying quietly for the last hour. "This is both remarkable and odd."

"Oh?" said Snoot, looking up from her drone catalog. "How so?"

"It's plans for a new drone featuring distributed intelligence and precursor elements of neural nodes, a device many think is impossible."

"We've been wondering about that."

"Yes, well, distributed intelligence is here. That man's drone—Haggis, was it?"

"Yes, Haggis."

"A clear example, however rudimentary."

"And the neural thingy?"

Loblolly frowned. "Everything I know suggests it's theoretical to the extreme, but here, in these plans and schematics, it's quite clearly shown as an element of the drone."

"And that means?"

"Someone cracked the code to bring neural nodes into reality, or someone was trying to sell someone else a bag of goods, probably for a ton of money."

"Probably the latter, don't you think?"

Loblolly shrugged. "Maybe, but then again, everyone poo-pooed the Flux Capacitor, and now it's a standard feature on flying cars."

Snoot nodded wistfully. "I've always wanted a flying car."

"Yeah, me too. But . . ."

"They still cost a bloody fortune."

Loblolly closed the folder and looked around the room, which was near empty save for one woman sitting a few desks away. Loblolly leaned across her desk and whispered, "Don't turn around, but who is the woman sitting at Detective Grave's desk."

Snoot didn't have to turn around and quickly whispered back, "That's Tilda Must, the retective assigned to this district."

Loblolly's eyes widened. "I've heard of those, but I've never actually met one."

Snoot chuckled. "Be careful what you wish for. Once we finish this case, she'll be on us like flies on a dead crab."

Loblolly gave Must one last glance and shivered. "Holy shit. Are you sure we should solve this case?"

Snoot snorted, which was becoming a frequent occurrence in their burgeoning relationship.

55

The team parted ways with assurances by all that they would complete their assignments and return to the station in time for the three o'clock meeting with Captain Morgan. Charlize and Smithers would stay in place, to interview Yul Brynner and as many of the other magnificents as they could in the allotted time. They'd then make a brief stop at Prissy Orville's home, so Charlize could gather an air sample containing Prissy's perfume. With any luck, they would also interview Right Orville, the victim's son.

Grave and Blunt would proceed to DroneOn to interview its owner, Chance Fortuna. But first, Blunt would take advantage of the buffet, scooping up Basque delights to take home to June.

Grave glanced at his watch. "Come on, Blunt."

The cloud that was Blunt floated down the buffet line and began scooping up another delight. "Sir, I'll only be a minute. Perhaps you should go ahead. I'll scoot this food home, pick up June, and meet you at DroneOn."

Normally, Grave would have objected to the delay, but having June with them would be a plus when it came to discussing distributed intelligence and neural nodes. "How long do you think that will take?"

"About forty minutes, I'd expect, depending on traffic."

Grave mulled it over. Forty minutes would place them at DroneOn just after 1:00 p.m., which would leave about ninety minutes for the interview and plenty of time to make it back to the station. "Okay, I'll see you there around one."

Blunt had worked his way down to the next steaming dish. "Fine, sir."

Grave left him to it, walking out of the room without another word, although he was sure he heard Blunt saying something else. *Was he laughing?* Grave paused briefly and wondered whether he should retrace his steps and find out what was so funny, but decided against it. Blunt would eventually figure out that he was talking and laughing in an empty room.

Grave continued on through the grand foyer and out the door to his waiting Austin Healy Sprite, sliding his long legs into its glove-like comfort with practiced contortions. Turning the ignition switch launched him and everyone within two miles into the wonderful world of high-decibel gospel music and the booming voice of the now-deceased Reverend Bendigo Bottoms. Hearing his voice gave Grave chills but reminded him of his promise to return to the Crab Cove Cinema Cemetery. Blunt's food run would give him just enough time to talk to the reverend and Victoria again before proceeding to DroneOn.

He slipped the car into gear and sped along the Orville's long, tree-lined driveway, scattering gravel as he went, the hum of the new electric motor completely lost in the sound of joyful voices. In seconds, he was making the turn onto the Coast Highway, or rather the Third New Coast Highway, its predecessors now highways for fish and crabs. It was a longer route, but at this time of day, the shortest routes would be filled with tourists in search of steamed crabs and Crab Cove tee-shirts.

Grave pressed the accelerator, speed be damned.

56

There was something magnificent about the magnificents, even now as they sat around the table in their non-Western, domestic-servant garb, curious to know what Charlize and Smithers would ask next. They had entered the room and taken their seats with a flourish, to the accompaniment of piped-in theme music to *The Magnificent Seven*. Yul Brynner, the butler, and head magnificent, had taken the lead in the interview, answering even questions directed at other magnificents.

Steve McQueen, who had played Vin Tanner in the movie and who now served as chauffeur, seemed to be a bit twitchy and restless, particularly when Yul spoke. Charlize remembered from her research on the movie and the cast that Brynner and McQueen didn't get along during the filming. Steve McQueen had tried his best to upstage Brynner in every scene they shared, using unscripted gestures and tics to draw attention away from Brynner.

The other magnificents played their parts equally as well. Horst Buchholz, who played Chico and now served as sous-chef in the Orville's vast kitchen, seemed to embody insouciant, boisterous, and naïve youth. Charles Bronson, who played Bernardo O'Reilly, seemed right at home as a burly caretaker and gardener. Robert Vaughn, who played Lee, was now the Orville's smooth-talking manservant, assisted by the jovial Brad Dexter, who played gold-seeking Harry Luck in the movie. It was not surprising to learn that James Coburn, who had played Britt, the knife-throwing expert, was the Orville's chef.

The early questions were standard meet-and-greet questions that any simdroid would ask another simdroid. What was your series number? When were you produced? Any special upgrades? What are your feelings about simdroid rights and suffrage? And so on. The magnificents, for their part, had questions about Charlize's getup as Sherlock Holmes, as well as Smithers' take on a country doctor named Watson. Charlize had told them of her love and admiration for the mythical detective, and all the upgrades she had had to give her the character's skills, or at least the ones she believed in.

The magnificents answers had been just as matter-of-fact, and not a single one seemed the least bit nervous, even McQueen. They were produced by Ramrod Robotics, through a special order by the Orvilles. They had each had subsequent Ramrod upgrades to smooth out their fine and gross motor movements, as well as their speech simulations. For the past few years, however, the Orvilles had taken over the upgrades, giving each of them specific skills in drone manufacturing, management, and their current domestic duties. None seemed concerned about their heavy workloads.

"There were some issues early on about energy utilization and battery life, but that was sorted out long ago," said Yul. "We can go for weeks now without a charge."

"Impressive," said Charlize. "Now, I know you are all very busy, so to speed things up, and with your permission, of course, I'd like to propose that Smithers and I be permitted to extract data from your memory cores—your simcortexes—for the days of the two murders. It would help us immensely in sorting out who was where and what happened when."

Yul seemed taken aback. "What murders?"

Now it was Charlize's turn. "What? Why, the murder of Wright Orville and Lachlan McLachlan. Surely you've heard."

Yul frowned and looked around the table. "None of us know what you're talking about."

Charlize described the time and place of each murder, which seemed to trigger something in Yul.

"Ah," he said brightening. "The gap."

"Gap?"

"The time period you referenced has been wiped from our memory banks. We couldn't tell you anything about those days. Where we were. What we did. Absolutely nothing."

Charlize pressed him. "And why is that, specifically?"

Yul shrugged. "Mr. Phizz said it was an experiment. He would erase a section of our memory, and then see if there was any way for someone else—a hacker, say—to retrieve the data. He said it was successful experiment."

"I bet he did," said Charlize.

Yul threw up his hands. "So, you see, I'd like to help—we'd all like to help—but your request is not possible. Our memory cores for those days are wiped clean. I may have once known the answer to your question, but I am incapable of responding now."

Charlize raised an eyebrow. "And James Phizz, the chief designer at C3, did this to you?"

"Yes."

"And when was this memory wipe initiated? Can you tell me that?"

"Um, last night, at our monthly checkups."

"And you didn't think this was odd?"

Yul shrugged and looked around the room at the other magnificents, who were shaking their heads. "I—*we*—didn't think to ask. He told us it was an experiment, and that's all. Listen, our checkups are something we look forward to. Mr. Phizz always has something new for us, something that makes us feel better or work better. We wouldn't think to question him."

Charlize nodded slowly. "I see. Well, then, this questioning may take a little longer than we expected. We'll have to work around your memory lapses and come at the problem from a few different angles."

Yul smiled back at her. "Ask away. We have nothing to hide." He paused, then added, "Except what's hidden."

"Right, then," said Charlize, fixing her gaze on James Coburn at the end of the table. "Mr. Coburn, would you be so kind as to surrender your knife to Mr. Smithers here?"

James Coburn blanched, a reaction that transformed his faux skin to nearly white. Charlize had never seen the like in a simdroid, even the latest models. She'd have to look into that.

He was incredulous. "My knife?"

"Yes, we'd like to test it for blood. And any other knives in your kitchen."

Coburn frowned, pushed back slowly from the table, and stood, his hand coming quickly forward as the stiletto sped through the air.

57

The sound of gospel music reverberated across the cemetery as Grave pulled the Sprite into a parking space near the path that led to the various sections of the graveyard. When he turned off the ignition, the gospel music continued on for some seconds in his head and then kindly stepped aside and made room for other thoughts, which came quickly and chaotically, as if they'd been waiting for the start of a Black Friday sale at New Walmart.

He thought of his father, Jacob, and his father's fiancé, Ida Notion. Would they ever set a date? Did he care? How many visions has she had today? Would the visions help solve either case? Was Mr. Bug really no better than a Magic 8-Ball? Was Wanda telling the truth? Was Frank? Were the magnificents involved? If so, how? Where in the world was Lachlan McLachlan's head? Would he be able to avoid Tilda Must's pursuit?

This last thought seemed to bring him abruptly back into the moment. He found that he had already climbed out of the car and made his way up the hill toward Victoria's bench in the old section of the cemetery. She was there and smiling brightly.

"Oh, Simon," she said with a giggle. "I'm so happy to see you. So much news."

He sat down next to her. "News?"

"Oh, yes. Firstly, the cemetery is undergoing a complete upgrade. All the clunky monitors are being replaced by the latest holographic platforms. I saw the first one installed just yesterday, for a man who was a juggler in life."

"A juggler? Seriously?"

"Yes, for a show called something or other." Sometimes Victoria was not as specific as she could be.

"Um," Grave ummed.

She put a finger to her lips. "Oh, I know. It was called The Most Amazing Last Circus Ever. An odd name, don't you think?"

"Yes."

"Anyway, it's quite marvelous. You can walk around it, view it from any angle. When you're at his back, you actually see his back. I'm quite taken with it. He wasn't much of a juggler—dropped a lot of balls—but still, it was magical."

"Sounds great," said Grave, clearing his throat with some emphasis, hoping she would take it as impetus to move on to other news.

"And there's more," she said. "Your Mr. Orville is here. Finally released from stasis."

Grave sat up straight. "What? Where? Have you talked with him?"

Victoria looked around. "I don't see him at the moment. He's still wandering around on one of the tours, I suspect. Getting used to things."

"But did you talk with him?"

She shrugged. "Well, of course I did. It's my job."

"And?"

"And, he's a real piece of work, that one. As I mentioned the last time you were here, he's not a very friendly person. The others are already calling him Mr. Grumble."

"Did you ask him about his death?"

"Yes, I always do. He says the last thing he remembers is falling on the wet grass and how wonderful it smelled."

Grave sighed. "No, I mean how he was killed. And who killed him."

"Oh, why didn't you just say so? Actually, he wasn't sure, although he suspected a gentleman named Eli Wallach had something to do with it."

Stranger than strange, thought Grave, *but kudos to Ida Notion.* "Do you know who that is?"

"Nope, not a clue. Should I?"

"No, not really. Too long after your life. He was an actor of some note."

"Oh, how wonderful. But he's not buried here, I'm afraid."

"No, he wouldn't be." He cleared his throat again, which had the desirable effect on Victoria.

"Now, as to your Mr. McLachlan. Oh, my goodness, what a delightful man. I am happy to report that he is here and has been reunited with his head."

"Seriously?"

"Well, sort of. Kind of. He has to carry the head around, which is quite amusing for us, and confusing for him."

"And have you talked to him?"

"No, not really. I mean, he tries to speak, but nothing comes out. He's very frustrated. I'm going to try paper and pen next time, although eye-hand coordination may be a problem for him. Perhaps if I hold his head, I could—"

"Yes, yes," said Grave, "that would be helpful. Tell me, how did his head arrive? Did someone else bring it?"

"A good question, but with no answer. He was just suddenly there with his head, walking around with the other new arrivals."

She suddenly stopped and laughed. "I must tell you. There is this wonderful new woman here. I've never seen her like. She puts glitter and these little cute stickers on everything, and draws faces on balloons, and is an absolute joy to be around. Her name is Nancy, and I'm sure you'd just love her. We all do."

Grave shook his head. "She sounds lovely, but perhaps another time." He looked down at his watch. He needed to move on.

Victoria grabbed his wrist and looked at the watch. "Why do you wear these things?"

"To manage time."

She laughed louder than he had ever seen her laugh. "Ha, as if it could be managed. It rolls on, sir, and nothing you do can stop it, not even for a second."

"Well, then," said Grave. "I'll count you among those who think time travel is impossible."

Victoria cocked her head and gave him an odd, appraising look. "Don't be ridiculous! Time curves and loops and has doors leading this way and that. Past, present, future—it's all one marvelous labyrinth."

"Seriously?"

"Sir, if you had a proper watch, it would be much too big for your wrist."

He looked down at his watch again. "Speaking of which, I'll have to stick to the time I understand. I need to see the reverend."

"Very well. Don't be a stranger." And with that, she was gone.

But to where, thought Grave, *or when?*

58

Charlize was capable of cheetah-like speed, but Coburn's action had caught her completely by surprise. She could only watch, mouth open, as the knife sped down the length of the table and embedded itself just in front of her.

The next few seconds were chaos, as Coburn was restrained by McQueen and Bronson, who wrestled him back down in his seat.

He was seething. "Go ahead, take the knife, take all of them. You'll find *nothing*."

Smithers was on his feet, cuffs at the ready, but Charlize motioned him back into his seat.

"I don't think that will be necessary," she said. "Will it, Mr. Coburn?"

He shook his head.

"As Britt, Mr. Coburn here has the skills to hit any target he aims at. If he were trying to hit me, he would have. Still, I must caution you, Mr. Coburn. Any further eruption will result in your arrest and possible dismantling."

Coburn's eyes grew wide. "You wouldn't."

Charlize cocked her head. "Oh, we would, sir. We really would." She looked around the room. "And that goes for everyone else as well."

She glared at each of them in turn, and each looked away, except for Yul, who seemed to be enjoying her performance.

"Now," she continued, "let's get back to the topic at hand: the murders."

Yul raised a single eyebrow. "But we know nothing."

Charlize nodded. "Of the events themselves, yes, and everything that happened those days."

Yul shrugged. "So, aren't we done here?"

"Not at all. We'll simply focus on the time periods just before and just after your memory gaps."

"And try to piece it together?"

"Yes." She looked around the table. Everyone was nodding. "Good."

She turned to Steve McQueen. "Mr. McQueen, I wonder if you would explain your household duties for us. What you do and how you interact with the Orvilles."

McQueen shrugged, twitched, scratched his head, and puffed out his cheeks. "Pretty simple, really. I drive people around."

"Which people, specifically?"

He puffed out his cheeks again, part of his programmed thinking mannerisms and consistent with his scene-stealing antics in *The Magnificent Seven*. "Any and all Orvilles, any time, any place."

"And these drives occur every day?"

"Um, not always. Sometimes, on a rainy day, say, everyone will opt to stay in place, keep their gunpowder dry."

"And does any family member use your services more than any other?"

"That would be Irving Orville. He's like me. He likes to drive fast. I mean, did you see me in *Bullit*?"

"Ah," said Charlize. "So, your programming is not limited to your role in *The Magnificent Seven*?"

McQueen beamed. "No, with me, you get the whole ball of wax. *Bullit*, *The Great Escape*, *Papillon*—even *The Blob*."

"Right," said Charlize. "Now then, have you ever had occasion to drive Wright Orville?"

He cocked his head and threw in a nuanced, noncommittal twitch for good measure. "Not really. He and Prissy and Right live in their own house across town. I'd only pick him up from time to time. Usually, to head to the airport with Frank Orville on business trips."

"So it would be unusual for you to have picked him up during the memory-gap period?"

He nodded, then smiled as if he had just stumbled on the right answer. "Yes, very unusual."

"And did you ever drive any other family member here to his house?"

He started to say *no* but then paused. "Well, now that you mention it, there was this one time, just last week. Mrs. Orville, Wanda, had me drive her to his house."

Charlize raised an eyebrow. "Did Mrs. Orville say why?"

"No, but she did seem more nervous than usual."

"Oh?"

"Yeah, she hates the way I drive, but it was more than that, like she was afraid to go, but had to go. Do you know what I mean?"

"Not really."

"Okay, it was like going to his house was the last thing she wanted to do. It was like she was being summoned, to be punished in some way."

"Punished?"

McQueen smirked. "Orville treated people like dirt."

Charlize nodded. "So we've heard. So tell me, Mr. McQueen, if I had asked you three days ago who would most want to kill Wright Orville, whom would you have said?"

The question seemed to have sent McQueen into a paroxysm of mannerisms, tics, and gestures as if he was trying to access and sort through every nuanced reaction that had carried him through his forty-four films. He settled finally on darting glances at each person at the table, followed by a slight jerk of the head, and nervous head-scratching. As he did this, Charlize noted that Yul Brynner was shaking his head and whispering, "Oh, Jesus, here we go again," to himself.

"Well," McQueen began, "that would obviously be a long list, but if I had to lay money on it, I'd say Irving Orville."

Charlize leaned toward him. "Oh? And why is that?"

McQueen selected a suitable shrug. "Because three days ago, the elder Orville was in a state. Screaming, hollering, throwing things across the room. Even threw a punch at his drone, Butch."

"Why was he so upset?"

"Um, I didn't catch it all—I had duties to attend to—but it seemed to be about C3 and its financial position."

"Do you know what set him off?"

McQueen gave her a quick smile. "Now that you mention it, yes. He had just taken a call from Brad Dingle, through Butch."

"The CFO at C3?"

"Yes, that's the guy."

"Did you hear anything specific? You know, something that would have set him off?"

McQueen shrugged. "Not really, although Mr. Orville did seem incredulous. He kept shouting, 'Worse? *Worse?*' You know, like that, like he couldn't believe it."

Charlize paused, thinking about what to ask next. McQueen, who had seemed to come to life during the questioning, as if he were rising to a new role that would both test and affirm his acting skills, settled back into his chair with a satisfied smile.

Charlize looked at him again. "I know this may be a stretch, but can you think of any reason why Mr. Dingle would call Irving Orville with such news instead of Wright or Frank?"

McQueen shook his head, then chuckled.

"What?" said Charlize. "What's so funny?"

McQueen looked around the room, searching for support. "Sorry, it's just that, in my experience, the only other family member Dingle talks to here is Mrs. Orville."

Charlize's eyes grew wide. "Wanda?"

McQueen nodded, which set off a wave of nodding and knowing smiles from the others.

Charlize took it all in. "What am I missing? What's the inside joke?"

Yul held up a hand to stop McQueen from replying. "Mrs. Orville has, shall we say, *many* outside interests."

"So you're saying she was having an affair with Mr. Dingle?"

Yul waggled his hand in the air. "Um, *affair* might be too strong a word. A dalliance perhaps. As they say, a butterfly needs many flowers."

Charlize looked around the room. "Are you all in agreement on this?"

They all nodded.

"I see. By any chance, have any of you overheard such calls between Wanda and Dingle?"

The magnificents looked back and forth at each other in a way that shouted *YES*, and then Charles Bronson raised his hand. "Last week."

"Last week what?" said Charlize.

"In the garden. I was tending the roses, and she was there with her drone, Crystal." He paused.

"And?"

"We were outside. There was no need to be whispering to her drone, but that's what she was doing."

"And you're sure it was Dingle?"

Bronson laughed. "Oh, yeah. She has a pet name for him: *Dingy-Wingy*."

The other magnificents laughed and shot knowing glances back and forth.

Charlize held up a hand. "Wait. Was this anything more than a flirtation?"

It was Bronson's turn to raise his eyebrows. "Oh, my. Yes, indeed. I couldn't catch it all, but I remember hearing the words *urgent* and *plan*."

"Interesting," she said. *Interesting, indeed*, she thought.

59

Grave had expected to see the Reverend Bendigo Bottoms before he left the graveyard, but the man's ghost was nowhere in sight and continued to be nowhere in sight for more minutes than Grave had left on his schedule. He had so many questions to ask him. Victoria had never been very helpful about what life after death—or whatever it was—was like, or even what dying and death was like. All she had said was that it was a *process*. *What does that even mean?*

Thoroughly daunted and disappointed, Grave reluctantly climbed into his Sprite and experienced the next best thing: the reverend at work, booming out another sermon bookended by gospel music. Grave remembered this old broadcast well. The reverend was trying, in his own unique way, to explain the burgeoning crab population in the face of an otherwise bleak period of an ever-warming planet. That god could focus on the needs of Crab Cove was particularly heartening to the reverend, who saw global warming as a small part of a larger plan.

Thus enthralled, Grave hardly noticed anything else on his way to DroneOn. In fact, he almost missed the turn to the Warehouse District, which would have been a terrible thing to do, because the highway abruptly ended 500 feet past the turn, with a fifty-foot drop-off to the bay, one of the few spots in Crab Cove where a person could actually fall more than a few inches.

Unlike C3's modern, gleaming facility of geometric perfection and architectural overindulgence, DroneOn's building was nothing more than a retrofitted old warehouse, featuring an ambiance of rust and decay. Grave had to cock his head to one side to make the building look straight.

Two blurs hovered at the warehouse's entrance, which Grave took to be Sergeant Barry Blunt and his wife, June Thursday, spokesperson for Ramrod Robotics. Their drones, Object and Friday, hovered near Blunt's police cruiser. Grave nodded at his drone, Barry, who knew immediately to join the other two. Leaving drones behind during interrogations was optional police procedure. Today, the last thing Grave needed was the constant humming of a drone, and the possibility of phone calls interrupting the proceedings. Still, Grave wondered what they did and talked about when they were alone. He had never liked cellphones, but these drones had a conspiratorial bent that made him uneasy. He sensed the drone era would not end well, but he wasn't sure who would be on the short end of it's unraveling.

"I hope I haven't kept you waiting," said Grave.

"Not at all," said June. "We just got here ourselves."

Blunt raised his arms to present the wonder of DroneOn. "Not exactly the Taj Mahal, is it?"

"Not even a Skunk 'n Donuts," said Grave.

"No," said Blunt. "No chocolate donuts here, I bet."

Grave laughed. "No." He turned to June. "How's my favorite little girl, Rippley?"

June's blur seemed to be frowning, but she said, "Oh, she's just fine."

Grave blinked, totally surprised by her curt response. Usually, he'd have to walk away from her to end a constant stream of news, good and bad, about her precocious tike.

She quickly added, "Look, shall we go in?"

Pleasantries thus exchanged, the three of them walked up the concrete steps, trying their best not to touch the rusted metal rail. Blunt pulled open the heavy, windowless gray door, and nearly fell backward. A gust of wind created by pressure differences in and outside the warehouse nearly pushed June back down the steps as well, but Grave grabbed her just in time, and with Blunt's help, pushed her up the steps and into the reception area.

A young woman in a glassed-in cubicle gave them an appraising, questioning look. "May I help you?"

Grave flashed his gold detective badge, but the flash seemed to have no effect on the woman, whom Grave now realized was a simdroid look-alike for actress Betty Booyah, who had risen to fame for her role in *Like Tubas for Trombones*, a 2047 remake of *Like Oboes for Bassoons*, which had swept the Oscars in 2031. In the remake, Betty had reprised the role of musician Tanya Bananya, a failed, down-on-her-luck Bassoon player who discovers she should have really been an oboe player. The producers of the remake had simply replaced the oboe with a tuba and the bassoon with a trombone. Rumor was that the switch was made to take full advantage of Betty Booyah's preternaturally puffy lips. Whatever the reason, the movie flopped, but Betty's popularity soared. She had made several other films, most notably the films *Lips*, *Tulips*, and *More Lips*, each featuring outrageous plots involving, well, lips.

Betty's lips seemed to be moving again. Grave wondered whether their movement had caused the gust of wind.

"I said, may I help you?"

Grave started to flash his badge again but decided against it. "I'm Detective Simon Grave, of the Crab Cove Police Force. I'd like to speak with Mr. Chance Fortuna."

Betty shrugged and picked up a microphone. "Visitor for Fortuna, visitor for Fortuna." The sound of her voice echoed throughout the building.

She set the microphone down and pointed at an old wooden bench along the far wall. "Have a seat. Someone will be out to get you momentarily."

"Thank you," said Grave, who turned and nodded at Blunt and June to join him on the bench, which was just large enough for the three of them.

Momentarily stretched on to eventually, with no certainty that finally would ever arrive, so each of them picked up a magazine to pass the time. Grave chose a two-year-old issue of *Crab Fortnightly*, which had a special feature entitled, "New Bay Seasoning: Out with the Old?" Grave gave it a quick glance. The gist of the article seemed to be "choose what you like", it's a matter of taste. Bored, Grave moved on, thumbing through the issue, his focus mainly on ads for various new crab harvesting equipment, including fleets of submariner drones capable of harvesting precise numbers of crabs of a specific sex and size to assure maximum yield and continued growth and sustainability of the crab population.

Blunt had chosen an ancient issue of *Popular Mechanics*, its yellowed cover shouting out the news: "Finally, Flying Cars!" Blunt chuckled louder and louder with each turn of the page.

As Blunt chuckled, June grumbled. Each page of her magazine, a recent *Drone Weekly* ("Is Your Drone Happy? Should You Care?"), was being turned with a ferocity approaching that of a slammed door. *What's up with June?* Grave thought.

The question went unanswered as two burly men entered the reception area. Grave's first thought was to arrest them immediately and figure out their crime later.

60

Detective Polly Loblolly tore down the crime scene tape and pushed into Lachlan McLachlan's house.

"Careful," said Snoot. "It's still a crime scene."

"Right, don't worry about that. We'll be in and out of here without so much as leaving a hair behind."

Snoot sighed. As much as she liked Polly, there were certain things she didn't like about her, first and foremost her arrogance. She tried to tell herself that Polly was just displaying supreme confidence, that any perception of arrogance was a misreading of the woman, by a woman without supreme confidence. *Still.*

Polly had insisted on coming back to the scene. She had seen something in the folder that gave her concern. Just what, she wasn't sharing. She had just said, "We have to get back to the scene," and that was that. She was out the door and climbing into the driver's seat of Snoot's hovercruiser. Perhaps that was a second thing she didn't like about Polly: her inability to grasp that she, and not Snoot, was the junior detective.

Snoot sighed again. "All right, out with it. Why are we here?"

Polly was already ten feet ahead of her, heading to the open door to what looked like a laboratory or office or office-laboratory, or at least some place where a man could tinker on this and that without interruption. There was tinkering equipment in abundance, including 3-D printers, microscopes, computers, what looked like a medical operating suite, and all manner of gizmos too technical even for Polly to identify. And sitting smack in the middle of all this were two large bird cages—doors open and bird free.

Snoot called after her. "What are you looking for?"

Polly turned away from the empty cages and waved the file folder at Snoot. "To see if we have a match."

"A match to what?"

"Handwriting, paper type, printed characters, sentence structure, his printer—*everything*."

"So you think—"

"He's been set up, yes. And if there's no match here, there will most certainly be a match elsewhere, in the den of our murderer or murderers."

Snoot smiled to herself. Maybe arrogance or self-confidence—or whatever it was—was a good thing. All Snoot could think to say was, "Ah, ah."

61

Sometimes the correct order is out of order, and such was the case with the rest of Charlize's and Smithers' interviewing day. Their initial thought was to proceed directly from the Orville Manson to the headquarters of C3, but it made more sense, at least geographically, to make a quick stop to see Prissy and Right Orville on the way.

By any measure, Wright and Prissy Orville's house failed to live up to the word *mansion*; it was just a large brick house plopped down on half an acre of land overlooking the bay. And from the looks of it, the bay was trying its best to make it over the grassy dunes and pay a final visit to the house.

The inside of the house was closer to a mansion, thanks to its furnishings, which suggested that someone who once lived in a mansion knew what the trappings and accoutrements should look like. Still, it was a step down from the Orville Mansion, or maybe even a dramatic plummet.

Charlize and Smithers followed Prissy into what she called her blackout room, a place where she could just be alone, away from the drone of the world and the drones of the world. Charlize was happy that Grave had warned her about Prissy's headphones and goggles. Otherwise, she would have had to simulate a guffaw.

Once seated, Charlize got straight to it, which was to repeat the same questions Grave had asked while she secretly took an air sample of Prissy's perfume, which was undoubtedly the floral bomb known as Day-Z-Dew. Prissy seemed annoyed by the questioning, of course, and the need to repeat what she had already repeated to "that strange detective."

Charlize persisted, and Prissy relented, and the interview was over before they knew it. The questioning of Right Orville, Wright's son, was another matter. Prissy at first objected to any interview at all, but with coaxing and concessions from Charlize and Smithers, she agreed to allow a five-minute interview with her son.

Unlike his mother, Right Orville embraced drones with gusto. For one thing, they kept his mother at bay, and for another, they provided hours of entertainment. Charlize and Smithers found him in his room, a swarm of tiny drones each no bigger than a bumblebee buzzing around his head in ever-changing patterns, their movements directed by the virtual reality mask on Right's head.

He was tall for his age, and lanky, with his mother's golden hair, but cut short and long and combed straight up to simulate an explosion. His eyes bulged in a way that suggested eternal surprise and were close-set over a nose that would have been the envy of Cyrano. As with most children of the drone era, his skin had a funeral home pallor, the result of extended time indoors playing games with his drones.

After some coaxing, Right set the mask aside and gave them an annoyed, questioning look. "Who the hell are you?"

"I'm Detective Charlize Holmes, and this is my assistant, Doctor Smithers-Watson."

Right cocked his head. "So you're role-playing?"

"Um, not exactly," said Charlize.

"More precisely," said Smithers, "we are sentient simdroids with the skills of our namesakes."

Right squinted at them like they were some new game to play. "Interesting. So how do we play this?"

"Ah," said Charlize. "Easy enough. We're investigating the death of your dad, and had a few questions for you."

Right's demeanor changed abruptly. Interest became disinterest. Friendliness became animosity. Synonyms became antonyms. "No," he said firmly and began putting his mask back on.

"Wait," said Charlize. "Yes, of course it's a game. We're testing your ability to match wits with the one and only Sherlock Holmes."

Right shook his head. "You don't look like Sherlock Holmes. You look like that old bitty in the hearing aid commercials."

Even beautiful actresses grow old, Charlize thought. "Well, don't hold that against me. So, shall we begin?"

Right nodded. "Maybe. What do I do? Should I talk loud so you can hear?"

Charlize ignored his demented chuckle. "Firstly, "I'll ask you a question."

"This sounds boring."

"But," Charlize continued, "but, if you don't like the question, instead of providing an answer, you can ask me a question, so long as that question is better than my question."

"This still sounds boring, and *stupid*."

"Come on," said Smithers, "give us a chance. Really, it will be fun."

Right shrugged. "Oh, all right. What's your question?"

"Good, good," said Charlize.

Charlize and Smithers went through the usual questions. Where was he at the times of the murders? (No problem, he was here in his room, and his drones confirmed it.) Did he kill his father? (He laughed, shook his head, and laughed again.) Did he know who might have killed his father? (*Get in line* was his reply.) Did he know of his mother's whereabouts then? (She never left the house.) Did anyone come to the house or leave the house during that period? (Yes, his father had left the house, and seemed to be in a hurry.) Did he drive his own car? (He didn't own a car.) Did you see the car that picked him up, then? (No, but it sounded like a hovercar.) Did your father call you or your mother after that? (No, of course not, he never brought a drone home from work, what with his mother's condition.) Really? (Yes, really. He was no fan of drones, although he wasn't as bad as Right's mother.)

Charlize thanked Right for his time and stood to leave.

"Wait," said Right. "I just remembered something. Perhaps it's important."

"Yes?"

"He was dressed for the beach, but it was already dark."

"Yes, we already know that."

He shrugged. "Then again, some sections of the beach have lighting, of course."

"Yes, that's right."

"I know, but that's not the oddest thing."

"Oh?"

"No, he had a folder with him. Who takes a folder to the beach, even if it is midnight?"

Perhaps someone with plans to meet a terrible bagpipe player thought Charlize.

62

Grave could barely keep his mouth closed as he studied the two men who had come to pick them up and take them to meet Chance Fortuna. One of these gentlemen would have been enough to boggle the mind, but two? The words *goons, thugs, bruisers, gorillas, hoods, strong-arms, tough guys, made men,* and *whatever* came to mind.

They seemed to be throwbacks to another era when black shirts and red ties were a thing for the criminal element. They seemed to be a burly matched pair, a frick and frack of muscle and intimidation. As Grave looked back and forth at them, wondering whether he should take advantage of his Hap Wadoo training and run away, he realized that the men were twins. Same beady eyes, same cleaver noses, same broad brow, same cleft chins, same pockmarks from excessive teenage face-picking.

The first Whatever seemed to be speaking. "So you wanna see Mr. Fortuna? What's your business?" His voice was deep and gruff.

Grave closed his mouth and flashed his badge, which forced the man to take a step back as if he were a vampire facing a cross. "Cops?"

"Yes," said Grave. "Detectives, actually, investigating the death of Mr. Wright Orville."

"Yeah, we heard about that," said Whatever Two. He turned to Whatever One. "What do you think, Buddy?"

"I don't know, Lemon. The boss will be sore if we don't get this right." Buddy's voice was higher and a bit shrill. It was as if each word had to pass by some barrier in the man's throat that wanted to keep words in.

Buddy turned to Grave. "Mr. Fortuna is in one of his moods today."

"Oh, is he?" said Grave.

Buddy just nodded at Grave, then turned to Lemon. "Ain't that right, Lemon?"

Lemon shrugged and rolled his eyes. "As always."

Buddy gave Grave another once-over and tried his best to make out the faces of Blunt and June, which remained elusive for all but the trained eye. "Jeez, I'd hate to have to pick you guys out of a lineup."

He turned and laughed in the direction of Lemon. "Ain't that right, Lemon?"

Lemon grinned back. "They could get away with anything."

Buddy nodded. "Am I right?"

Lemon nodded back. "You're right, Buddy."

"All right, then," said Buddy. "I guess you guys are okay. Come on, follow us."

And with that, Buddy and Lemon turned and began walking into the depths of the warehouse. Grave, Blunt, and June followed, trying to take in as much information about DroneOn as they could along the way.

The floor was humming with activity, much of the hum coming from new drones lifting off the assembly line on their first flights. Not that all the drones achieved flight. Some made it a few feet above the assembly line before crashing down, and others just rolled off the line and fell to the floor without so much as a final buzz.

"I can see why Mr. Fortuna might be in a mood," said Grave to the back of Lemon's and Buddy's heads.

Lemon and Buddy issued twin grunts and just kept walking.

Grave looked back at the line. Men, not simdroids, were operating it, so there was no look of quiet efficiency. It was more like chaos with obscenities as each man accused the next of screwing up the process. Meanwhile, the carnage at the end of the line had reached a point where any sane man would punch a red emergency button and bring the whole line to an abrupt halt. And a loud alarm confirmed there was at least one sane man along the line.

Lemon and Buddy turned their heads to have a look and issued synchronized *oh shits*.

Lemon followed with, "The boss is not going to be happy."

Buddy nodded and turned to Grave. "You sure you want go through with this? The boss is going to be pissed."

"Not a problem," said Grave. "Most suspects are *in a mood*."

Buddy's eyes grew wide. "*Suspect?* Shit, don't call him that."

"No," said Lemon. "We ain't had nothin' to do with that Orville business."

Grave held up a hand. "Of course you ain't—er, I mean of course you didn't. *Suspect* is just a generic term."

Lemon screwed up his face. "Generic? What in hell is that? I think I'd rather be a suspect."

Grave didn't know what to say to that, but realized that Lemon may have earned his nickname from the way he screwed up his face, which suggested someone sucking a lemon.

"Whatever, whatever, let's stop this suspect talk. Mr. Fortuna is right in here." He pointed at a door with a frosted glass window that announced in black-trimmed gilt *Chance Fortuna, CEO*.

Lemon and Buddy paused to adjust their suit jackets and ties and smooth back their greasy black hair.

Lemon caught Grave looking. "Mr. Fortuna can't abide slobs."

"Ah," said Grave. "Shall we go in, then?"

"Yes," said Buddy, "but let me introduce you. Mr. Fortuna likes that formal shit if you know what I mean. He's very particular."

"No problem," said Grave.

Buddy took a deep breath, nodded at Lemon, who did the same, and then put on a practiced smile of greeting and pushed open the door.

Grave was not prepared for what happened next. As soon as they opened the door, a small man in a blue seersucker suit rushed by them, waving a revolver. "Who the fuck turned off the line," he screamed.

Everyone froze except Lemon, who chased after the little man.

"I told you," said Buddy. "He's in one of his moods."

"Well, I hope he has a license to carry that old relic," said Grave.

Buddy dismissed Grave's comment with a wave of the hand. "Ah, it's just an old theater prop. Shoots blanks."

"A prop?"

Buddy chuckled. "Yeah, yeah, but the workers don't know that. Let me tell ya, it keeps 'em in line."

"I bet," said Grave.

As if on cue, the sound of shots came from the production line, followed by a string of obscenities beyond the ken of mortal seamen, followed by the sound of the line resuming operation.

Seconds later, the little man burst back into the room, followed by an exhausted Lemon, who had been trying his best to calm his boss down.

Buddy smiled at them and waited patiently as the little man took off his jacket, tossed it on a nearby table, and then climbed into a grand leather chair behind a large rosewood desk.

Buddy cleared his throat. "Mr. Chance Fortuna, may I present Detective Simon Grave. Detective, Mr. Chance Fortuna."

Chance Fortuna nodded at Grave, then squinted at Blunt and June. "And who might these two be? Jesus, they look like they're trapped in white cotton candy."

Grave could see that Blunt was struggling to reply, so he jumped in. "This is Sergeant Barry Blunt and his wife, June."

Fortuna nodded, then took out a handkerchief and wiped his brow. "It's frickin' hot out there."

Even sitting behind a desk, or possibly because he was sitting behind a desk, Fortuna seemed preternaturally small, particularly his hands, which looked like doll's hands. Grave couldn't quite calibrate the man's height. He certainly wasn't a dwarf or a midget, but he was barely taller than either. But for the cigar that stuck out of his mouth, Grave would have taken him for a young boy of six or seven.

Fortuna stared at Grave with eyes as black as his slicked back hair. "So, what do you want?"

Grave was happy to begin. "We're here to talk with you about the death of Wright Orville."

Fortuna slapped his hands down on the desk and laughed. "Ha, I heard about that shit going down. Good riddance to him. Good goddamned *riddance*."

Grave sighed. "I understand he was a competitor."

Fortuna waved a hand in front of his face. "Wait a minute, wait a minute." He turned to Lemon and Buddy. "Okay, you're done here. Go check on the line or something."

Lemon and Buddy turned and left the room. Fortuna waited until they had closed the door behind them and then turned back to Grave. "Dumb shits."

"Excuse me?" said Grave.

"Those two, the Franchisi twins. Not a brain between them." Fortuna noticed that he was still holding the revolver and quickly set it aside. "Now, then, I thank you for the news of Mr. Orville's death, which I already knew—good news travels fast, eh?—but I can't imagine why you're here otherwise."

"Ah," Grave continued. "We're interviewing people who knew Mr. Orville, people who might have information about his death."

Fortuna took the cigar out of his mouth and gave Grave a blank stare. "What?"

"We're looking for Orville's killer."

Fortuna came back to life. "And you think I had something to do with it?"

"I didn't say that."

"Well, you're here, aren't you?"

"Well—"

"Listen, Mr. Detective, everyone knows I hated that bastard, but it wasn't like I was the only one. I've got at least ten former C3 workers on that line out there who would've slit that man's throat for a dime."

Grave was about to tell Fortuna that he understood that fact full well, but the unmistakable sound of the line shutting down once more entered the room and said howdy to Chance Fortuna, whose eyes grew wide. "Shit, shit, *shit*," he screamed, picking up the revolver once again and racing from the room. He may have been short, but he was fast.

Grave looked back and forth at Blunt and June and tried his best to suppress a giggle. "Holy shit, he's like that old cartoon guy Yosemite Sam."

The sound of gunfire erupted from the direction of the line. Yosemite was on the warpath once more.

63

The door to Jim Phizz's laboratory closed behind Charlize with a pressurized click, although click was not the right sound; it was more of a sucking sound, something between a *fwoop* and a *shwoop*, and clear evidence that the door was now by-god sealed tight. In any case, Charlize realized at once that she was in the inner sanctum of C3's chief designer, Mr. James "Sloe Jim" Phizz.

The room was easily a hundred feet on a side and filled with the latest scientific equipment and tools. Charlize estimated that the room represented 33.75 percent of the entire building's footprint, give or take 0.737 percent. Quite a percentage for the work of one man. She couldn't help but think of Smithers, who loved a good percentage or two and who was now cooling his already cold and lifeless heels in the reception area, prohibited by Phizz from entering. *Rules*, Phizz had said.

Charlize sniffed at the air, which smelled almost medicinal, save for a trace of Day-Z-Dew perfume.

"Quite a laboratory," she said, looking around while surreptitiously taking an air sample.

Phizz had been studying her with interest. "Are you a real detective?"

Charlize smirked. "Yes, of course."

"But you're a simdroid, yes?"

"Yes, which is an advantage, don't you think?"

"Oh?"

"Yes, as a simdroid, I'm dispassionate. For example, if I were a woman, I might be distracted by the way you've been looking me up and down since I arrived, or your scan rating of 9.63 on the handsomeness scale."

Phizz looked away. "Oh, I didn't mean, I mean I—"

Charlize cut him off. "Oh, you did, Mr. Phizz. You did."

Phizz started to speak, but Charlize held up a hand.

"It's okay. Now, also as a *simdroid*, I am smarter than most detectives, and to the point, have been programmed with the most sophisticated abilities in criminal investigation."

She paused, listening for a gulp from Phizz, who readily complied. Her scans detected a look of worry and concern on his face.

"So," she continued, "think of your favorite best fictional detective—Cross, Wimsey, Marple, Poirot, Ramotswe, Dibney, Chan, Wolfe, Fletcher, Mars, Columbo, Holmes, Clouseau, even the amazing Dirk Gently, or *whomever*—and tell me that you shouldn't be mighty careful about what you say to me right now. Because I have the skills of each and every one of those detectives, so if you hold back or vary from the truth, I shall surely sniff it out."

In pointing out her skills, Charlize failed to mention a critical flaw in her programming; namely, the fact that she approached every investigation as an almost uncontrollable committee of more than a hundred fictional detectives, some well known, some obscure, and each offering disparate, conflicting views of what they were seeing or hearing. It was all she could do to suppress this intractable committee in favor of her idol, Sherlock Holmes. In some ways, this made her even less effective than Grave, who may or may not have had a committee in his head.

Phizz sighed, which her scans indicated was a sigh mix of concern and resignation. "So that explains your Sherlock Holmes costume."

Charlize cocked her head. "Yes, I guess it does."

She turned away from him and walked over to a large stainless steel table topped by a partially assembled drone. "And what do we have here?"

Phizz, alarmed, raced to the table and threw some kind of space-age quilted silver blanket over the drone. "Sorry, that's secret, I'm afraid."

Charlize grabbed the blanket and whipped it off. "There are no secrets between us, remember?"

"But—"

"For example," she said, shutting him down. "*For example*, there is no need for you to pretend that you haven't been having an affair with the boss's wife. Wanda, I think she's called."

Phizz blanched and took a step back.

"Ah," said Charlize, poking a finger softly into his chest. "You see now why I'm dressed as I am, and know what I know."

Phizz seemed to lose his fizz, deflating before her very eyes.

This was going to be fun, she thought. She detected a smattering of applause from the committee.

64

Detective Loblolly had the back of Mr. Bug wide open, revealing circuit boards you couldn't find now at a Larry's TechnoJunk City. They were that old, and to Loblolly's mind, utterly useless. Still, she had promised the captain a go at Mr. Bug, and she still had a few tricks up her sleeves.

"I can't promise anything, sir," she said in the general direction of Captain Morgan, who was slumped behind his desk, barely paying attention. All he was interested in was the time, a source of anxiety that had gone from a four-beat walk to a two-beat trot, to a canter, and was now in full gallop.

"Mmph," he said, which pretty much covered his appreciation of the situation.

"Keep at it," said Detective Snoot, who was sitting across from the captain, playing with Fred, who seemed to be a bottomless pit of affection. She knew she was going to keep him.

Loblolly pressed on. "You see, sir, the way the engineers linked board 34C with board 87F should have been a big red flag for them. How they missed it, I'll never know."

"Mmph."

"Exactly, sir. They should have linked 34C with *78F*. Perhaps a dyslexic mistake, perhaps not. Anyway, their mistake created a logic loop, which is never a good thing, is it?"

"Mmph."

"Right, so it's like a person who can't make up his or her mind and then, in frustration, just throws a dart at the wall for an answer."

"Mmph."

"So, by redirecting 34C to 78F, we should see a whole new Mr. Bug. We might even see accuracy slightly above 50-50."

"Mmph," Morgan began, but then his brain seemed to lock on to the word *accuracy*, waking him from his slumber. "What did you say about accuracy?"

Loblolly smiled at him. "It should be much improved."

Morgan sat bolt upright. "You don't say? Well, then, let's get on the horn with Charlize and Grave. Have them input whatever data they have, so we can make our meeting as productive as possible." He glanced at the clock. "And hurry."

"Will do, sir. And should I input the data about the content and source of the information in the McLachlan folder as well?"

"Yes, yes, that too."

He glanced at his watch again. The horse seemed to have slowed a bit.

65

Jim Phizz had been cooperative but not helpful. His affair with Wanda had been as brief as it had been frustrating. She had invited herself into his lab just a week ago, on the pretext of supplying him with what she called important information from Frank. But there was no such information, which soon became unimportant to Jim, who had been enthralled with her beauty for months and fell instantly into her welcoming arms.

Phizz had described in perhaps too much detail their in-laboratory, week-long coital adventures, which seemed to leave no surface untouched, however challenging. And then just yesterday, after a one-last-time appeal from Phizz, she had abruptly ended the affair. He couldn't figure out what he had done wrong, or any reason for her sudden change in emotions.

Whatever the cause, he had firm, irrefutable alibis for his whereabouts during the murders, as confirmed by security cameras and several drones.

That left Charlize with one last interview, and if she hurried, she might just pull it off and get back to the station in time for Morgan's meeting. Phizz had been more than willing to escort her out of his lab and down the hall to the office of the CFO, Brad Dingle, who seemed annoyed by her arrival.

"Do we have to do this now?" he said. "I've reports to do, for Mr. Orville." He glanced at his watch. "Really, this is most inconvenient."

"I assure you this will not take long," said Charlize, sniffing at the air in his office, which seemed to have given up all hope of freshness. Still, there was a hint of cologne and more than a few parts per million of Day-Z-Dew. The perfume did not surprise her—Wanda's scent seemed to be everywhere, and the magnificents had said there was an affair in progress—but the cologne seemed odd for a man well into his fifties, even for one having an affair. Perhaps he lacked confidence.

Not that he seemed old for his age, or unconfident, even with his baldness and less-than-handsome aspect. Despite the worn black suit and stained tie, and a demeanor suggesting he had been bowed and eaten away by numbers, she could tell that he balanced his sedentary work-life with vigorous physical activity. He might have even been a gym rat given the way his biceps bulged under his suit, and his neck stretched the limits of his tie. Put him in a professional wrestler costume, and you'd never think he was a man who spent his days sitting behind a desk.

Dingle squinted at her, not quite believing. "All right, but let's be quick about it. I have to get the monthly financials to Frank—Mr. Orville." He turned to his drone, who had been buzzing behind his shoulder. "Malcolm, run along and tell Mr. Orville there may be a brief delay."

The drone wobbled a bit unsteadily and then buzzed through the open door and accelerated down the hallway.

Dingle closed the door, then motioned Charlize to a chair in front of his desk, and sat back down in his. Charlize wondered whether his chair had been special-ordered to accommodate his width. The man was a bull.

"I have a few questions for you, Mr. Dingle." She pointed at the bar charts on the wall behind him. "Things don't seem to be going all that well. What's the problem?"

Dingle frowned, which seemed to be his default expression. "I'm afraid that's a bit too technical, even for a detective such as yourself."

"Ah," said Charlize, "not true. In my first iteration as a simdroid, I was a financial auditor."

Dingle's eyes grew wide. His gulp seemed to echo throughout the office. Charlize detected a new scent: *fear.*

66

Captain Morgan sat behind his desk, mentally checking off members of his team as they arrived for the three o'clock meeting. Detectives Loblolly and Snoot were the first to arrive, no doubt because they had been at the station, helping him with Mr. Bug, who was already in a whirl of buzzing and flashing lights, doing his newly fixed best to make sense of the disparate input from the teams.

Loblolly and Snoot had apparently hit it off right from the start. They chose seats next to one another and began whispering and giggling like schoolgirls about something. In all his time with Detective Snoot, Morgan had never so much as seen her smile, and now this. Loblolly was clearly a transformative influence on her, and to Morgan's mind, a positive one.

Charlize and Smithers were next to arrive, and after polite nods of recognition to Morgan and Snoot, and handshakes with Loblolly, they took the next available seats next to Loblolly and Snoot. Morgan had to admit that the addition of Charlize and Smithers, even with their ridiculous costumes and arch impressions of Holmes and Watson, had been one of his best ideas.

Next came Detective Grave, Sergeant Blunt, and what appeared to be Blunt's wife, June. Morgan had learned to recognize the cloudy image of Blunt, but June was still a challenge for him. As Morgan expected, Grave had immediately fixed on the comely Detective Loblolly, who seemed to return his awkward flirtations of greeting with equal eagerness and interest. Morgan could already sense where this might be going, and just hoped Grave didn't screw things up so badly that Loblolly would resign and flee.

Morgan looked at his watch. *Where in the devil is Polk?*

He scanned the outer office. Simdroid officers scurried about, working on other cases. Several tourists sat on a bench, waiting for loved ones to be released into their custody after being booked for minor beach crimes. The coffee pot remained empty, as did the donut box. And hovering just outside his office window, drones Barry, Object, and Rum seemed to be in an intense conversation with Loblolly's drone, Pine Cone. Fred the dog, nose pressed to the glass of Morgan's door, drew his attention with occasional futile scratches at the glass. Next to him stood Retective Tilda Must, whose nose may as well have been pressed up against the glass. Her frustration at not grabbing Grave before he made it into the relative safety of Morgan's office was palpable. Morgan briefly imagined her scratching at the glass, then turned back to his waiting team.

Everyone was now looking at him expectantly. "Um," he began. "Let's wait a couple of minutes for Polk."

He glanced over at Mr. Bug, who was now vibrating like an unbalanced washing machine, again.

"Perfectly normal," said Loblolly. "He'll settle down in a minute. A lot to digest."

"Yes," said Morgan. "I've seen him do this before. Just hope he comes up with a better answer this time."

Morgan noted Smithers' sudden interest in Loblolly. "Yes, Smithers, Detective Loblolly here has had a look at the old boy, and fixed something or other."

"Oh," said Smithers, "was it cross-wiring?"

Loblolly nodded. "Yes, the 87F-78F problem."

Smithers nodded appreciatively. "Classic."

"Yes, pretty much textbook. We'll find out soon enough, I guess."

"Fine," said Morgan, "fine." He looked at his watch. "I don't know what in blue blazes is keeping Polk."

"Ah," said Charlize. "I dropped off some air samples for him to analyze. I think he may be delayed a bit."

Morgan sighed. "All right, then, let's begin. With any luck, he'll arrive before the television crews take over the parking lot."

Grave groaned loudly, which made Morgan chuckle. "Yes, Grave, she'll be here."

Loblolly raised her hand. "Who, sir? Am I missing something?"

"Ah," said Morgan. "Of course, you wouldn't know. I'm talking about a certain TV anchorwoman, Claire Fairly."

Loblolly smiled. "Oh, I just *adore* her."

Grave groaned even louder.

Morgan shook his head, a knowing smile on his face. "Keep that thought as long as you can, Loblolly, but keep your guard up. Fairly is not always fair—or balanced."

The other team members laughed.

"Now," Morgan continued, "let's begin with the Orville case, shall we? Grave, you're up. And for the benefit of our new detective, please provide as much detail as possible."

Grave nodded, stood, and walked over to Morgan, who patted him once on the back and sat down with his usual grunt.

From his new vantage point, Grave could see the team's collected drones hovering near the glass. They seemed to be agitated about something. Perhaps it was the presence of Tilda Must, who was standing next to them, her cold stare directed at Grave and Grave alone.

He cleared his throat and directed his attention—and comments— in the direction of a friendlier face, Detective Polly Loblolly.

He almost melted when she smiled back at him.

67

Some say that the devil is in the details, but Grave knew the true saying involved an angel, not a devil. And for every detail he provided, an angel—Detective Loblolly—beamed back at him, eager to hear the next detail and the next.

Grave ticked off the salient points at the crime scene: the position of the body; the multiple lacerations from multiple sources; the opinion and conclusions of medical examiner Jeremy Polk, still absent; the arrival of Charlize and Smithers, and her quick identification of the body and traces of Day-Z-Dew perfume, suggesting the presence of a woman; and the testimony of an eye witness, Lachlan McLachlan.

Loblolly's hand shot up at the mention of McLachlan. "By any chance did he mention the folder we found with his body?"

"No," said Grave. "We talked for quite a while, but he never mentioned it."

"So it's possible he didn't know about the folder until the night he was killed."

Charlize was about to interrupt, but Captain Morgan held up a hand. "Hold on, Loblolly. And you, too, Charlize. We'll get to that. Just bide your time, please."

Loblolly sighed heavily but nodded her assent. "Yes, of course. Sorry for the interruption. Please go on, sir."

Grave smiled at her. A smile was not necessarily called for; in fact, it may well have been inappropriate, but Grave never did have much in the way of impulse control.

"Very well," he said. "So, the *folderless* McLachlan said he was drawn outside by the commotion and saw a man running for his life, being chased by what he described as a demon hound."

Snoot's hand shot up. "Sorry to interrupt, Grave, but we've determined why he would have thought that."

"Oh?"

"Yes, the so-called demon hound was glowing."

Grave gave her a confused look.

"Glowing, sir, as in phosphorescence, from the clay in the caves, and the glowing beast was Chester Clink's dog, Baskerville."

Grave nodded. "So Clink was using the dog as a watchdog."

"Yes, exactly. And Baskerville was just doing his job, chasing Orville away."

"That doesn't explain why Clink had McLachlan's head, though," said Charlize, which had Morgan out of his seat.

"Wait, wait. Let's not go off on tangents. Keep to the sequence, all of you." He turned to Grave. "Continue."

Grave cleared his throat. "Well, then, let's get back to my interview with McLachlan, who was a very strange man indeed."

Loblolly beamed back at him. "Yes, yes he was."

Grave was almost certain he heard an angel singing, albeit an angel with a deep, sexy voice. Unfortunately, he chose that moment to look in the direction of Morgan's door, where Tilda Must stood, a devil in her own right, staring back at him through the glass with unwavering menace.

68

Retective Tilda Must stood outside the glass door to Captain Morgan's office and watched as her elusive target, Detective Simon Grave, droned on about his current case. If she had been programmed to sigh in any meaningful way, she would have sighed deeply at this moment, but that just wasn't possible. What was possible was a flat affect coupled with an icy stare, which her creators thought would be two mannerisms of extreme importance to someone intent on getting at the truth.

It had worked on many a detective, and she knew it would work on someone as obviously weak-minded as Grave. She just had to get the dolt into a locked interrogation room for fifteen minutes, and he'd be singing her song.

The question was how to accomplish that. The man was slippery and seemed to sense her presence. She thought and thought. And thought some more. But the fact was she had exhausted every programmed technique of apprehension and entrapment. The man had foiled each and every one of them.

She would need something new. She could ask headquarters for help, of course, but her failure to close the case on her own would be duly noted in her file, which could lead to dismissal and reprogramming, as what, she had no idea. Perhaps as a meter maid, perhaps as a restroom cleaner, perhaps even as a saltwater taffy puller down on the boardwalk. Or a crab picker. She cringed. No, she couldn't involve headquarters. And then it came to her, the perfect solution.

Most *ah-hah* moments come with a smile suggesting some element of glee, but smiling was no more an option than failing for Retective Tilda Must. She noted a slight rise in body temperature and a thinning of her lubricant, which was more than enough evidence for her to realize that her plan was perfect—and foolproof.

She just needed a fool.

69

Grave tried to shake off the image of being chased in the dark by a glowing mastiff. No wonder the poor man had had a heart attack.

He noticed that everyone was staring at him, waiting for him to move on. "Oh, right, so as I was saying, McLachlan saw our demon hound chasing—and he thought, killing—Wright Orville. And he also saw a car."

"And the woman, right?" said Charlize.

"Um, no," said Grave. "He didn't mention a woman. Just the dog and the car."

"Wait," said Loblolly. "Surely he had a drone with him?"

Grave shrugged. "There was no mention of it."

"I can explain that," said Charlize. "His son, Right, said his father hated drones, only used them at work. And as for the missing woman, we know she was there. She just must have left earlier, before the murder."

Loblolly frowned. "But the car was still there. How did she leave? Were there two cars?"

"A good question," said Grave, giving her a smile that may have gone too far for the moment. "And hold that thought; it could be important."

Loblolly brightened and eased back into her chair.

"Now," said Grave. "Let's move on."

He glanced back at Morgan's door again. Retective Must was nowhere to be seen, but he could see Polk headed their way.

"Wait, here's Polk."

Polk pushed into Morgan's office with a smile on his face that suggested a cat and a thousand swallowed canaries. "Sorry I'm late. I have some results, but don't let me interrupt you."

Grave shrugged. "We were just getting ready to discuss suspects, but—"

Morgan was on his feet. "Let's hear what Polk has to say."

Polk beamed back at him and pulled out a sheaf of papers from his briefcase. "Results from the samples. Day-Z-Dew is in all seven of them."

Charlize was now on her feet. "Seven?"

Polk smiled. "Yes, seven. The sample taken at the scene of the Orville murder, the three samples you gave me, Charlize, the sample provided by Blunt here, and the two samples given to me just a while ago by our newest team member, Detective Loblolly."

Everyone turned and looked at Loblolly, who smiled back nervously. "Yes, from inside McLachlan's house and on the folder and papers found with his body."

Morgan smiled appreciatively at her. "Well, now."

"And my sample was from DroneOn," said Blunt. "June said she thought she smelled perfume, so . . ."

Morgan was beyond excited. "Well, out with it, man. What did you find?"

Polk paused for as long as he felt he could. He loved these moments when all attention was on him, and he could revel in the glow of his expertise. "We have a match. No, in fact, we have six matches."

Morgan was losing his patience. "Who then? Who?"

"We can eliminate Prissy Orville because the perfect match in all six instances is Wanda Orville. We can place her at the scene of both murders."

"I knew it," said Charlize. She turned quickly to Loblolly. "I mean about the first murder. Kudos on the second."

Loblolly beamed back at her.

"Well, then," said Morgan. "I guess we best suspend this discussion and pick her up. Nothing like having a suspect in custody in advance of a news conference."

Grave nodded. "Blunt, let's go."

"Me, too," said Charlize. "And Smithers."

"What about us?" said Snoot.

Morgan pounded a fist on his desk. "Wait a gosh darn minute. Yes, we need to pick her up, but what about this new revelation? How is DroneOn connected?"

Loblolly spoke up. "Um, I think I know that, sir."

Morgan was about to coax the answer out of her, but Mr. Bug, who had been vibrating with some energy, suddenly stopped, all his lights flashing.

"Hold on a minute," said Morgan. "I think Mr. Bug has finished his analysis."

Everyone crowded around the great analyzer to read the message on his screen: *Eli Wallach.*

Morgan shook his head in disbelief. "Eli Wallach?"

Snoot snorted as a disappointed Morgan turned back to Loblolly. "Sorry for the interruption, detective. Please continue."

Loblolly opened her mouth, but the next words seemed to come from nowhere. A child's voice, screaming with delight.

"Wah-lick, Wah-lick, yesh!"

Just as suddenly, a cloud appeared, which slowly resolved into a young girl.

70

According to the *Oxford Dictionary of Emotive and Denotive Arts*, there are no fewer than thirty-seven ways a human can gasp, regardless of their native tongue. There are gasps for joy, anger, spiders, tax bills, tax returns, and all manner of situations. There is also a gasp, so rare many consider it purely theoretical, in which the gasper, unable to decide among thirty-six available gasps, will choose all of them, concatenating them in a way that suggests a balloon inflating in quick bursts. Unless stopped, so the theory goes, the gasper will yield to paroxysm and death.

Every human in Morgan's office seemed to have chosen that deadly course except Sergeant Blunt and June, and it was June who brought them back from certain death, or at least certain breathlessness, much to the relief of Charlize and Smithers, who were confused by the sudden display of gasping. They just weren't programmed for that.

"Everyone, Rippley," said June. "Rippley, everyone."

Loblolly was the first to find voice. "Oh, my, she is so *cute*. I just love her freckles."

Others quickly recovered and joined in.

"Look at that red hair," said Snoot.

"She reminds me of Pippi Longstocking," said Morgan.

"No, more like Orphan Annie," said Grave.

"How marvelous," said Smithers. "See the way the air ripples around her?"

"That's why we call her Rippley," said June with more than a hint of parental pride.

Blunt beamed. "Isn't she something?"

"She is," said Charlize, "but more to the point, why is she here, and how would she know about Eli Wallach?"

"Yes," said Morgan. "What's going on, Blunt?"

"I'm not sure, sir, but she's been with Grave and me all day."

Grave gave Blunt a look that suggested an impending gasp. "What? You mean *everywhere*?"

"Yes, sir. She sat in on the interviews, wandered about on her own, did some snooping here and there. Completely invisible, of course."

"Not my idea," said June, shooting a disapproving look at her husband. "He was just supposed to bring her to the station for a meet and greet. That's all."

Caught in the middle of this adult maelstrom, Rippley did what any 750-day-old girl would do—she began to sniffle and cry.

June reacted quickly, scooping her up in her arms and rocking her as the little girl went from visible, to blurry, to cloudlike, to vapor-like, to completely invisible. "There, there," said June. "It's all right."

"Me sorry."

Blunt bent down beside June, guessing at the approximate location of his daughter's head. "Honey, everything is okay. Just tell daddy where you heard about Eli Wallach."

Rippley slowly became visible and looked around the room. "You not mad?"

"No, honey. We all think it's wonderful that you know about Eli Wallach. We just want to know how, when, and where you heard about him."

Rippley sighed. "Everywhere. At big house. At stinky warehouse."

"Very good," said Blunt. "Now, *who* was talking about Eli Wallach?"

"Mish Wander, and men. Many men."

"*Many* men?"

Rippley held a finger to her lips. "Yesh, in whispuhs. But me hear."

71

Gasp followed gasp, but less and less, as Rippley unfolded her story. Captain Morgan, for one, was in awe of her ability to remember details and describe situations. If she were older, he knew he would hire her on the spot for undercover work. At the same time, he was concerned that her testimony would be inadmissible in a court of law. Whatever she told them would have to be corroborated in other ways.

And told them she did. At the mansion, she had seen Wanda whispering to a simdroid dressed as a chauffeur, which everyone quickly deduced was Steve McQueen. And while Grave, Blunt, and June had waited in the reception area at DroneOn, she had run straight onto the warehouse floor, where she saw Wanda talking to three men who were clearly Fortuna and the Franchisi twins. And that's where she had seen a drone that Wanda and the others kept referring to as Eli Wallach. It was a funny looking drone, and huge, with a face painted on it that could only have been the bandito Calvera, as played by Eli Wallach. It even had a sombrero on top.

"And awful teeth," said Rippley. "Like he did not brush morning or night. And then they covered him up with a terp."

"I think you mean *tarp*, dear," said June.

"Yesh, *tarp*." And with that, she crossed her arms and sat back down in June's lap. "That all, mommy."

Grave was shaking his head in disbelief. "Well, I must admit I didn't see that coming. Wanda, yes—her alibi just didn't smell right—but Fortuna and the twins? How does this all fit together?"

Loblolly spoke up. "I think I have a clue, sir. I took the liberty of analyzing the documents in the McLachlan folder, particularly the handwriting, which didn't match McLachlan's at all. I think we'll find that the handwriting will match Wanda's or Fortuna's. Maybe even one of the Franchisi twins."

"Good work," said Morgan. "There's still a lot to do, of course, but the first thing we need to do is bring in Wanda and the others. Sort out the known *knowns*, the known *unkowns*, and the unknown *knowns*. You know, and this handwriting business, too."

"Um, right," said Grave. "Blunt and I will take DroneOn."

Charlize chimed in. "And Smithers and I will take C3. I have a funny feeling Phizz may also be involved."

"Could be," said Grave. "From what I saw at DroneOn, they're not capable of assembling a drone like the one little Rippley just described."

"Exactly," said Charlize.

"Okay, then," said Morgan. "There's still the matter of Wanda."

Snoot was on her feet. "Loblolly and I will take the mansion and bring in McQueen and Wanda, if they're there."

"Either or both could also be at C3 or DroneOn," said Charlize. "So I think we're covered."

June stood up, Rippley still in her arms. "And I'll take *Detective* Rippley home, if you don't mind."

Everyone laughed, including Rippley.

"Me 'tective," she squealed.

"All right," said Morgan. "And while you're all doing that, I'll work on postponing the news conference. We're also going to need warrants eventually, so I'll work on that as well. But for now, let's just bring them in. Okay, get to it. And take as many officers as you need for backup."

As everyone scrambled out of his office, Morgan slumped back down in his chair and smiled at Mr. Bug. "Well, fella, you did it. You finally did it."

An unexpected voice responded. "Well, I can see I'm no longer needed here, or maybe *anywhere*."

"Oh, Polk, I thought you had already left."

The small man uncurled himself from his chair and moved toward the door. "I mean, why do I keep doing this when all the credit goes to psychics and invisible children?"

"Well—"

"Not to mention machines with the IQ of a Magic 8-Ball."

"Jeremy, Jeremy, Jeremy."

"And simdroids playing dress-up, and that damned Grave."

"Well—"

"Whatever happened to forensics and procedure and logic, Hank?"

Morgan knew that whenever Polk called him Hank, he was in for a long conversation. He motioned Polk back into his chair and slumped back into his.

Mr. Bug made a burping noise, which made Polk roll his eyes and begin shaking his head with the precision of a metronome.

Morgan could only shrug. "Interesting times."

72

Speed was of the essence, by the essence, and for the essence, so Grave hopped into Blunt's hovercruiser, which though it lacked gospel music, was much faster than the Sprite.

Grave checked his watch. "Don't go through town."

"Tourists?"

"Yes, take the Third New Coast Highway. It's longer, but faster."

Blunt threw the car into gear and immediately kicked in the turbo booster, sending the car hurtling out of the parking lot with ever-increasing speed. Grave could feel himself being pressed into his seat as the G-forces grew, and the world outside became as blurry as the man driving the car. Buildings flew by, and then the world on the right turned greenish-blue as they sped down the Third New Coast Highway.

"Should just be a minute," Blunt said.

"Good," said Grave. "That's quite a little girl you have there."

"Thank you, sir, but again, my apologies for not bringing you in on what she was about."

Grave sighed. "I should be angry, but it appears she's at least put a crack in both cases."

"Yes, sir. What do you think about this business with the folder? How does that fit in?"

Grave immediately thought of Loblolly and the way she had held the folder. Her hands. *Oh, my god*, he thought. *Those lovely hands.* "I don't know, but I'm confident we can tease that out of Fortuna or one of the twins. Play one against the other, probably."

"Yes, sir."

"We'll want Loblolly in the room, of course."

Blunt smiled knowingly, albeit in a cloudy way. "Of course, sir, of course."

The hovercruiser slowed, then slowed some more as Blunt turned it into the parking lot outside DroneOn. The building looked exactly the same, with one exception. There was a sign on the entrance that read, "Closed."

Grave checked his watch. "On a workday? At this time?"

"Something's afoot," said Blunt.

"Oh, more than afoot, I think," said Grave. "More like six little feet on the run. Come on, let's see if there's anyone about."

They climbed out of the car and headed for the building, but then Blunt suddenly stopped. "Wait, where's Object—and Barry?"

Grave looked around. "I don't know. I assumed they followed us out of the station, but maybe not."

"They were acting strange back there. What do you suppose is going on?"

"I haven't a clue. Come on, let's go."

They climbed the steps to the entrance, Grave taking the lead, testing the door. It wasn't locked.

"Come on," he whispered to Blunt, then slowly opened the door and walked into the reception area. He could see through the inner glass door that the manufacturing floor was dark, but the lights were still on in reception.

Then a small voice said, "May I help you?"

He wasn't sure where the voice was coming from, but the voice was helpful in that regard. "Over here," said the voice.

Grave scanned the reception area, finally noticing a hand waving from behind the receptionist's counter. And then the hand became an arm attached to a woman: the receptionist.

"What are you doing?" said Grave.

"Oh, just cleaning up some odd bits before I leave."

"Where is everyone?"

She didn't appear to be at all concerned. "Oh, the workers are on holiday. If you call a complete shutdown a holiday."

"And Mr. Fortuna and the twins?"

She shrugged. "Also on *holiday*."

"Do you know where they might be on this holiday?"

"Oh, yes, they've been talking about it for days. They're going to Mars."

Grave was stunned. "Mars?"

"I wish I could afford it," she said. "I'd be there in a flash. They say the sunsets are to die for."

Grave was slowly recovering. "Okay, okay, Mars. When did they leave?"

"Just a few minutes ago. If it's important, you can probably catch them at the Mars Terminal. I think Mr. Fortuna said gate six." Her last words were yelled at Grave and Blunt, who were already halfway down the stairs.

Mars!

73

Charlize and Smithers had received two head shakes from the receptionist so far—neither Wanda nor McQueen were on the premises of C3—but as disappointed as Charlize was, she was still game enough to ask about Phizz.

The receptionist nodded, happy to finally get to yes. "He's in his laboratory, as usual. Please follow the escort drone."

With that, she lifted a drone no bigger than a baseball into the air. "Take them to sector six, door four, code 3785."

The drone seemed to nod at the receptionist, and then a tiny arm appeared from its side, directing Charlize and Smithers to follow it.

Charlize remembered the way, but dutifully followed the drone down long glass hallways, past office after office. When they passed by Brad Dingle's office, she could see that it was empty. The downward-trending bar chart behind his desk seemed to have taken a further drop. His desk, which had been heaped with papers the last time, was now pin-neat. She wondered about that briefly, but not enough to stop and consider the situation further.

The little drone suddenly stopped, punched in a code, and announced the presence of Charlize and Smithers to the unseen occupant of the laboratory. Unknown to it, at least.

Seconds later, the door eased open, and an obviously morose Jim Phizz peered out. All the fizz had gone out of him.

"Oh, it's you again."

Charlize got right to the point. "I think you know why we're here."

Phizz did his best to cover. "No, no idea."

Charlize cocked her head. "Come on, you must know we're here about Wanda and the drone."

Phizz crumpled. "The drone, yes."

"Tell me about it. Did you build it? Did you help with Orville's murder?"

Phizz was taken aback. "The murder, no, *never*. I've already told you. I had nothing to do with that."

"But you *did* design the drone?"

"Yes, but I was tricked. Wanda said she wanted to surprise Irving Orville with a drone to go along with his Magnificent Seven."

"So you designed a new drone to look like Eli Wallach."

Phizz shook his head. "No, yes, sort of. There wasn't enough time to design a new drone, so I modified one of our military prototypes, an elite K-9 drone. Really, nothing more than adding a face and a ridiculous sombrero."

"But a drone that could kill."

Phizz gave her a sheepish look. "It shouldn't have been able to. I reprogrammed it to prevent that, but—"

"But anyone with knowledge of drones could have switched it back."

Phizz nodded. "Yes, but it was a birthday gift, so I never thought—"

"No, I suspect you didn't, what with your love for Wanda."

His lip began to tremble. "Love? I was *used*. I thought we had something, but it was Dingle all along."

Charlize held up a hand to stop him. "The seven mentioned something about that."

"Yes, it was always those two. Well, the hell with them both, and good riddance."

"What do you mean?"

"I thought you knew. They just left—for Mars. She didn't even say goodbye."

The news hit her like a sudden power spike in her circuits. The sheep was trying to tell her that the murderers were on the lam.

"Mars!"

"Yes, surely you passed them on your way in. Picked up by McQueen in that old Mustang of his, a 390GT 2+2 fastback."

Charlize didn't answer. She grabbed Smithers by the arm and began running. "Get on the horn to Morgan. Notify everyone. Come on, hurry, we have to get to the Mars Terminal."

Smithers tried his best to keep up—he was a water buffalo to her cheetah—but he managed to make the call while keeping her in sight.

74

Loblolly pulled the hovercruiser into the long driveway to the Orville Mansion and hit the brakes, startling Snoot, who was thumbing through another drone catalog.

"What the—"

"Look, up ahead."

Snoot turned her attention to the mansion. Another police hovercruiser was parked in front, and what she saw next startled her further. "Must? What is Retective Must doing here?"

"Exactly," said Loblolly. "I thought she was only supposed to get involved in past cases, not current ones."

"Why do you suppose she's with Yul Brynner?"

"*Shit*, and why are they shaking hands? What's with that?"

"I don't know, but let's find out. Come on, punch it."

Loblolly slammed the power pedal to the floor, and the cruiser lurched forward, its rotors spraying gravel in all directions.

"She's spotted us," said Snoot.

"Good, the worm turns."

Snoot was only half listening. Her focus was on Must, who was now running for her own hovercruiser, but the odd expression snapped her back. "What? Worms?"

"Oh, sorry, an expression my grandma used to use," said Loblolly, slamming on the brakes. "I'll explain it later."

"Come on," said Snoot, throwing open the door and scrambling out.

But it was too late. Must was speeding by them, headed for the highway.

"Shit," said Snoot. "*Shit.*"

Loblolly climbed out of the hovercruiser, along with her drone, Pine Cone, and watched Must make the turn out of the driveway and speed away. "*Jesus.*"

Pine Cone would have commented, but she was interrupted by a call that forced her to use the All-Points Bulletin ring tone, a deafening high-pitched warble, and proceed with the message in a voice not hers. "All stations, all stations, proceed at once to the Mars Terminal. Multiple murder suspects attempting flight. Proceed with caution but with full speed. Note, suspects may be armed and should be considered dangerous. End of message."

Loblolly looked at Snoot. Snoot looked at Loblolly. Pine Cone shuddered in the air, trying to shake off the unexpected voice. "I hate when they do that."

They scrambled back into the hovercruiser and sped away.

Mars!

75

The bodies, or what was left of them, were lined up for all to see—a female and four males—but Loblolly wasn't done yet. She lifted the mallet and brought it down on a leg, hard, and smiled at the satisfying crack.

Snoot rolled her eyes. "You really need to learn how to eat crabs, Polly."

Loblolly looked down at Snoot's expertly picked crabs and smiled. "Yeah, I guess, but these are delicious, even mangled."

"Nothing better than crabs at Bob's Crab Shack, even this early in the morning."

Loblolly looked around. The place was filled with table after table of tourists, each with a pile of fresh steamed crabs in front of them, the smell of Old Bay and New Bay intermingled with butter and corn. Beyond the tables, on the pier, several boats had docked and were unloading bushel after bushel of just-caught crabs ready for the steam pots. Overhead, drones of every shape and size whirred and buzzed and hovered over the tables. And above them, in numbers Loblolly had never seen before, hundreds of seagulls soared and screamed.

"Thanks for this," she said. "It's been a wild couple of days."

"We both needed a break, and for me, there's nothing better for soothing the soul than diving into a bushel of crabs."

Loblolly smiled at her, then frowned. "Do you think we could have solved the case without the help of that little girl?"

Snoot was surprised at the question. "Of course. No doubt. We had your work on the folder, for one. That linked Orville and McLachlan and their murders, and pointed a big fat finger at Fortuna and the twins."

"I guess you're right."

"Of course I am. Just take Charlize and the perfume. Nailed that bitch Wanda as the woman at the scene. And at the center of both murders—*everything*."

"And her dismantling of Brad Dingle in interrogation. I had no idea she knew so much about accounting."

Snoot chuckled. "Remember the look on his face when she said *embezzlement*?"

"He cracked like an egg."

"Spilled his guts to her."

Loblolly nodded and reached for another crab. "Yes, I thought it would stop at money, but it didn't."

"Nope, Dingle wanted the money, and Wanda wanted the plans—the *real* plans—for the neural nodes and distributed intelligence developed by McLachlan and Wright Orville."

"And she persuaded Fortuna into thinking he would get those plans, when her plan all along was to pull the big switcheroo, saving the real plans for herself, while doctoring the file to implicate Fortuna. Brilliant, really. "

"Yeah, she seemed to be working everyone. And we know Fortuna got the Eli Wallach drone and the head of Haggis. My guess is he planned to reverse engineer them both to create next-generation drones or who knows what and capture the market."

"Did Fortuna admit that yet?"

"No, but Charlize is working on him now, so it won't be long before she cracks him, too."

"Gotta love her."

"Indeed."

Loblolly raised her mallet and slammed it down into the middle of another crab.

"Jesus, Polly, that's not the way to do it."

"Sorry, old habits."

Snoot sighed. "Anyway, the twins sang without much coaxing."

"Yeah, they didn't realize that Orville's heart had given out, so they and the drone had their way with the body. And they couldn't refute the EverEye evidence, so they folded—fast."

"Gotta love the EverEye, too. The images of McLachlan and Haggis. I mean, they really put up a fight."

Loblolly slammed her mallet down on a claw, which sprayed juice everywhere. "Hey, let's not forget Polk. His work nailed both of them and their knives. No question."

"He's such a sad man," said Snoot. "Maybe he's been on the job too long."

"Morgan, too. Do you think they'll retire?"

Snoot rolled her eyes. "Polk, maybe. Morgan, probably not. I swear that man will go on forever. He and that damned Mr. Bug."

Loblolly snorted and pulled a big hunk of meat from the claw. "Ha, look at this."

Snoot smiled. "Impressive."

"Still, it's a shame we didn't catch Wanda. There's still a lot that doesn't quite fit together."

Snoot shook her head. "Oh, no, she's caught. She's just on a three-year round trip to Mars. We'll get her back here and interrogate her."

"Three years? Wait, I thought we were going to intercept them at the lunar orbital refueling station."

"The LORS? Nope, only old freighters use that anymore. Passenger flights are direct."

"Well, crap."

"Indeed."

Loblolly sighed. "Anyway, you have to admit, she really planned this right down to the last detail."

Snoot nodded. "The McQueen thing?"

"Yeah, having the foresight to have McQueen detain Dingle while she raced through customs with the money and the plans. I tell you, it wouldn't surprise me one bit if she had a plan for getting off that Mars shuttle and disappearing."

Snoot had to admit she might be right. "Maybe. She's a beautiful woman with a track record of turning heads and gaining advantage. She bested her husband, Dingle, Phizz, Fortuna and his goons—even the magnificents."

"The memory gap thing."

"Yeah, brilliant."

Loblolly pushed her little piles of crab parts into a single pile and moved it aside with both hands. "Now, one more thing."

Snoot didn't know where this was going. "What?"

Loblolly looked her in the eyes. "Tell me about Grave."

Snoot recognized the dreamy look. *Oh, shit, she's smitten.*

Snoot tried to change the subject. "Shouldn't we really be talking about Chester Clink? The Coast Guard has identified several cave systems we need to check out."

Loblolly was insistent. "Nope. Tell me about Grave first."

Snoot sighed. "Oh Polly, Polly, you really don't want to go there. Let's talk about the chocolate donut plan instead, huh?"

But Loblolly just raised her eyebrows and leaned toward Snoot. "Tell me. *Now.*"

Snoot sighed. "All right, but promise me one thing first."

"What's that?"

"That you'll never show Grave the tattoo you got last night—*ever.* Or tell him that I have the same one."

Loblolly thought about the location of her new tattoo, a little red crab on her inner thigh, and sighed. "Well . . ."

"Come on, Polly, swear."

Loblolly knitted a hem to a haw. "I don't know."

"Then you hear nothing about him from me. Nada."

Loblolly rolled her eyes. "Oh, all right. I swear."

Snoot extended her arm across the table, folding away all the fingers on her hand, save for her pinky, which she curled in front of Loblolly's face. "Pinky swear."

Loblolly shook her head in disbelief. "A pinky promise? What are we, thirteen?"

She grabbed Snoot's pinky with hers and shook on the deal. On the other hand, which she held behind her back, two fingers crossed to nullify the deal. *Yes,* she thought, *perhaps we are thirteen.*

"All right," she said. "Tell me. Tell me *everything.*"

Above them, the sound of seagulls rose a notch, and then another notch, as if they didn't want to hear about Grave or listen to the natter of humans and the clatter of crab mallets, or anything other than themselves. Whose world was this, anyway?

Epilogue

Grave looked back at the reverend, who had picked a dandelion and was admiring the morning dew on its golden blossom. "Reverend, you told me once that life was like a tuna fish sandwich."

The reverend looked up from the dandelion and smiled at him. "Indeed, I did."

"Well, given your current situation, do you still agree with that?"

The reverend chuckled and eased closer to him on the bench. "You know, the biggest thing I'd change would be the bread. I'm sure I told you wheat, but now, given my *situation* as you say, I'd have to go with rye, or maybe one of those artisanal breads with the seeds that stick in your teeth. And maybe throw in some more Old Bay with the tuna, Simon. You know, there's something to be said for spice."

Grave looked him in the eyes, which were as golden as the dandelion and seemed to swirl with the power of the universe. "And what about *death*, reverend?"

The reverend cocked his head, a little surprised at the question. "Death? Well, I'd have to say that death is quite the entrée."

And then the reverend laughed with all he had, a laugh immortal, a laugh worthy of a gospel choir singin' for all they were worth, on a great, gettin' up mornin' in Crab Cove.

And then, just as suddenly, he was gone, leaving Grave alone in the cemetery.

An entrée, he thought. *Well, that's one entrée I don't want to taste. At least not yet. Probably tastes just like chicken.*

He looked around one last time. "Shall we go see Victoria, Barry?"

Barry waggled in the air. "Sir, don't you think you've talked to yourself quite enough for one morning?"

Grave smiled. "I guess. Okay, Barry, let's go home."

"Yes, sir. Sounds like a good idea."

The ride home was quick and loud, the gospel music shaking the leaves on the trees as he pulled into his driveway and turned off the motor. His father and Ida were on the porch, waving frantically at him. They seemed alarmed about something.

He climbed out of the Sprite and headed for the porch, the last persistent echoes of gospel music replaced by the unmistakable theme music from *The Magnificent Seven*, rising in the air and growing louder by the second, seemingly coming from all directions.

And then there they were, revealing themselves in turn, surrounding him: Brynner, Vaughn, Coburn, even the just-released McQueen. All seven of them, guns drawn, closing in, with an eighth simdroid wearing a sombrero and a gotcha grin.

Retective Tilda Must.

Grave tried to back away, but the circle grew tighter.

"Take him," she said, but before they could move in, Barry suddenly started warbling in a high-pitched tone.

"Attention, Attention," a voice not Barry's said. "All officers proceed immediately to the boardwalk. Tourists and drones under attack by seagulls. Repeat, proceed at once."

Tilda sighed and dropped her chin to her chest. "*Shit!*"

Grave and Barry didn't need coaxing. Seconds later, they were in the Sprite, gospel music taking them to battle. *Onward, Crab Cove Soldiers!*

They drove on, through a town caught up in the present, tangled in the future, and wedded to the past—and, apparently, at the mercy of seagulls.

Grave couldn't help smiling to himself. *God, I love this town.*

Other Books by Len Boswell

Simon Grave Series:
A Grave Misunderstanding
Simon Grave and the Curious Incident of the Cat in the Daytime

Other Mysteries:
Flicker: A Paranormal Mystery
Skeleton: A Bare Bones Mystery

Memoir:
Santa Takes a Tumble

Creative Nonfiction:
The Leadership Secrets of Squirrels
Stick Figures: The Life and Art of Len Boswell

Note From The Author

Word-of-mouth is crucial for any author to succeed. If you enjoyed the book, please leave a review online—anywhere you are able. Even if it's just a sentence or two. It would make all the difference and would be very much appreciated.

Thanks!
Len

About the Author

Len Boswell is the author of six additional books, including *Simon Grave and the Curious Incident of the Cat in the Daytime*, *A Grave Misunderstanding, Flicker: A Paranormal Mystery, Skeleton: A Bare Bones Mystery, The Leadership Secrets of Squirrels,* and *Santa Takes a Tumble.* He lives in the mountains of West Virginia with his wife, Ruth, and their two dogs, Shadow and Cinder.

Thank you so much for reading one of
Len Boswell's Simon Grave Mystery novels.
If you enjoyed the experience, please check out our recommended
title for your next great read!

A Grave Misunderstanding by Len Boswell

"The Bottom Line: A truly hilarious mystery in the tradition of Janet
Evanovich, Thomas Davidson and Rich Leder." *–BEST THRILLERS*

View other Black Rose Writing titles at
<u>www.blackrosewriting.com/books</u> and use promo code
PRINT to receive a **20% discount** when purchasing.